Goldengrove

HARPER

An Imprint of HarperCollins*Publishers*
www.harpercollins.com

FRANCINE PROSE

Goldengrove

A NOVEL

GOLDENGROVE. Copyright © 2008 by Francine Prose. All rights reserved. Printed in the United States of America. No part of this book may be used or reproduced in any manner whatsoever without written permission except in the case of brief quotations embodied in critical articles and reviews. For information, address HarperCollins Publishers, 10 East 53rd Street, New York, NY 10022.

HarperCollins books may be purchased for educational, business, or sales promotional use. For information, please write: Special Markets Department, HarperCollins Publishers, 10 East 53rd Street, New York, NY 10022.

FIRST EDITION

Permission for "My Funny Valentine" lyrics TK

Designed by Jessica Shatan Heslin/Studio Shatan, Inc.

Library of Congress Cataloging-in-Publication Data is available upon request.
ISBN: 978-0-06-621411-5

08 09 10 11 12   OV/RRD   10 9 8 7 6 5 3 2 1

In memory of my mother, Jessie

Margaret, are you grieving

Over Goldengrove unleaving?

Leaves, like the things of man, you

With your fresh thoughts care for, can you?

Ah! as the heart grows older

It will come to such sights colder

By and by, nor spare a sigh

Though worlds of wanwood leafmeal lie;

And yet you will weep and know why.

Now no matter, child, the name:

Sorrow's springs are the same.

Nor mouth had, no nor mind, expressed

What heart heard of, ghost guessed:

It is the blight man was born for,

It is Margaret you mourn for.

—GERARD MANLEY HOPKINS,
"Spring and Fall: To a Young Child"

Goldengrove

One

WE LIVED ON THE SHORE OF MIRROR LAKE, AND FOR MANY YEARS our lives were as calm and transparent as its waters. Our old house followed the curve of the bank, in segments, like a train, each room and screened porch added on, one by one, decade by decade.

When I think of that time, I picture the four of us wading in the shallows, admiring our reflections in the glassy, motionless lake. Then something—a pebble, a raindrop—breaks the surface and shatters the mirror. A ripple reaches the distant bank. Our years of bad luck begin.

That was how Margaret would have thought. My sister was the poet.

I was Miss One-Thing-After-the-Next. Which is how I remember what happened.

But that's not how it happened at all. One thing happened, then everything else, like a domino falling and setting off a collapse that snakes out toward the horizon and spills over into the future.

• • •

IF ALL THE CLOCKS AND CALENDARS VANISHED, CHILDREN WOULD still know when Sunday came. They would still feel that suck of dead air, that hollow vacuum created when time slips behind a curtain, when the minutes quit their orderly tick and ooze away, one by one. Colors are muted, a jellylike haze hovers and blurs the landscape. The phone doesn't ring, and the rest of the world hides and conspires to pretend that everyone's baking cookies or watching the game on TV. Then Monday arrives, and the comforting racket starts up all over again.

Even before that Sunday, I was glad to see the day end. It wasn't that I liked school so much, but the weekends lasted forever. The loneliness, the hours to fill with books, homework, computer, watching old films with my sister, if she was in the mood. Silence, then the Sunday sounds of our house by the lake. My mother playing the piano, my dad's prehistoric Selectric.

That Sunday, that first Sunday in May, was so warm I couldn't help wondering: Was it simply a beautiful day, or a symptom of global warning? Even the trees looked uncomfortable, naked and embarrassed, as if they were all simultaneously having that dream in which you look down and realize you've forgotten to put on your clothes.

Two Cleopatras in our royal barge, my sister and I reclined and let our little rowboat drift out onto the lake. Margaret arched her shoulders, flung one arm over the side, and trailed her fingertips in the water. It was one of those actressy gestures she'd copied from the classic black-and-white movies to which she was addicted. She liked me to watch them with her, and we were allowed to stay up, because our mother said we would learn more from *Some Like It*

Hot than from a year of school. It was often hard to tell what our mother meant, exactly, except that we learned to flutter our lashes and say, "What's a girl to do?" in breathy little-girl whispers.

One thing Margaret and I had in common was: we could do imitations. We knew whole scenes by heart, like the end of *Flying Deuces*, when Hardy is killed in a plane crash and then reincarnated as a horse with a black mustache and a bowler hat. Laurel's so happy to see him he throws his arms around Ollie—that is, the horse possessed by Ollie's grumpy spirit.

Sometimes Margaret would do a gesture or line and ask me what film it was from. Her silvery laughter was my prize for getting it right. The only rowboat scene I knew was the one in which Montgomery Clift pushes Shelly Winters into the water. And I was pretty certain that wasn't what Margaret was doing.

Margaret said, "This is heaven."

I wished I could have been like her instead of the kind of person who said, "Don't you ever worry about the polar ice caps melting?"

"Debbie Downer," said Margaret. "Give yourself a break. It's Sunday, Nico. Take a day off." Squinting, she aimed her smoke rings so that they encircled the sun like foggy auras.

Margaret had promised our parents she wouldn't smoke. Mom's parents and Dad's father had all died young of smoking-related causes. Both of our parents used to smoke. Their friends had started dying. The new weapon in the arsenal of Mom and Dad's War on Smoking was some bad news we'd gotten that fall: Margaret had a heart condition. A mild one, but I worried.

She'd fainted the first and last time Mom talked us into doing yoga with her. I still have a photo my father took that day on the lawn, of the three of us doing downward-facing dog or some other mortifying position that, our mother had convinced herself, was helping her arthritis. Margaret, Mom, and I are bent till our heads nearly touch the ground, like those snakes that, Margaret told me, bite their tails and roll after the children they swallow whole. Planted apart for balance, our legs take up most of the photo, downward-facing croquet hoops of descending sizes. What the picture doesn't show is that, seconds after it was taken, Margaret collapsed in a pile of leaves. At first we'd thought she was joking.

Our pediatrician, Dr. Viscott, ran some tests and said that Margaret should eat well, exercise, don't smoke. That stutter on her heart graph was something they'd keep their eye on.

Margaret knew she could smoke around me. Smoking was the least of the things she trusted me to keep secret.

From across the lake, we heard our mother practicing the spooky Chopin waltz that always made me think of ballroom dance music for ghosts. She kept making mistakes and starting over again. She'd wanted to be a pianist, she'd gone to music school, but she changed her plans when she met my dad and they ran off to be hippies. Margaret had found a snapshot of them picking soybeans on a commune in northern California. Long hair, overalls, bandannas, a Jesus beard on Dad.

For years our mom had had a job writing liner notes for inserts in classical CDs. Now her fingers were sprouting lumps, but still she tried to learn whatever piano piece she was writing about.

"You know what's crazy?" I said. "Every time you blow a smoke ring, Mom hits a wrong note. Maybe she does have ESP."

"Maybe *I* do," said Margaret.

Our mother often boasted about her mind-reading powers. I think she meant it to scare us out of doing anything she'd disapprove of. She liked to say her own ancestors would have burned her at the stake. Both our parents were the rogue only children of starchy New England families, so naturally they'd fallen extra hard for the whole peace-and-love agenda, even though, by the time they joined, the hippie movement was mostly over. They'd counted on the world becoming one big organic farm, and when that didn't happen, they'd sort of had to scramble.

Our house had been Mom's parents' summer place. She'd inherited it when her father died, just before Margaret was born. Puritan family portraits decorated the upstairs bathroom. Mom thought it was funny to hang them there, but the glowering dead men and women had delayed my toilet training until Dad figured it out and briefly turned their faces to the wall.

"There's a lot Mom doesn't know." Margaret let another smoky ring slip from between her lips. "Okay. Who am I, Nico?"

"The caterpillar from *Alice in Wonderland*?"

"Beautiful," Margaret said.

I braced myself for the crash that came when Mom made so many mistakes she banged her fist on the piano. Then heavy silence weighed on the air, scooping out a depression I imagined filling with the rattling of Dad's electric typewriter.

It was pitiful how the computer age had bypassed our father completely. He couldn't even swipe his card at the supermarket checkout. Margaret and I had to do it for him, while the checkers smiled sweetly and wished we were dead so they could be our handsome father's wife or girlfriend or daughter. Oddly, Dad's backwardness was never counted among the traits that Margaret, the lover of everything old—films, jazz songs, vintage postcards and clothes—inherited from him. Margaret said she was born too late, and it did seem a little strange, to live in the twenty-first century and long for the 1930s and '40s and '50s.

In our family, everything was neatly divided up. Margaret and Mom were the musical ones. Margaret and Dad were the beauties. Margaret and I were the mimics. Dad and I were the thinkers. I got A's in math. I liked knowing why things happened and the order in which they occurred. My teachers said that I might be a scientist some day. Or so they learned from the aptitude test they'd made me take in sixth grade. It was true that when I surfed the Web, I liked following the links that led from marine biology to ecological disaster.

No one had ever suggested that Margaret take an aptitude test. Everyone knew she was going to be a singer. My father used to say that he and I always wanted to know what everything meant, but that my mother and Margaret only cared about how it sounded.

Goldengrove, Dad's bookstore, was on the corner of Main and West Street. His female customers worshipped him, they'd buy anything he suggested. His real ambition was to write. Ever since I could remember, he'd spent evenings and Sundays working on a book about how people in different cultures and eras imagined the end of the world. He said he planned to call it *Eschatology for Dummies*.

Water kissed the side of the boat.

"Sing something," I told Margaret. In the fall she was leaving for Oberlin with a full scholarship in music.

"Like what?" she asked, as if she didn't know.

At the Senior Show, she'd sung "My Funny Valentine." She'd

sung it half-speed, smoky, low. She'd gotten a standing ovation. Mom was the first one out of her seat and the last to stop applauding, even though she hated the song and had lobbied hard against it.

"Why *that* one?" Mom had asked Margaret. "There are plenty of beautiful standards. Sing 'Little Girl Blue' if you really want to depress the shit out of everyone, honey. But 'My Funny Valentine'? Some patronizing jerk telling the poor ugly duckling he doesn't care if her mouth's a little weak. *Laughable. Unphotographable.* He's doing her a *favor*, even though *her figure isn't Greek?*"

"What does that mean?" I'd said.

"It means she has a body," said Mom. "A normal female body."

Margaret said, "It's a love song, okay? It's not what *I* think love is. Or you, Mom. It's what one person thinks love is all about."

"One *person?*" said Mom. "One *guy*. Don't kid yourself."

I didn't care if Mom liked the song. I'd heard it as a promise. Some boy would come along some day and love me for myself, even if I was unphotographable, or a few pounds overweight. Being somebody's laughable valentine was better than being no one's, funny or not.

Margaret eased down her bathing-suit straps to get a head start on her tan. I was wearing the sort of one-piece suit that magazines called slimming. I yanked the elastic over where my white, dimpled thighs popped out.

"Am I fat?" I asked Margaret. "You have to tell me."

"You're perfect, Nico."

I said, "You didn't look."

"I don't have to," she said. "I know what you look like. I looked like you do when I was your age."

"You were fat four years ago? I don't remember that."

"You. Are. Not. Fat," said Margaret.

"So what you're saying," I asked, though I was pretty sure she wasn't saying that at all, "is that in four years I'll look like you?"

"Trust me on this," Margaret said. "Whether you want to or not."

People told us we looked alike, but I couldn't see it. Margaret was the beautiful sister, willowy and blond. The lake breeze carried her perfect smell. She smelled like cookies baking. She claimed it wasn't perfume. It was her essence, I guessed. I was the pudgy, awkward sister. I still smelled dusty, like a kid.

Our parents had given us the wrong names. Margaret should have been Nico, I should have been anything else. They told us they'd named Margaret after a line in a poem. They claimed they'd just liked the sound of Nico, but I didn't believe them.

Dad still had his record player and his record collection. That was how Margaret discovered the Velvet Underground and Nico with her chalky, disappointed voice. It was strange how she sounded like Margaret, only hollow and checked-out, and with a foreign accent that made it seem she was learning the words as she sang them.

Margaret had rented, on DVD, a documentary about Nico, and we'd watched the sad story of the German superstar who flamed out after her fifteen minutes of fame. My sister was silent, all the way through. I didn't like how she sat jackknifed forward, studying, taking lessons.

When I'd asked Mom if they'd named me after *that* Nico, she'd hesitated, then said, "Do you really think Daddy and I would name our child after some Wagnerian zombie junkie? By the way, that's another hideous song. Don't be anyone's mirror, darling."

I leaned over and felt the water. *It* knew that summer wasn't here.

"Please," I asked Margaret. "Sing 'My Funny Valentine.' Just for me, just once."

With a crisp, thumb-and-forefinger flick she'd learned from some '40s detective, Margaret skipped her cigarette across the lake. Then she let her eyelids droop and began to sing.

She always sang it differently, but it was always pure sex. When she sang, "*Stay little valentine, stay,*" it sounded like honey, like grown-up female code-speak for "Please, have sex with me, please." I'd wondered how she could have sung it like that in front of the whole school, and how the teachers and parents could have given her a standing ovation. Near the end, someone's disgusting father actually sobbed out loud. Didn't it cross their minds that she could never have sung it that way unless she was having sex with her boyfriend, Aaron?

Maybe they weren't applauding Margaret, but rather the chance that someone from Emersonville might have the talent to leave the last place on earth where no one had a cell phone. Ever since 9/11, yuppie families had been fleeing the city, buying houses around the lake. They said they had to get used to it, but they'd learned to love the country: no cell phones, no BlackBerries, a slower way of life. Throughout the civilized world, teenagers lived on their phones and text-messaged from room to room. But the nearest towers were in Albany or Pittsfield, and my sister and I and our friends at school were stuck in a time-warp bubble. No wonder Margaret was obsessed with the past. We lived in it, in a way. Some day, I promised myself, I would move to Boston or New

York. Margaret and I could handle the city, even if our parents couldn't.

"*Yet you're my favorite work of art.*" Margaret sang to the lake and the trees and the sun. I knew that, in her secret heart, she was singing to Aaron. It was strange, how the music changed everything, so that, note by note, Mirror Lake began to look like one of Aaron's paintings.

At the same Senior Show, Aaron did a PowerPoint presentation of his paintings of the lake in different lights and seasons. The first painting was of the Fourth of July, of colored stars exploding and wobbling in the black water. Somehow everyone recognized that they weren't ordinary landscapes, but something special and new, as if an old master had decided to paint on velvet. The audience gasped each time a new image appeared, until they heard themselves and giggled. Aaron waited, then clicked on the next image, and the crowd gasped again.

Margaret was the singer, Aaron the artist. They were the glamour couple, their radiance outshone the feeble gleam of the football captain and his slutty cheerleader girlfriend. They were superheroes with superpowers. Aaron saw more than a normal person. Once, when he and Margaret and I were riding around, he'd braked and shown us a grove of orange mushrooms like fingers wriggling out of the moss. Margaret was always the first to hear thunder, or a mouse in the wall, or some amazing Billie Holliday phrase I'd never noticed even though she'd played me "God Bless the Child" a thousand times before.

"*Is your figure less than Greek?*" Margaret sailed the line over the lake, and I tried not to think about how our mother had mocked it.

Margaret and Aaron were in love. I was their alibi. Margaret would tell my parents she was taking me to the movies, and I'd go to the theater, and she and Aaron would pick me up when the film was over.

On the way home I'd tell Margaret about the film, in case Mom or Dad asked. But they never did. They always said lying was worse than whatever the lie was about. I already knew that even if they were right, you couldn't live in a family without a lie or two as a cushion between you and the people you loved. If you were lucky, you might not need a big lie, maybe not even one as large as Margaret smoking and having sex with her boyfriend.

The first time Margaret and Aaron went out, Aaron came in to meet us. Mom and Dad intercepted him at the door, a body block they intended to seem welcoming and friendly. He shook hands, starting with Mom, who winced. An electrical current arced between Aaron and my father, sparking with more information than either wanted the other to have. By the time Aaron got to me, his palm was so wet that I had to stop myself from wiping mine on my jeans.

The next morning, Dad said, "There's something squirrelly about the guy. As if he had a secret acorn stash, and the thing he really gets off on is not telling the other squirrels where he's got it hidden."

Margaret said, "You say that about every guy I go out with. Every guy I bring home, it's like *Romeo and Juliet*." In fact she'd only dated one guy, junior year, and it hadn't lasted. A senior with a bolt through his ear who made everyone call him Turbo. "Maybe you think that any guy who would want to hang out with me must have something wrong with him."

"Quite the opposite," said Dad.

Mom said, "I know what your father means. The kid's too good-looking. Little Adonis carries himself like a vessel of some precious oil he'll drip on you if you're lucky."

Margaret said, "How strange that someone who married Dad should hate someone for being handsome."

"We don't *hate* him," said Mom. "*Hate* is a little extreme, dear."

"That's enough," our father said. "The kid's got a screw loose, is all."

It embarrassed us when our dad used lame, old-fashioned phrases like that. Something's not somebody's cup of tea. That's how the cookie crumbles.

"*What* screw loose?" Margaret asked.

Dad said, "I don't know, sweetheart. The one that holds it all together."

"*Is your mouth a little weak, when you open it to speak, are you smart?*"

Margaret's voice rose and lingered lightly on "smart." She made it sound like fun, like flirtation, not like a list of qualities some guy is telling his girlfriend she lacks.

Mom and Dad told Margaret she couldn't smoke, but not that she couldn't see Aaron. They always said it was a mistake to forbid kids to do something, unless you wanted to make it their heart's desire. They often talked as if all four of us were involved in some group child-raising project, as if treating us like semi-adults would make us do what they wanted. But they gave Margaret such a hard time about Aaron—Little Adonis this, screw loose that—that it was easier to pretend that Margaret and I were going to the movies.

Besides, Margaret liked conspiracies, codes, secret signals, her version of the tactics with which the brave Resistance couriers outfoxed the Nazis in her beloved French World War II films. We had a system worked out: Margaret and I would drive most of the way to town in Mom's car and meet Aaron at a designated spot. We'd park Mom's car behind a barn and get into Aaron's van, and they'd drop me off at the mildewy-smelling, fake-retro Rialto.

"Don't change a hair for me, not if you care for me." Our little rowboat caught a current and turned, then stopped turning.

Sometimes I tried to see Aaron from our parents' point of view. *Squirrelly* didn't seem like the word for a sweet-tempered guy who, like my sister, seemed to throw off a golden light. *Screw loose?* Margaret was right. Our parents would have hated any boy she brought home.

Aaron often had paint on his jeans and his hands, and once, when he showed up with a comet of blue across his forehead, I nearly reached over to wipe it off, but Margaret got there first. Aaron treated me like a person, unlike the boys in my school, to whom I was a window through which they kept looking for a hotter girl with bigger breasts.

After the movie, Aaron would ask me to imitate the stars. My Julia Roberts, especially, cracked the two of them up. He called me "kid," which he'd probably got from a film he'd watched with Margaret. They liked the same things—jazz, old movies, art—though I never knew if Aaron had before they'd started going out.

"Stay little valentine, stay."

Lazily, the boat revolved, until Margaret's blond hair was back-lit. When I looked into the sun, my sister blazed like a candle. Her eyes were shut tight, and I could tell that her mind was empty except for the music.

The last wisps of that *"Each day is Valentine's Day"* hung over the water, like the haze of heat and mosquitoes that would shimmer there when it was really July instead of this fake summer day.

I said, "Are you seeing Aaron tonight?" I wondered what was playing at the Rialto. Margaret and I listened to Mom practice so long without a mistake that I almost relaxed.

"I don't know," Margaret said. "We had a fight this morning on the phone."

"A serious fight? About what?"

"Nothing. Nothing important. Aaron can be a little nuts."

"Nuts meaning . . ."

"Freaky," Margaret said. "You've got to watch out for him sometimes."

"Freaky how? Watch out how?"

Margaret had something she wanted to say, but she wasn't going to say it.

"A screw loose?" I said.

"Right. A screw loose." It was a relief to be off the subject of Aaron and onto the subject of Dad.

"Anyway," she said, "how serious can it be? Aaron and I are out of here in September. He'll fall in love with the first girl who takes off her clothes in art class."

"Won't you miss him?" I asked.

"I already miss everyone. You, Mom, Dad. Aaron, I guess. And I'm not even gone yet."

I said, "Then shut up about it, okay?"

"I'm sorry. You know I'll miss you, Nico. You know I'm sad about leaving."

I had decided to forget about Margaret leaving and just enjoy the summer. Last summer, I'd been an intern at my old nursery school, and the summer before that, I'd gone to the town's recreation program and a week of soccer camp. This summer, I planned to read, watch movies, go swimming with Margaret, maybe catch a fish or two that Dad could cook for dinner, and not waste one precious minute before she left me alone with our parents.

With our eyes closed and the sun on our eyelids, I felt I could ask a question I could hardly let myself think, face to face.

"Can I ask you something?"

"Surprise me," she said.

"Are you and Aaron having sex?"

She lit another cigarette. I was sorry I'd asked.

"I thought I said, 'Surprise me.' "

"Well, are you?"

Margaret spun a smoky doughnut from between her parted lips. Finally she said, "Yes. But you knew that, Nico."

We'd certainly never discussed it. She and Aaron never even held hands when I was around. Sometimes I'd imagine them making out, until I'd begin to feel a strange sensation, like something inside me dissolving from the center out. Was that sex? I didn't know. I liked it, and I didn't. I knew it was sick and perverted. Not the feeling so much as the thinking about my sister and her boyfriend.

For a moment I was distracted by the red branches inside my eyelids. The sun was trying to trick us into believing that the afternoon would last longer than it would. With the first hint of dusk, Margaret would want to go inside. Once she told me that twilight was when the spirits of the dead surfaced from the lake and made party plans for the night. She loved telling me ghost stories. I knew, that is, I *usually* knew, that she was trying to scare me. But what made it scary was that part of her believed it.

"What's it like?" I persisted.

"What's what like?"

"Sex."

"God, Nico. I can't believe you're asking me this."

After a long time Margaret said, "You know how when we go out for ice cream, you never know which flavor you want?"

After they picked me up at the theater, we'd drive to the Dairy Divine. I always took forever deciding, until I'd finally give up, give *in*, and settle on something awful. I knew it was only ice cream. But the lumpy cherry vanilla and the gross butterscotch mocha raisin seemed like a frozen symbol of everything wrong with my life. Aaron and Margaret never got impatient or made me feel rushed or embarrassed. Margaret said there was something holy about indecision and regret. She told me the French expression—the spirit of the staircase—for the voice that catches up with you, minutes after the fact, to make fun of whatever you said and come up with the perfect answer you didn't think of. We even had our own code phrase: SOS, we called it.

Margaret always ordered pistachio, which tasted like dish detergent. She thought the color was funny. She liked the way the maraschino-cherry green dye stained her lips and tongue, and when she finished, she'd smile at us, leaving me and Aaron to marvel at how someone could look so beautiful with a green mouth and teeth. Sometimes the kid behind the counter would offer her a napkin as if he wanted to ask her to sign it.

Aaron ordered coffee swirl, sometimes butter pecan. Margaret let him taste hers, and she'd have small bites of his. Something about the easy, intimate way they traded tastes was what first made me begin to think they'd had sex while I'd been at the movies.

When had we switched from talking about sex to talking about ice cream? I said, "I know it drives Aaron crazy. Even though he's nice about it, he really hates it, right?"

Margaret shrugged. "Sex is the opposite of not being able to make up your mind. You don't *have* a mind. You don't have to think. You know *exactly* what you want."

What could Margaret possibly mean? She was getting like Mom. I thought, I'll never eat ice cream again.

I said, "We forgot the sunblock."

Margaret said, "You look good with a tan."

"Mom will have a fit," I said. "Skin cancer, remember?"

"Mom will have a fit for a change." Margaret leaned over the boat. "Can you see the bottom? Look, Nico. Look at that."

I looked until we almost tipped. A dark shape flitted by.

"See what that was?"

"Yes," I lied.

"You didn't," she said. "But so what. Did you know there's a lake in Macedonia where the fish are seventy million years old? Maybe if we saw all the way down, we'd see fish that have been here that long."

"Each fish lives seventy million years?" Ever since we were little, she'd made up scientific facts. She told me that if everyone in the world wore their watches upside down, time would run backward. She said that turkeys were so stupid they drowned in the rain, and that you could sharpen your hearing by walking around with your eyes shut. The problem was, some of it was true. Maybe there *were* fish that old living in a lake like ours. Maybe that was why I was drawn to science. I liked the idea of an authority I could go to for a ruling on the stories my sister told.

Margaret sighed. "The species, Nico. Not each individual trout."

"Joke," I said.

A shadow darkened the water. Last summer, algae had begun to grow—Dad pointed out the obvious irony—on the surface of Mirror Lake. By last August, it was an eco-threat, and now the town was watching to see if the bloom would return. In a few weeks, they were having a town meeting about the pond scum. The *phytoplankton*. It was a word I liked knowing.

"Not if the phytoplankton chokes off their air supply," I said.

"Listen to you." Margaret exhaled through her nose.

This turn in the conversation was making me feel gloomy. I would never be poetic and beautiful like Margaret. I would never find a boy to call me his funny valentine.

I told myself to keep quiet. I said, "You shouldn't smoke."

"Why not? One cigarette's not going to kill me. God, you *do* sound like Mom."

"That's three," I said. "Three cigarettes in an hour."

Margaret gave me a long, unreadable look. Was it anger? Affection? The sun in her eyes? She stood. The boat rocked slightly.

"Smoke this." She smiled and gave me a funny salute she'd copied from Ginger Rogers. Then she dove into the water.

I watched her swim toward the landing. I thought of the seventy-million-year-old fish looking up toward the light and seeing the sleek graceful dolphin streaming just above it. I would have to row home by myself. Exercise was good for me if I wanted to look like Margaret. I needed to rest a while first. Sunspots ticked the back of my eyelids.

I sat up and looked for Margaret. Usually, she lay on the dock, sunning herself and waiting to help me tie up the boat. Maybe she'd gotten a phone call. Something made me shiver, as if I'd floated over a cold spot.

I rowed in as fast as I could and, panting, dragged the boat onto the bank. Our mother was still practicing that spooky Chopin waltz. I couldn't find Margaret anywhere. Still a little breathless, I kept on calling her name.

I had to walk around in front of our mother and wave both arms until she noticed and stopped playing.

I said, "Have you seen Margaret?"

"No," she said.

"I can't find her," I said.

"I'm sure she's fine," she said. "Why wouldn't she be?"

"I can't find her anywhere." The jagged edge in my voice tore away the cobwebby trance she'd been in.

Mom stood up from the piano bench. She said, "Where *is* she, Nico? Go *find* her."

Two

❧

NONE OF US KNEW. NO ONE KNEW. THAT WAS WHAT EVERYONE
kept saying. First we didn't know what had happened, then we
didn't know *how* it happened, and then we still couldn't understand why, why Margaret, why our family, though it wasn't *like
us* to say, "Why us?" What did it mean to be *like us*? What did *us*
mean without Margaret?

They searched for Margaret, they dragged the lake. Parked
beside the water, the police car kept flashing its beacon. It wasn't
night, it wasn't dark, they weren't speeding to a crime scene.
Maybe the spinning light was meant to reassure us. Help was on
the way.

All the time the divers were working, my parents didn't let me
go outside. We sat on the porch, listening to the men shout from
boat to shore and watching a trick of the light that made the red
beacon seem to revolve on the white porch ceiling. My parents
each held one of my hands with a steady pressure: half comfort,
half restraint. They were afraid I'd see something that might scar

me for life. But I was already scarred for life, and I couldn't look at the lake. I couldn't imagine letting my skin touch its filthy water. I'd been planning to go to the town's algae-problem meeting and show off what I'd learned on the Internet. Let the phytoplankton bloom. Let the fish strangle and die.

We watched the beacon until my father said the light was driving him nuts and went to ask the cops to turn it off. Even after the light blinked out, a red shadow stained the ceiling. Some time later my father came in, and we took one look at him and knew that they had found her.

Still, every breath I took was a prayer. Let my sister be alive. I would devote my life to saving the lake if it didn't kill her.

I kept hoping it was all a mistake, that she'd gone into town to meet Aaron. But I knew that hadn't happened. Mom had suggested we phone him. Just like that, she'd said, "We should probably call Aaron." What had all that play-acting been about, those sisterly trips to the movies? That my parents had known all along made me furious, for a second. A second was all we could afford. We had to be good to each other.

"I'll call him," I'd said. I didn't want him hearing that Margaret was lost from someone who thought he had a screw loose.

"Wait a minute," Aaron's mother said when I'd asked if he was there. She'd shouted his name, as if across a distance. It took him a while to come to the phone.

I said, "Have you seen Margaret?"

"Kid?" he said. "No, I haven't. What's up?"

"You haven't seen her anywhere?"

He heard the pleading in my voice.

He said, "Should I come over?"

The truth was, I would have liked him to. But I said, "Better not."

Almost as soon as they found her, the doorbell started ringing. The neighbors who brought over food had the grim, determined expressions of people seeing loved ones off on a journey. There were platters of sandwiches, casseroles of mac and cheese, bowls of tempting salads and fruit, but we weren't tempted. Dad cooked, it helped him, just as it helped my parents to focus on me, just as it helped me that I had them. They were careful of me, they protected me. I never once heard the word *autopsy*, though I was pretty sure it happened.

My mother and father expanded into larger versions of themselves. The decisions they made, the small things they did, made me glad that they were my parents. They never even considered the corny funeral limo. My father would drive us in his Jeep, just the three of us without some stranger in black eyeballing us in the mirror. The only bad move they almost made was: Dad wanted to play a tape of Margaret singing "Amazing Grace." It was part of her application portfolio for a college that seemed to want students who could smoke beloved hymns into smoldering torch songs.

Mom said, "Are you out of your mind? They'll have to wheel us out on gurneys." I was relieved when my dad backed down. I couldn't have stood hearing my sister sing about how she was lost, but now she was found.

I was surprised when my mother told me I didn't have to go. She said, "Nico, it's up to you to decide whether or not you want to say good-bye to your sister that way." I was still bursting into tears when anyone said the word *sister*. And when someone said *your sister*, I wanted that person dead. I didn't want to go, but what would I do? Stay home? Go to the movies and wait for someone to pick me up?

The day of the funeral was windy and cold. I imagined Margaret stage-managing the scene for maximum tragic drama. I wondered if the newly dead were allowed to control the weather as a consolation for never again feeling it on their faces.

All day, my parents and I clung together. We'd been hugging more than we had in our whole lives until then. Not hugging so much as leaning. We were so physically *tired*. I kept wanting to tell Margaret how goofy Mom and Dad were acting, until I'd remember why.

My clearest memory of the day is of my father's scratchy jacket. I burrowed into it so hard that the wool left welts on my face. The graveside ceremony was conducted by the minister from the Unitarian Church, to which my parents went a few times and then quit because Mom liked to sleep in on Sundays. I kept my eyes shut the whole time and blocked out the service by chanting nonsense inside my head. I tried to imagine a beautiful place. Margaret had taught me to do that when I went to the dentist. But nothing worked, there was nowhere to go. Not the lake, not the rowboat, not Times Square, not Paris.

Everyone said, "I'm sorry." Everyone hugged me and wept. My best friends, Samantha and Violet, were practically sobbing their eyes out. I wanted to tell them to quit it. They couldn't have known that their tears were contagious. The minute I stopped crying, I'd look at them and start. Mom told me that all I had to say was, "Thank you for coming." I repeated it like a tourist who knows one phrase of a foreign language.

We were heading toward our car when our path was blocked

by a tall, good-looking, blond kid wearing a tan suit. His face was blotchy, his eyes were the rubbed raw pink of pencil erasers.

"I'm so sorry," he said.

"Thank you for coming," I said.

Only then did Aaron emerge from his smeary disguise. As he turned to shake my father's hand, I was afraid that my parents would be as mean to him as they were when Margaret was alive. I was less concerned about Aaron than about what *I* might do. Aren't you *sorry?* I'd have to ask. Don't you wish you could have back your little problem of not liking Margaret's boyfriend?

My mother threw her arms around Aaron, Dad thumped his shoulder, and I had to walk away because it was so much worse than what I'd imagined. I leaned against the car and focused on a bottle cap glinting in the wet parking lot gravel. Who'd drunk that Diet Coke? A mourner? A cemetery worker? Cheating couples? Goth nerds who haunted the graveyard for fun? That was Margaret's new social life, the people she got to hang out with.

Someone distracted Mom and Dad, and Aaron came over to me. Without my parents around to complicate things, I was simply glad to see him. He hugged me for a second, then backed off and patted my arm as if it were a puppy that might bite.

He said, "I promise not to ask how you are if you don't ask me."

"Deal," I said.

Now, it seemed, *my* tears were contagious. I looked down at the bottle cap. When I looked up, Aaron was leaning on the Jeep. At the same moment, we noticed our backs were soaking wet. We tried to stand on our own, but we were both too tired, and we slumped against the car and let the water seep through.

I said, "I heard you torched your paintings. I thought that was totally cool."

My mom's friend Sally told her that after they found Margaret, Aaron stacked all his paintings of Mirror Lake in his backyard and squirted them with charcoal lighter.

"Thanks," he said. "I couldn't look at them. It was like living with the portrait of the serial killer who murdered your whole family. I mean, *my* whole family."

I said, "I understand. It was genius."

He said, "I wish you'd say that to my parents. They're trying to make me see a shrink."

"I heard that, too," I said.

"A *grief counselor*." Aaron sneered. "Some asshole who never met Margaret."

I wished he hadn't said "grief." Or "Margaret." I looked over at my parents, embracing another stranger.

Aaron said, "I went once. Just to shut them up. There's a guy here in Emersonville. The dude was wearing a lab coat. He looked like a *vet*. He asked if I wanted to talk about my feelings. I said no. We sat there with the clock ticking, and then he said we had to wait until I was *ready* to talk. He'd see me in a week. In your dreams, I thought. But here's the crazy part. As I was leaving, the guy said, 'I feel I have to tell you, I heard your friend sing at the Senior Show. My daughter is in your class.' "

"Who's his daughter?" I asked.

"Who cares?" Aaron said. "Are you getting this, Nico? The guy said he'd never heard anything like the way Margaret sang 'My Funny Valentine' at the Senior Show. He said it moved him to tears. He told me he'd actually sobbed out loud."

"Wait a minute," I said. "Tears? The *pervert*? They sent you to see the pervert dad who cried at the Senior Show?"

Aaron nodded. "You got it. I *ran* out of the guy's office. I couldn't wait to tell Margaret about the insane coincidence of their sending me to see the slob who'd blubbered during her song. I imagined her saying maybe he wasn't a slob, maybe he'd been really moved. Maybe it was the power of art, maybe he would have cried if he'd heard Billie Holliday. I was halfway to my car when I remembered why I couldn't tell her."

I said, "You imagined her saying all that?"

"Word for word. But of course it wasn't her. So where was it coming from? Me? Or *was* she talking to me?"

I said, "Stuff like that happens to me all the time."

Aaron said, "The worst part is, there's no one I can tell."

I said, "You just told *me*."

"That I did," he said.

We saw my parents approaching. Aaron started talking faster. "Listen. One day this summer, let's go for a ride. Hang out."

That would be nice, I would have said, if I could have spoken. That was what the staircase spirit told me I should have said. The spirit whispered, "By summer, he won't recognize you on the street."

I nodded like a bobble-head doll as Aaron backed away. Then my parents scooped me up, and we got into the car.

Aaron faded into the rainy background, speckled with the blossomlike faces of kids from Margaret's school. I despised them for being alive when my sister was dead. A winnowing had taken place, like picking teams for a game. Everyone else had wound up on the team of the living, leaving Margaret behind, chosen last, to play on the larger but more unpopular loser team of the dead.

"Poor kid." My mother meant Aaron.

"Poor everybody," said Dad.

I DIDN'T HAVE TO GO BACK TO SCHOOL. MY PARENTS WORKED IT out so I could skip final exams and get the A's I would have gotten anyway.

Samantha and Violet called to tell me again how sorry they were. I knew they meant it, they cared about me. I hated the sound of their voices. Every time the phone rang, I still thought it might be Margaret.

They were the ones who told me that Margaret's graduation had featured a blown-up portrait of her onstage, an angel beaming at everyone who came up to get a diploma. Her friends and teachers and Aaron all gave tearful speeches, and they showed the video of her performing "My Funny Valentine" at the Senior Show. It seemed like an odd song to sing at your own memorial service.

The principal had called to invite us and ask if we wanted to speak. Everyone said they understood why we didn't go, we needed to heal our own way. Some people probably thought we were weak. But I was glad not to have to sit there, trying not to turn and stare at everyone trying not to turn and stare at us.

The summer yawned before me, a pit of boredom and pain. A dull pressure knuckled inside my chest, and I began to wonder if heart problems ran in our family. Sometimes at night I woke to a hammering inside my chest, as if my heart were trying all the exit routes from my body. I pictured my parents coming in to find I'd died in my sleep. I was glad the idea of a heart attack frightened me so badly. As much as I missed Margaret, I didn't want to join her.

My father cooked our favorite meals. He'd always been a good cook, but now the less we ate, the harder he worked. He made chicken pot pies with buttery crusts, lamb with flageolet beans, swordfish pounded thin and fried with bread crumbs, capers, and lemon. He never complained when the food went back to the kitchen untouched. Everything tasted like Styrofoam, and we had to sit perfectly still if we didn't want to catch sight of Margaret's place at the table. There was always too much food and not enough air in the room. Our efforts at conversation were punctuated by sighs that were partly sadness and partly just trying to breathe.

One night at dinner, Mom said, "Nico, darling, why do you keep touching your chest?"

"My heart hurts," I said, and everything stopped, as if I'd dropped a heavy plate, still rattling, on the table.

"Everyone's heart hurts, honey," said Dad.

Mom silenced him with a look.

"Your heart?" she said. "Your actual *heart?*"

"Right here," I said. "I think so."

"We'll get it checked out," she said. "I'll ask Dawson to recommend a specialist." Dawson was the doctor in Albany who'd diagnosed Mom's arthritis. "I need to talk to him, anyway. I think my hands are getting worse."

She held up her hands and rotated them: palms out, palms back. Her knuckles were swollen, but they didn't seem worse than before.

"Give it a few weeks," Dad said. "This may not be the best time to tell about your hands."

My mother said, "I think I can distinguish one kind of pain from another."

Dad said, "Actually, there was a piece on the news about that medication Dawson prescribed."

"It's dangerous, I hope," said Mom.

"How much are you taking?" Dad took off his glasses and rubbed the bridge of his nose.

"Not enough," said Mom. "He never gives me enough to help."

Dad said, "Be careful, Daisy. They've taken a lot of that crap off the market. The good news is, you lose the joint pain. The bad news is, you lose your life. The stroke, the blood clots, the—"

My mom said, "The pain in my hands *is* my life."

"What medicine?" I said. "Stroke? Blood clots? Mom shouldn't—"

"Don't worry, she won't," Dad said.

Mom said, "Maybe he can switch me to something safer. Anyhow, I'll call him. He can recommend someone for Nico."

Dad said, "The chances of something happening to Nico are statistically less than lightning striking twice in the same place."

"Lightning *does* strike twice." I said. "It hits the highest point. If there's one tree in a field—"

"You're fine," said Dad.

"I'm *not* fine," I said.

"That's not what I meant," Dad said.

"It was treatable," said Mom. "Henry, my God, it could have been treated."

That was something I hadn't known, and wished I hadn't found out.

"If we'd only paid attention," Mom said. "If we'd only been more aggressive . . ."

Aggressive was the last word I would have used about my parents. They could have prevented this. Margaret would be alive.

I said, "Why don't you make an appointment for me to see a real doctor in the city?" I was sorry as soon as I said it. I didn't want to know.

"There's nothing to worry about," said Dad.

"Okay," said Mom. "I'll get a name. We'll make an appointment."

We went back to not eating. Dad had made edamame. I unzipped a pod, and teased the membrane off one bean, then another. I was getting thinner, but it wasn't what I'd wanted when I used to stand in front of the mirror, inhaling till my ribs ached.

My mother said, "Speaking of health concerns . . . Nico, aren't you losing a little weight? The last thing we need around here is some life-threatening eating disorder."

My father put his hand on her arm.

"Daisy," he said. "Relax."

"Relax?" she said. "You're kidding."

"No one's eating," he said. "We don't have to torture Nico about food. We didn't when—"

"When what?" I said.

"Radishes?" my father said. "Remember the radish diet?"

So they'd known about that, too. How could I have thought it was a secret when for days I ate nothing but radishes and ramen noodles for dinner? My parents never even glanced at what I put on my plate. Maybe it was part of their theory that anything they forbade would become our heart's desire. And maybe they were right, because the diets never lasted. Mom and Dad often mentioned how twisted our society was for making young women want to be thin. They'd pretended that they were just talking and not giving us warning advice.

"It's not like that now," I said. "I'm never hungry."

"Make sure you drink plenty of water," said Mom.

"I do," I lied. Then we sat there.

What had we talked about before? Margaret had done all the talking. Now there was nothing to say. We were the wallflowers left behind when Margaret waltzed away.

Finally, I said, "You know what Violet told me? At graduation, the picture they used was Margaret's yearbook photo. You know the one." I bugged my eyes. "Margaret despised it. She told me that the photographer had gotten the kids to focus by saying, 'Look at my hand!' and every portrait caught the person at the moment of noticing that the guy was missing two fingers."

My parents pretended that Margaret hadn't told us the story. Because that was what we did then. We talked about Margaret as if all the old family stories were news. It made us feel as if our connection with her was ongoing, as if our knowledge of her was susceptible to revision. Every so often, I almost slipped and said something that might have led to the subject of Aaron. Then Margaret's face floated before me, silencing me with a fierce look that I was already forgetting.

Dad said, "Daisy, remember the time we took her to church and she pretended to be sick so we'd have to leave, and all the way home she did that perfect little-kid imitation of the minister preaching 'God is not a BMW'?"

Mom said, "What made you think of that?" It was a trick question. Poor Dad. The minister was the same one who'd spoken at Margaret's service.

My mother speared a green bean and stared at it as if she'd never seen a bean or a fork. I focused on the impaled bean. I hated seeing them cry.

She said, "I can't stop thinking about the last argument she and I had. It started about smoking and escalated. We both said things we didn't mean, and I never got to take it back. Isn't that the worst horror? That your child could die like that before you got to make up?"

My father walked behind her chair and held her by the shoulders. He said, "You loved each other. How could you have a teenage daughter and not have a little fight now and then? She'd been on permanent eye-roll with you for the last five years."

"It wasn't a fight," Mom said. "And it certainly wasn't a *little* fight."

"I'm sorry," said Dad. "I—"

I said, "She was smoking that day in the boat. I told her she shouldn't. She got mad, that's when she dove in. I should have let her have the cigarette—"

I caught myself in mid-sentence. I never told on my sister. But you couldn't tell on the dead, you couldn't get them in trouble.

"You told her not to smoke," said Mom. "You wanted her to live."

One thing I would never tell them was that Margaret's last words were, "Smoke this." That was her special present for me, the hair shirt she'd left me to wear until time and age and forgetfulness laundered it into something softer.

Somehow, I managed to get my feet and walk around the table. The three of us clumped together. My father squeezed us so hard that Mom's shoulders rattled against my chest. My tears kept dripping into her hair, which presented a logical puzzle until I realized that somehow, at some point, I'd grown as tall as my mother.

Three

❧

EVERY NIGHT, I DREAMED ABOUT MARGARET. SHE WAS ALWAYS
alive and well. I had one of those recurring dreams that trick you
into thinking you're awake, then plunge you into another dream,
more brutal than the first because the fake awakening makes the
second dream seem more real. I dreamed I heard my sister's voice
and followed it to the kitchen, where she was sitting with Aaron at
our red enamel table. She was eating Cheerios from the box and
blowing smoke rings. I thought, Mom and Dad will kill her!

She and Aaron were talking and laughing. But when I
walked in, they fell silent. Aaron gave me a funny look. Why
had I told him that Margaret was dead when she so obviously
wasn't? I shrugged. I must have gotten it wrong. She hadn't
dived into the water, or maybe they'd found her and saved her.
Margaret smiled and touched her lips, entrusting me with another secret.

That was when I awoke, seasick, drenched, and shipwrecked,
as if the knotted sheets were a sail on which I'd washed ashore. I

longed to slip back into the dream in which I might catch up with Margaret.

I counted the hours till morning, then the minutes and seconds, until I got dizzy and lay there thinking of how Margaret and I used to play those little-kid games of pain and endurance, twisting one another's arm until the loser cried out. Now I was playing against myself, but even so, I gave in. I got out of bed and wandered through the house, tripping over the books and shoes no one bothered to pick up, as if there was no particular spot where anything belonged.

Our house had always been neat before, but now our possessions had taken advantage of our moment of weakness. In the dark, the house grew more corridors and corners, and blackness scrambled the map of how one room led to the next. Margaret had told me that the woman who owned the house before Mom's parents saw a ghost that warned her she would die if she stopped building on additions, which eventually she did.

I used to be scared of the house at night, not of killers or ghosts, but of my own power to imagine something watching me from the shadows. Those fears were gone completely. What could the shadows be hiding? Now I wished I could meet a ghost with a message from my sister. I loved the mysterious creaks and groans. I hurried toward them on the chance that the mouse in the wall might be Margaret's spirit. Margaret had always loved ghost stories, and now our lives had become one. But it was a ghost story in reverse, a ghost story in which the living were praying to be haunted.

It didn't matter how much noise I made. I knew that no one was sleeping. Insomnia was our language. We'd worked out a kind of system—an etiquette, you might say. When one of my parents roamed the house, the others would stay in bed and let my mother sit at the silent piano or leave my father to open and shut the refrigerator door. But if I was awake, alone, one of them would get up and find me in the dark.

The only semi-comforting part was that we didn't have to talk. They'd been dreaming about her, too. The mystery of death, the riddle of how of you could speak to someone and see them every day and then never again, was so impossible to fathom that of course we kept trying to figure it out, even when we were unconscious.

Eventually we'd go back to our rooms and lie in the dark and pretend, for the others' sake, to sleep. Which, I vaguely remembered, was how you *fell* asleep. First you pretended, then you were. The tricky part was that thinking about pretending to sleep meant you were still awake.

One night, I heard Margaret knock on the wall between our rooms. I got up, as I always had, to see what my sister wanted. I was halfway out the door before I realized that a whole new dream had found a way to torment me.

I waited for dawn, but only because I had forgotten how hard mornings were. For a second, I'd feel normal. Then came the dim awareness of something off, out of place. Then the truth came crashing in, and that was it for the rest of the day. Sunlight was a reproof. Shouldn't I feel better than I had in the dead of night?

I couldn't remember simple words, the purpose of household objects. I used to like helping my father cook, but now I'd stare into a drawer and wonder which one was the garlic press and which one was the corkscrew. I'd go to the living room, only to find myself pointing the mobile phone at the TV and pressing and pressing and pressing.

Violet and Samantha phoned to ask if I wanted to go somewhere. It took me forever to recognize their voices. I'd forgotten why I'd liked them and what we used to do. They'd mention movies, a party. Violet's parents were going away. Samantha's mom had offered to drive us to the mall. I'd think, Their mothers told them to call. Samantha had a sister, so I hated her more.

When I said I didn't want to go out, they sounded a little annoyed, as if I was acting princessy and spoiled. Why didn't I appreciate the good deed they were doing? They seemed relieved when I said no and they could hang up before I changed my mind or started crying. Naturally, they sounded strange. They weren't talking to the same person. I was no longer Nico. I was the dead girl's sister.

After a while they stopped calling, which was fine with me. What we would have talked about? Boys? School? MTV? Complaining about period cramps? My friends were silly and boring. I wanted to be with Margaret.

There was nothing I wanted to do in place of the things I *couldn't* do now, the everyday things I'd hardly noticed before. I had a mental list, like the one near the lifeguard's chair at the lake, when they *had* a lifeguard, before the town got too cheap. A bottle, a diver, an unleashed dog with red diagonal slashes.

1. No cookies. They smelled like my sister. I even avoided the baked goods aisle in the supermarket.

2. No lake. I kept my curtains drawn so the sight of it wouldn't

sneak up on me. Every so often, I made myself look, searching for the spot where Margaret dove in. It was like staring at
the sun, dangerous and searing.

3. No Margaret's room. Once in a while, I heard my mother
rattling around, opening and shutting drawers. I fought the
urge to tell her to leave, Margaret wouldn't like it. I worried
that Mom might start getting rid of Margaret's stuff, but I
should have known better. Sometimes she ran out of Margaret's room, leaving the door open, until Dad came along and
closed it. Until he did, walking down the hall was like passing
an accident scene. I turned my head, I tried not to look, but I
couldn't help it.

Margaret's room had been a work of art, an installation in
progress. She was always tacking up pictures of jazz singers and
movie stars, vintage snapshots and hand-tinted postcards, and taking them down when she lost interest. She made altars with photos
and candles to her rotating personal gods. One day it was Carole
Lombard, the next day Gandhi or Marlene Dietrich, Malcolm X,
Bono, or Saint Francis. Every time Margaret went to town, she'd
find a treasure—a mismatched pair of mannequin limbs, a case of
Mardi Gras beads, antique hatboxes stickered with labels, a cruci-
fix made of popsicle sticks—though we lived in a town in which,
I'd thought, no one threw out any interesting garbage.

I couldn't stand it that Margaret's room would never change
again, not unless my parents gutted it. What would it become? A
guest room? We never had guests, and we certainly wouldn't now.
I'd read about cultures and countries where people made shrines

to their dead. But an altar to Margaret would have been redundant. All we had to do was not dismantle the one she'd made to herself.

I tried not to look, but I'd find myself staring at Margaret's bed. How could it be there without her? I could picture her so clearly, her long limbs sprawled on the fraying thrift-shop quilt made from satin neckties. I used to sit against the pillows, my head turned away from the slightly smelly stuffed animals she'd had since she was little. I'd listen to her practice a song, or I'd help her choose an outfit before she went out with Aaron.

She'd say, "Nico, be honest. Does the green jacket look better than the blue?" Green or blue, who cared what I said? Margaret always looked perfect.

Sometimes we'd lie with my head on her stomach, listening to music. I felt the music run through me as she hummed the melody line or sang the low harmonies to gospel songs, or the country heartbreak ballads she made fun of and adored. She'd point out slight variations between two recordings of *The St. Matthew Passion*, the clumsy stress on a single word that ruined the entire chorus. A James Brown yelp or the way Nina Simone rolled a note around in her mouth before she spit it out.

There was almost nothing Margaret wouldn't listen to, nothing she couldn't learn from. I remembered her playing hip-hop so loud that both our rooms bumped to the beat. She knocked on the wall, and when I went to see what she wanted, she was punching the air along with the bass line. She said, "Don't you love how the guy uses his voice as a rhythm instrument?" The only song she hated was the theme from *Titanic*, which brought up the next item:

4. No music. If I'd heard "My Funny Valentine," someone would have had to shoot me. It wasn't only good music that hurt, songs Margaret might have sung. Bad music was worse, in a way. Once, I went with Mom to the health food store, and the theme from *Titanic* was playing. I glared at the other shoppers as if they were witnesses to a crime. They were stuffing their carts with cereal to keep their families healthy. Without Margaret, there was no one to protect me from the cardboard granola and the syrupy Hollywood sound track. Which reminded me:

5. No old films. No movies of any kind.

One night, my parents decided to go to the movie theater in Albany, the only place for miles around that showed anything foreign or indie. Margaret and I used to joke that Mom and Dad wouldn't see a film unless it was Taiwanese or Iranian and put you to sleep before the opening credits.

"Come with us," Mom begged me. "It'll be . . . fun. It's . . . suspenseful."

"What country is this one from?"

My parents exchanged guilty looks.

"Korea," my mother admitted. "God, Nico, it doesn't exactly make you seem smart to roll your eyes when someone says Korea."

I said, "I don't have to *seem* smart."

"Girls," said my father. "Please. Daisy, leave her alone. Come on, Nico, honey. Come with us."

"Not a chance," I said.

My father said, "How about this? If you don't like it, we'll pay you the cost of the ticket. It's a win-win situation."

I said, "You don't have to bribe me just because you're afraid to leave me home alone."

"That's not true," said my father.

But we all knew it was. They were terrified by those three little words: Only Remaining Child. The phrase had started lurking in back of their minds and popping out like a jack-in-the-box the minute we left one another's sight.

I liked the idea of time on my own. What scared me was the thought of sitting through a boring movie. Boredom was dangerous now that every empty second was an invitation to gaze into the abyss and think how sweet it would feel to jump. Dangerous, because in those days, there was *only* boredom and grief, like two visitors, dressed in black, refusing to go home, no matter how we yawned and squirmed and kept looking at our watches.

"Mom, Dad, you can go to movies," I said. "Nothing bad will happen to me."

My mother knocked on wood.

"Have fun," I said. "I'll be fine."

I felt as if they were kidnappers who'd been holding me hostage, and now I could chew through the duct tape. But where would I escape to? Solitude and silence. The minute they left, I turned on the TV, as loud as it would go. Even though it was something I sometimes did with Margaret, I poured myself a shot of Dad's high-end tequila. I sipped it and settled into the couch.

Within seconds I realized I'd made the wrong decision. I ran to the window, but my parents were already gone. The remote was a demon magnet dragging me toward the old movie channel.

I clung to the harmless sitcoms. I tried one, then another. I didn't understand what anyone was saying. Actors sat around waiting for someone to burst through the door and detonate the laugh track. I switched to the news: a Baghdad street, the two charred truck skeletons offhandedly tossed into a ring of campfires. Flash, flash, the portraits of boys Aaron's age, wearing uniforms and brave smiles to convince us that they didn't mind being dead. Their faces had always saddened me, but now I imagined being their sister.

I hit the mute button and watched a senator work his mouth like a sucker fish as his face turned redder and redder. On the Discovery Channel, a scientist was talking about building an outer-space umbrella to shield our planet from UV death rays. Once, I would have been interested, but now I turned off the TV and picked up a paperback mystery Mom had been pretending to read. The few drops of tequila had misted my brain like frying-pan spray. Every sentence slid out even as I read it.

How long had Mom and Dad been away? Why *couldn't* lightning strike twice?

I shut my eyes. I awoke to the sound of my parents' car—I *hoped* it was their car—pulling into the driveway. I jumped up and rinsed out the tequila glass and swished water around in my mouth. I found the cartoon channel, turned down the TV, and tried to do a convincing imitation of myself chilling at home.

I needn't have bothered. My parents looked like patients who had just heard that some promising new treatment had failed in clinical trials. They'd brought their own weather inside, the way that people carry winter into a warm room. I could tell they'd been arguing all the way home from the theater.

"How was the movie?" I said.

Mom said, "My God, Henry, how the hell was I supposed to know it was a horror film about drowning? Your dad seems to think I would purposely take him to a film about girls disappearing under the water—"

"It's called *The Lake*," Dad said. "What did you expect? And there's no need to involve Nico in this."

"I'm sorry. I wasn't thinking," Mom said. "I can't always do the thinking for both of us."

"Maybe you think too much," said Dad. "Maybe that's your problem."

"All right," I said. "All right." I imagined Margaret saying, "At least it was Korean."

Dad said, "Nico, are you okay? Were you all right, alone here . . . ?"

I said, "I was fine. I had a nice time."

The truth was, I couldn't breathe. I was trying to see Margaret's face, but I'd forgotten what she looked like.

Which reminded me of the final rule:

6. No photographs. Why had I never noticed that our house was a Margaret museum? I couldn't walk into a room without seeing two little blond girls preserved under glass, beaming from my mother's piano or my father's desk. Every time I opened a kitchen drawer, Margaret smiled up at me from a nest of receipts and rubber bands.

I'd made these rules for my own protection. But every so often I broke one just to see how it felt.

One afternoon, in the supermarket, I faked a craving for cookies. My father was so thrilled that I was showing any interest in food, he handed over the shopping cart and said, "Go. Fill it with every delicious, teeth-rotting baked good they have."

Marigold-colored biscuits, marshmallow mounds, sandy discs swirled with hibiscus, beckoned to me from the shelves. I opened a package and inhaled, playing to the security cameras. Let them get this on tape! The box smelled like baked chemicals, but nothing at all like Margaret. I'd thought I could recapture her smell, but it was gone forever. I couldn't imagine asking my parents if they remembered what she'd smelled like. I stretched out my arms, as if to lean back on the evil waves that the cookies were transmitting to innocent baby brains.

As we pulled out of the supermarket parking lot, Dad said, "Nico, is something wrong?"

"You've got to be kidding," I said.

"I mean, did something happen in the store? You seem . . ."

"Nothing happened," I said.

"You didn't find any cookies you liked?"

"They were gross," I told him.

We were passing Golden Oldies, where Margaret used to make Mom and Dad stop and buy things for the house. Our red kitchen table, a giant orange floor lamp—stuff that my parents didn't really like because it reminded them of their childhoods, but that they'd bought to please Margaret, who convinced them that mid-century modern was beautiful and cool. The shop was owned by a guy named Brad, Mom's friend's Sally's ex-husband. I purposely averted my eyes until we passed the store. Everything was a timed grenade set to explode on visual contact.

After a silence, my father said, "There's this new book that's selling really well. It's about wizards and magic. Harry Potter for grown-ups. I never understood why so many people were buying it until . . . all this . . . this thing with your sister." Dad couldn't bring himself to say *Margaret*, he couldn't make himself say *death*. "But now it makes perfect sense to me why someone would want to escape. And now when someone asks for the book, I always wonder if that person is suffering like I am, and if they're just pretending to be normal."

I said, "That's what *we're* pretending. Sometimes, walking down the street, I'll see somebody and think, Someone that person loved has just died."

"I love you, Nico," my father said.

"I love you too, Dad," I said.

Dad said, "I always felt that Goldengrove had a sort of, I don't know, semi-social-work function. Someone would come in with a problem, and I'd think I could find that person a book that might actually help."

"Peace and love." I spread my fingers in a V sign.

"Don't be cynical," said Dad. "It's unattractive in a person your age. A customer would limp in on crutches, and I'd say, 'You should read *A Voice Through a Cloud*.' "

I thought, *A Voice Through a Cloud: The Story of Dad.*

"What's that?" I said, only because he expected me to.

"It's a great book about a guy who gets hurt in a bicycle accident. I don't know why I thought it would help. Or why *anything* would help."

"The point is, Dad, you were trying," I said. "You *wanted* to help."

"Thank you, sweetheart," Dad said.

Back home, I stood outside Margaret's door. I closed my eyes and concentrated so hard it was like praying. Whom was I praying to? Margaret, I guessed. I did that sometimes in those days. Give me the nerve to walk into your room and go through your things, which you would have hated.

Once, I'd walked into Margaret's room and found her nude, in front of the mirror. She didn't seem embarrassed, which may have been why it felt less like seeing a naked person than like seeing a girl in a painting. I watched the naked, painted girl turn in tiny increments, like a rotisserie chicken

"It's a wretched morning," she was saying. "I'm so bored with my face. I wish I had someone else's face. But I suppose you get the face you deserve."

"What's that from?" I said.

Frowning into the mirror, Margaret said, "Nico, how about knocking?"

I'd learned my lesson so well that even now I knocked on the air. I don't know how long I stayed in the dark hall with my fist raised until I found the courage to inch open the door.

Margaret always liked it when I noticed what was new, what image or fresh piece of junk she'd added to her collection. I'd learned to do it so well that even now I looked for what was different until I remembered why nothing would be.

I made myself stand up straight. I said aloud, "There is no afterlife." Where was heaven? In the sky? How were the dead transported after their Houdini escapes from their coffins? I knew kids who went to church and believed that after death you and your family sprouted wings and played instruments, like at some eternal band picnic. I envied them. I wished I believed that some day I would be able to tell Margaret everything that had happened since that last afternoon on the lake.

I repeated, like a spell, "There is no afterlife." So why had I been trying to contact her, to pick up some sort of signal? I liked it when my right knee ached, because that was her weak point. I would have settled for any indication that she was at peace, or better yet that she missed me or needed me to do her a favor. I wanted her to appear in a dream and say, "Nico, go burn a candle at my Billie Holliday altar." My logical mind had been invaded and possessed by the spirit of a superstitious lunatic. I thought about Margaret helping me, pulling strings from beyond. But what did I want her to do except not be dead, a miracle that, even I knew, was beyond my sister's powers?

I stood, very still, in her doorway. Then I crawled into her bed. The pillow smelled like Margaret. Not like cookies, exactly, but cookielike. Purely her. I inhaled, and it was like sucking on one of those plastic pipes that help asthmatic kids breathe. The lump in my throat dissolved enough for me to get some air, but only for a second, and I was choking again. Maybe I did have a heart condition. I rolled over onto my side and curled up into a ball.

When I opened my eyes, I was staring into a snow globe on Margaret's night table. I'd always loved it and wished it were mine. I used to imagine that if I stared into it hard enough, I could dissolve into atoms and pass through the scratched plastic globe, and a miniature version of me would reassemble inside it, twirling in the storm beside the tiny ballerina that I realized, only now, was a figure skater.

One summer, when I was a toddler, we rented a summer cottage. In the kitchen was a wall-sized '70s photo mural of a meadow in the Rockies. My parents told me that I used to scoot my walker across the room and get a running start and hurl myself against the wall, trying to break through to the wildflower field. It was the same with the snow globe. I'd shake it, longing to enter that other dimension, staring and staring until Margaret ordered me to stop.

Now I shook the snow globe and watched the miniature skater stalled in mid-pirouette by the storm of cottony flakes bigger than her yellow head. How wintry Margaret's room was! My fingertips were frozen. I pulled the tie-quilt up to my neck. I must have slept, because I woke with that ravenous nausea that can follow a restless nap. I dragged myself out of bed and walked over to the closet. I touched a feather boa, a sequined vest, an organdy skirt I couldn't remember Margaret wearing, until I was stopped by the sight of Margaret's favorite vintage T-shirt, dark blue with a silver shooting star trailed by a glitter comet.

As I pushed the shirt toward the back of the closet, Margaret's Hawaiian shirt pitched itself straight at me. Pineapples, bunches of coconuts, splashy purple orchids, grew from palms with fronds like the arms of the hula girls swaying beneath them. Margaret was generous with her clothes, but she would never lend me that one. She claimed it was some ancient synthetic that disintegrated, like Dracula, on contact with the sun. I didn't see how that could have been true, because Margaret wore it day and night, especially when she went out with Aaron.

I tried on the Hawaiian shirt. The rayon was cool, almost slimy. I was thinking the unthinkable: I could have anything Margaret owned. My parents would let me, they'd *want* me to take whatever I wanted. How angry Margaret would be if she came back and discovered what I'd done. But she wasn't coming back. I felt lightheaded, almost weightless.

I didn't want Margaret's snow globe *or* her clothes. I wanted to see her, just once.

I looked at myself in the mirror. And I saw her. With each step, Margaret's ghost expanded. Gingerly, I touched the glass. I thought of those fairy-tale mirrors that show you your dearest wish in return for some terrible price. Mirror, mirror on the wall. Your firstborn son for straw woven into gold, a glimpse of your drowned sister for something more expensive. Margaret filled the mirror and floated off the edges, and by the time I'd backed away far enough for the glass to contain her, Margaret had vanished, and there I was, wearing her hula shirt.

The girl in the mirror still wasn't me, but the creature that would have been produced by swapping half of my cells for half of Margaret's. Maybe it was the weight loss, or the fact that I'd grown taller, but for the first time I understood why Margaret used to say that some day I'd look like her. No one, not even Margaret, could have known it would happen so soon.

I was glad to see Margaret in me. It was proof that she still existed, even if some part of me must have had to move over to make room.

I went next door and took off the Hawaiian shirt and hung it in my closet. I would save it to wear, like a magic cloak, for those especially dangerous moments when I most needed its help.

Four

SUNDAYS WERE UNBEARABLE, LONELIER THAN BEFORE. TWO, THREE Sundays since Margaret's death, I knew the count from the moment I woke. Weeks would turn into months and years, but the meter would keep ticking.

Margaret's death had shaken us, like three dice in a cup, and spilled us out with new faces in unrecognizable combinations. We forgot how we used to lived in our house, how we'd passed the time when we lived there. We could have been sea creatures stranded on the beach, puzzling over an empty shell that reminded us of the ocean.

Occasionally, I'd find my parents in unexpected places: Dad in the middle of the stairs, Mom in the garage, as if she'd gone out with a purpose that got vaporized by the paint fumes. She took on massive housecleaning projects that she left half done. She ordered a paper shredder, and on Sundays, instead of music, I'd hear the hum of Mom making confetti from ancient tax returns she'd found in the attic.

She never again played that Chopin waltz she was playing that afternoon. She took a leave from writing liner notes. She hardly played at all.

She did keep going to yoga class. From my window, I'd spy on her, balanced on one leg with her hands joined as if she was praying to the lake. Or I'd see her arched over the grass like an upside-down lawn chair. When she stood up, she stumbled. Her arthritis was getting worse.

She asked if I wanted to join her. She still claimed that it helped. But I couldn't see how standing on my head would change what was inside it, or how it would help to hear Mom's friend Sally remind her to relax her shoulders and tuck in her butt.

Sometimes, after yoga class, Sally would follow Mom home in her car, and they'd hang out in the study where my mother used to write. I'd smell Sally's cigarette smoke wafting down from upstairs, though before, Mom had never let anyone smoke in the house.

Margaret never liked Sally. She said Sally was an example of how, given enough vanity and money, you could make your face look like a junior-high sewing project. Margaret was hardly ever mean like that, so it must have been something else. Sally always seemed wary of Margaret. But she'd treated me with a sly, flirtatious weirdness, as if we were coconspirators keeping secrets from the grown-ups. She'd ask how I was and then laugh and say, "You don't have to answer." Then we'd both laugh, embarrassed, because she'd thought she was rescuing me from teenage conversational hell, when all I was *ever* going to say was, "Fine."

Now, for my mother, yoga had become like the piano. She tried and failed and lay on the ground and got up and tried again, and got steadily more anxious instead of more relaxed.

Once, I watched from the upstairs window as Mom crumpled to the grass and Sally went around to the back of the house, where Dad was weeding a patch of bee balm. The afternoon sun picked out the gold streaks in Sally's hair. I wondered how much time and money she'd spent to make the sun do that. She looked up. I stepped back from the window. I moved closer again as she leaned toward my father, and Dad leaned away. I could tell she was saying she was worried about my mother.

That night, at dinner, Dad said, "I don't know what it is, Daisy. Instinct, maybe. There's something vampiristic about how Sally is feeding off our . . . situation. Remember that friend of your mom's? The one who showed up at the end and wouldn't leave her bedside? You said there were people like that. Human buzzards, you called them."

Dad must have been really serious. In those days, we never criticized, never complained, never mentioned other deaths, certainly not that of my mother's mother, who died just before I was born. For my father to call Sally a vampire was to stray perilously far from the narrow path we were walking from minute to minute.

"Whom *do* you trust, dear?" my mother said. "You didn't trust poor Aaron. Who knows how things might have turned out if we hadn't listened to your so-called instincts."

"Meaning?" said my father.

"Aaron's a fabulous swimmer," she said. "The kid with the screw loose, remember?"

She couldn't mean what I thought she did. Was my mother suggesting that if they'd let Margaret go boating with Aaron that day, he could have saved her? Unlike me, who'd taken a nap and let my sister drown. Did Sally tell my mother that Aaron was a swim-

mer? Was it even true? Neither he nor Margaret had ever mentioned that. I might have said so, if I hadn't been afraid that they
might ask why I was such an expert on Aaron. But it didn't matter
compared to what Mom had said. Somewhere inside my wise, loving mother was a furious child who blamed my father and me for
my sister's death.

The three of us mimed eating, until finally my mother said,
"Sally had a suggestion."

"Those are four scary words right there," Dad said.

"Very funny," said Mom. "She suggested it might be helpful to
go see Dr. Viscott and ask how he could have missed what was
wrong with Margaret."

Our pediatrician had come to the funeral, then phoned a few
times to see how we were doing. Until one night my mom grabbed
the phone and told him to stop calling. He'd been my doctor since I
was born. I'd always liked him. He had video games in his waiting
room and a model train that ran on a track. We'd learned to believe
him when he said that something would only hurt for a minute. But
lifelong pain, apparently, was not his field of expertise.

"He doesn't know," said Dad. "He never did. How would that
be *healing*? How would that make you feel better?"

"Well, Sally didn't mean *better*." A coleslaw speck had attached
itself to my mother's bottom lip.

"Advice from Sally . . . ," my father said. "Watch out, world."

"She meant it was something I might do to—"

Dad said, "The guy's a year from retirement. He's a broken
wreck. It's *our* fault for taking the word of some country doc.
What do you care what he admits? How's that going to change
things?"

He looked from my mother to me and back. There it was. *Our fault.* We dissected our cornbread-coated catfish and stone-ground grits.

"I think we should make Viscott pay. Not a fortune. But something. Something for what he did. For what he *didn't* do."

Dad said, "Do we really want to spend all that time with lawyers, pumping out all that venom? I know it's a cliché, but it won't bring Margaret back."

"*I know it's a cliché.*" Mom's flash imitation of Dad was precise and fiendish, and her tone had a reckless, razory edge I'd never heard before.

After its echo faded, Dad said, "You should try playing the piano, Daisy. Just try."

Mom said, "Did I ever tell you about my great-aunt Maeve? After her daughter died, she developed an allergy to music. She was always crying in elevators, and when you went to a restaurant with her, you had to call ahead and ask them please, no background sound track."

Dad said, "Daisy, I *knew* your great-aunt Maeve. She was nothing like you. Try, just give it a shot. Maybe if you noodled around for half an hour a day—"

"Noodled?" Mom spat the word back at him. "Sir, yes sir! Noodle. Relax. Any other instructions?"

Dad said, "I'm not telling you what to do. I'm just making a suggestion. Work's the only thing that helps."

"Nothing helps," Mom said.

My father said, "I know that. But we need distraction and time. Distraction to get us through the time between now and then."

"Between now and when?"

"The future," my father told her.

"Ah, the future," my mother said. She pondered that for a while. Then she said, "Actually, come to think of it . . . I already went to see Dr. Viscott."

"I see," my father said.

I didn't. Why had Mom fake-casually brought up the possibility of something she'd already done?

"How did it go?" asked Dad.

"Very nice, actually. Very apologetic. Very eager to help. He gave me a new medication for my hands."

"What kind of new medication?" asked Dad.

"Did I say *new*? I meant old. Something older. Time-tested. And you know what? It seems to be working."

No one said anything for a while as we watched Mom pick at her food.

"How's your book coming along, Dad?" I asked, to cut the silence.

"Okay, I guess," he said. "Yesterday I read an article that said the scientists feel pretty sure that the planet's got maybe five billion years left."

"That's a comfort," said Mom.

"It is, in a way," said Dad. I think he found it consoling to imagine having all that company when the world ended. Otherwise, it was all so isolated and pathetic. One death, one family, one grief at a time.

MY FATHER MUST HAVE BELIEVED THAT WORK COULD BRIDGE THE gap between the dark now and the slightly brighter future. He was spending every spare moment working on his book. Or maybe he was writing more because he had to do *something*, and he could barely make himself go into the bookstore.

One day, I went to Goldengrove with him to find something to read. But I'd forgotten the logic of how one word followed another. The sorts of books I used to like—fantasy, science fiction, world civilization compressed into the history of salt or cotton or tuna—seemed pointless, incomprehensible. Why would anyone care?

As I rejected book after book, I saw what my poor father had to endure. His customers practically walked on their toes as they approached the counter. They asked how he was getting along and began sniffling before he could reply. Or they'd tell him how sorry they were and gaze into his eyes, their own eyes brimming with puppylike adoration. Their literary Romeo, he was everything their husbands weren't—a reader, a listener, sensitive and handsome. Now that he'd been wounded, they took on his injury as their own. Every one of them could have healed him, and she knew just how she would do it.

Dad and I learned to brace ourselves whenever the doorbell sounded. After an hour he fled to his office at the back of the store.

With my father gone, I could stop pretending to look for a book and just hang out with Elaine. Elaine had worked at Goldengrove almost since it began. She knew how to use the computer, order from the distributors, keep accounts and pay taxes. Along the way she'd managed to read practically every book worth reading.

When you read a hundred books, you could join Elaine's Groucho Club and have your picture taken in a Groucho mask, which you got to keep. One wall was plastered with Polaroids of every kid in town in a mustache and glasses and a huge plastic nose—everyone except Margaret and me. Margaret read her hundred books but declined to be photographed wearing the Groucho face, and later I did the same, because my sister had. Which turned out to be fortunate, because now I could go to the bookstore without having to see her photo. Even so, I searched for her, as if I could still be surprised.

Elaine hugged me, pressing my face into her mane of bristly, colorless hair. Then she held me at arm's length. I let her look. I trusted her not to ask how I was feeling.

"Honey," she said. "I don't want to upset you. But you're starting to look more like your sister."

I said, "You couldn't upset me any more than I already am. Anyhow, I know. The other day the strangest thing happened. I looked in the mirror, and I saw Margaret."

"Eek," said Elaine. "*Persona*."

"What?" I said.

"Ingmar Bergman," she said. "Swedish. Black and white. Subtitles. Dull. You'd hate it."

Old films were a passion that Elaine and Margaret had shared. You couldn't mention an old movie Elaine hadn't seen. Not only did she know all the stars and directors, but she had a mental filing system so that, if you told her about a conversation you'd overheard at the supermarket or some incident at school, she could name a film in which something similar happened.

"What's *Persona* about?" I asked.

"Never mind," Elaine said. "Just promise me you won't watch it for another ten years."

"Okay," I said. "I promise."

Elaine loved to make us promise her things: Promise you won't smoke pot or have sex until you're twenty-one. Swear you won't smoke cigarettes ever. Margaret found it easy, because she'd already done all those things, just as I found it easy because I believed I never would.

Drugs and sex seemed like open invitations to confusion and shame, two emotions I dreaded long before I'd been forced to take our school's useless antidrug program. Our DARE instructor was a uniformed cop named Officer Prozak, which the parents thought was hilarious. Once a week, we'd listen to her ramble on about the ways in which various substances would destroy us. Maybe the accident of her name was why she seemed to expect to be doubted or mocked, and why her manner veered from cringing to hostile. Everyone said *she* was on drugs, and as she stood before us, chalking the back of her uniform against the blackboard, her terror of us—of everything—rubbed off onto her subject so that even tne kids who smoked dope daily were temporarily worried. Just say no, we'd chanted with her. Say no to the recurring hallucinations, the car wrecks, the crack-addled murders, the dried-chestnut brains.

Sex was scarier than drugs. Drugs could only drive you crazy. But sex meant getting naked in front of another person. I'd seen lots of Hollywood sex, perfect people with peachlike skin tumbling with balletic grace in the flattering light. I understood the biology. But textbooks didn't explain why you would *want* to take off your clothes with someone you hardly knew.

I thought about kissing, or at least about a boy saying he wanted to kiss me. In sixth grade, there had been a party at which the girls and boys paired off and went into a closet. Twice it was my turn, and both times the boys asked if we could just pretend to have kissed. Once might have been about the boy, but twice had to be about me. Plenty of kids had offered me joints, but not one boy had ever hinted he wanted to hold my hand. How did you know what boys wanted? I would never find out, unless the impossible happened and I became someone's funny valentine.

After we'd promised Elaine not to smoke or have sex, she'd say, "And if you *do*, promise me you'll make the guy use a condom."

Once Margaret asked if that was how Elaine wound up having Tycho, and Elaine went all dreamy and said, "That's another story."

I was encouraged that a guy had wanted to have sex with unglamorous Elaine. Maybe he'd even loved her for her many admirable qualities. Elaine knew lots of tricks involving pennies, matches, paper napkins you burned with cigarettes until a coin dropped into a glass. She called them bar games, which suggested a sketchy youth of playing strangers for drinks in seedy dives.

Sometimes Margaret and I visited Elaine at her apartment, which she'd decorated with shag rugs, plastic bucket chairs, *Sputnik* radios, clocks in the shape of spaceships. Margaret laughed about Elaine's excessively organic, tree-hugging style, but even so she saw Elaine as a cool adult, as proof that you could grow up and even have a kid without turning into our parents. I'd catch Margaret eyeing Elaine the way she watched a film from which she was planning to copy a gesture or snappy line.

Elaine had asked me something. What were we talking about? I vaguely remembered promising her not to see some Swedish movie.

"How's Tycho?" I said.

"Fine, I guess," said Elaine. "Any day he doesn't chew through an electrical cord is a good day."

Tycho was always a funny kid. I could still picture him as a frowny, superintense little baby with zero interest in the normal goo-goo games. When he finally learned to talk, his voice rasped like a kazoo. He'd gotten more peculiar since his diagnosis. Every so often he'd bang his head against the wall, and at stressful moments he'd bite his hands all bloody.

I'd known him so long that it hardly startled me when he'd yell for no reason, or ask loud, inappropriate questions, like did I have hair under my arms? Sometimes you could feel the pressure build, and he'd ask if he could go rock, then he'd bounce himself into a trance on his large rubber ball, a cross between a beach toy and some kind of Pilates equipment.

Elaine had ways of distracting him and talking him down from his obsessions. *Perseverations*, she called them, a word I'd come to love. My response to Margaret's death had been one long perseveration, so I felt even closer to Tycho than I had before.

Elaine said, "When do you think is the best time to give your dad some bad news?"

"Bad news?" I said. "What could bad *be* at this point?"

"Not *that* bad," said Elaine. "Oh, honey, I keep telling myself how important it is to remember the difference between a tragedy and an inconvenience. If only we could keep that in mind every minute of every day—"

"I do," I said. "Every minute of every day."

"I know," said Elaine. "I know you do. But you won't always. No one can. No one could live that way. No one would want to."

"You just said you wished you could."

Elaine said, "Let's take it from the top. My babysitter quit, so there's no one home after one o'clock when Tycho gets back from his mind-blowingly expensive special-needs day camp. That someone's going to have to be me. I'll have to take off until I find a replacement *me* to stay with him. Which isn't easy."

"Bring Tycho to the store," I said. "He can play his Game Boy."

"Not an option," said Elaine. "He can rip the covers off the whole manga section in the time it takes me to go to the bathroom."

I said, "Dad can handle the store on his own for a while."

Then, just to prove me wrong, Mrs. McPhail from the post office came in and wanted to know if we had the new P. D. James mystery. She asked if Henry was around, and when Elaine said he was taking a break in back, Mrs. McPhail said, "How is he?" Her voice caught, and a micro-sob hiccuped down in her throat.

"You see?" Elaine said, when Mrs. McPhail left. "With all the best intentions in the world, they'll chew your dad up and spit him out in little pieces. He needs to hire a kid to run interference for him until—"

"Until when?" I said.

"Until I find someone to stay with Tycho."

"*I* could stay with Tycho," I said. "We get along great. We could play video games all day." In fact, it seemed like the perfect way to get through the rest of the summer.

"It's not that I don't trust you," said Elaine. "But it's always a crap shoot with Tycho." Elaine was being kind, as usual. She didn't say I was having enough trouble taking care of myself.

In theory, it should have been easy to find a temporary Elaine. School was out, and working in Goldengrove was every high school book nerd's dream. But when Dad put a sign in the window, not one person applied. A cloud hovered over the store. It was one thing to stop by, flirt with my dad, have a good cry, go home with a new book. But to be there all afternoon would have been like buying a house on an earthquake fault or a flood plain. Misfortune could rub off on you. Your odds rose if you were around us.

After that, my father went in every day and came home at six. I hated thinking of him there, alone with the customers, each of whom imagined that if he would just ditch Mom and me and move in with her, her tears would wash away his grief and they'd have their own little book club.

One morning, Mom and Dad came into my room.

"Your mother had a brainstorm," my father said. I rolled over and faced the wall.

Mom said, "How about working afternoons in the store with Dad? Keep him company. You can be at the counter, he can write in his office. We'll pay you."

"No," I said. I knew they were worried about me. Lately, almost all I'd done was lie on the couch and sigh.

"Why not?" my mother asked.

"Because I don't want to go anywhere or do anything. Anyhow, aren't you afraid that someone might come in and rob the place when I'm there?"

"In Emersonville?" said Dad.

"Main Street," I said. "Serial killers drive through."

Mom said, "Here's the choice. Bookstore or we medicate you." Dad and I shot her quick looks. She laughed to make sure we knew she was joking, and I laughed too, not because it was funny but because for a moment she'd sounded like herself.

"Medicate me, *please*." I sat up and stretched both arms out in front of me. "Turn me into a zombie."

"That's it," said my mother. "The new choice is bookstore or bookstore."

"Bookstore," I said. "How much?"

They could have said nothing or a million dollars. Money was one of the things I'd forgotten the use for.

"Five bucks an hour," said Mom.

"Make that ten," said Dad.

"Fine," I said. "When do I start?"

The truth was, I was glad for a reason to get out of the house. Mom was beginning to scare me. Sally was spending more time up in my mother's study. I'd hear my mother's ragged new laugh, together with Sally's bark. None of us were laughing then, and for a while I imagined that any laughter was an improvement.

Mom seemed fine in the mornings. But by afternoon, she seemed to have blurred around the edges. She alternated between moody silence and chatty monologues I'd heard before, anecdotes about all the crazy people she'd known in her twenties: nudists, junkies, cross-dressers, Charlie Manson wannabes. Partway through a story, she'd forget what she was saying.

One night, Dad and I watched Mom sculpt her grilled scampi and mashed potatoes into a pyramid. She sat back, contemplated it, and said, "Don't you think that food has been underrated as an art medium? Henry, remember *Close Encounters*?"

"Unfortunately," said Dad.

"Remember that conceptual artist who used to eat cookies and throw up? Wasn't he the pet artist of the shah of Iran?"

"I don't know," said Dad. "I think it was the shah's sister."

"Whatever." Mom layered what remained of her food into a Leaning Tower of Shrimp.

"It's not art, it's dinner," said Dad. "Maybe you should *try* a bite instead of playing with it."

Mom rose from her seat. Her mouth opened and shut, like a marionette's. She left the table, left the house. We heard her car pull out of the driveway. What if we never saw her again? My father tried not to look worried.

"Maybe I'd better go find her," he said. "She shouldn't be driving." But before he could locate his car keys, Mom reappeared.

She said, "I can't remember why I went out. Or what I was going to get."

"Killed," my father muttered.

"What?" said my mother.

"Nothing," he said.

My mother knocked on wood.

In the past, she'd been proud, even boastful, about her memory. She used to say that music was yoga for your brain cells. She liked us to appreciate it when she went to town with a long mental list of errands and got every detail right and came back with everything that we'd asked for.

But now she often drove off and returned, sometimes twice, for her wallet or glasses. Her driving had gotten erratic: too slow, too fast, too slow. The light changed from red to green, and she'd sit there till someone honked, a rare event in the country. Lines of traffic snaked behind her.

I felt I should mention this to Dad. I wasn't telling on Mom. I was concerned about her safety. I was afraid that Margaret's death might have damaged my mother's brain. A few times she mentioned that she'd been having constant déjà vus. She hoped it wasn't a symptom of a tumor or early-onset dementia. I wished she wouldn't talk that way. What if Mom or Dad got sick?

I waited till one evening when my father was peeling carrots to ask, "Dad, have you noticed anything odd about Mom's driving?"

My father dropped the carrot and the peeler. He sat down at the kitchen table and put his head in his hands, a gesture as clear as speech.

I thought he said, "I'll talk to her." But I couldn't really hear, and I couldn't bring myself to ask him to repeat it.

Five

ONE MORNING, A FEW DAYS BEFORE I BEGAN WORKING AT Goldengrove, Mom said she was going for a haircut and asked if I wanted to come along.

Margaret had always cut my hair. The first time, she hacked off my baby curls with cuticle scissors. My parents had been horrified, but my sister was so gentle I don't think I even knew that the feathers sifting down had been attached to my head. After that, she'd practiced on herself, and she always looked so beautiful that eventually I asked her to cut mine, too.

We'd steam up the bathroom and mist the air with Mom's sandalwood oil. My sister wore her bathing suit, and her bare stomach brushed my arm as she danced around me, a half-naked sprite I watched in the mirror she squeegeed with her hands. Margaret was always so pleased with the result that her confidence convinced me, even when I was pretty sure I'd looked better before. In photos from that time I often seem to be wearing a pale, crooked helmet beneath which my round face bulbs out like a shiny plum.

For years, she'd been snipping my bangs short and straight across. Margaret said nerdiness was stylish, but I suspected her of overdoing it with me. She'd worn her own hair in a shaggy cap— an *homage*, she said, to Jean Seberg in *Joan of Arc*.

Our father used to joke that Margaret could always cut hair if the singing didn't work out. Usually Mom laughed at his jokes, funny or not. Margaret said that Mom was conditioned from birth to respond to male humor. She never seemed to get our jokes, and her own were so deadpan that you couldn't tell if she meant to be funny. But when Dad joked about Margaret cutting hair, Mom never even smiled. Her plans for Margaret didn't include a future in cosmetology.

Mom wore the same hairstyle she'd worn in her soybean commune days. Margaret said it was a '60s thing. You couldn't get them to change their look. The only thing that consoled me for not being beautiful like Margaret was seeing how her beauty caused a crackling in the weather between her and our mother. Once I overheard them arguing about Mom's hair. Margaret said Mom should let her cut it. She'd do a better job than the butchers Mom went to at the mall.

"Only one butcher, dear," our mother said, "and strictly speaking, *near* the mall."

Frank's was where our mother went. Frankenstein's, Margaret called it. Sometimes when Mom scheduled a haircut on our way to somewhere else, I'd have to leaf through the dimpled magazines and try not to stare at the women there, who did look like Brides of Frankenstein in their tinfoil antennae.

It was cruel of my mother to remind me of something that Margaret and I would never do again because my sister had left me to the mercy of butchers like Frank.

"We can get there when Frank opens," said Mom. "I'm sure he can fit you in."

"No, thanks," I said. "That's okay."

My mother's expression combined pure sympathy with the suggestion that I might want to go look in the mirror. Who *was* that person across the sink? A taller, thinner version of me, a stranger who needed a haircut. Mom wasn't trying to hurt me. She was trying to make me feel better.

"Sure," I told her. "Why not?"

Mom seemed to be looking forward to it, as if a trip to Frank's eggy-smelling salon was a comforting mother-daughter bonding rite, a test of faith that would involve entrusting ourselves to a guy with a comb-over who specialized in hennaing old ladies into redheaded Elvis imitators.

I liked the idea of going somewhere with Mom, at least in the morning when she was still clear. It was easier to talk in the car, with no eye contact required and the changing scenery constantly wiping away the gummy residue of whatever we'd just said.

But Frank couldn't take us till afternoon, and by the time we left, Mom was drifting in and out, like a radio station on the edge of its broadcast range.

She said, "So . . . are you looking forward to working . . ." I monitored her turn onto Route 9. "In the bookstore?"

"Yeah," I said. "I guess so."

I'd become the squirrelly one. My grief over Margaret was the hard little acorn I clutched to my chest. Knowing that my mother missed her too only made me feel more alone. Why couldn't she help me first and do her own suffering later?

We passed a tree in outrageous white bloom. A catalpa? An acacia? I couldn't believe I'd forgotten. My mother whistled a classical melody that dribbled out of tune.

"What should we talk about?" she said.

I'd always known my parents loved Margaret more. Like everyone, they'd brightened when she walked into the room. I knew they loved me, loved being with me, but there wasn't that same excitement. I'd never blamed Margaret. It wasn't what she would have chosen. But I *did* blame my parents, at least for not hiding it better. It served them right that they'd lost her, and now they were stuck with me. But I knew that was foolish, because I'd lost her, too.

It was a challenge to make conversation with Mom's car drifting into the oncoming lane. The first time, I let it go. The second time, she was heading for a red pickup truck. I screamed, "Why are you driving this way?"

"Which way?" said my mother, swerving at the last minute.

I waited a beat. "Remember you said you were having all these déjà vus?"

Mom said, "Hang on. Didn't this happen before?"

I twisted around to stare at her.

"Only kidding," she said.

When we got to the parking lot, she said, "You want to go first?"

I'd caught Mom's forgetfulness, like a cold.

"Haircut," my mother said.

"Oh. Right," I said. "Sure. Frankenstein can practice on me."

Frank said he was sorry for our loss. I flopped into his chair. His looked apologetic, but competent and determined, like a veterinarian getting ready to mercy-kill a child's doomed pet.

"Don't make it too short," I pleaded. Frank smiled as if the child was instructing him on how to put Fluffy to sleep.

I watched the sheets of hair drop. Frank ordered me to pick up my head, but I kept my eyes closed. I was afraid to look in the mirror and see Margaret dancing around me in our tropical, fragrant bathroom. When Frank leaned in to snip my bangs, I clenched my face like a fist.

At last, Frank sprayed on a coat of shellac and hardened it under the dryer. As he stepped back to admire his ugly-duckling-into-swan miracle, I looked at my reflection. I hadn't just gotten a haircut but a sex-change operation. The fish boy masquerading as me swam away, and I saw my mother staring. Her expression extinguished all hope that it wasn't as bad as I thought.

"You look lovely," said Mom.

"Thanks." I glared at her. Was she satisfied? Happy now?

"So?" Frank said. "Bellissima, no?"

"Bellissima," I agreed. What did it matter, really? I'd left the world in which people cared about bad hair days.

While my mom got her standard trim, I lost myself in a magazine devoted to which starlets wore which evening gowns to which Hollywood events. I glanced up from a story about the miracle Beverly Hills fertility doctor responsible for a whole generation of celebrity babies. Mom was grinning at me—all done!—and looking the same as before.

"Bellissima," I said, fighting tears. I told myself, It's only hair. It grows back. But I didn't believe it. Because like everything else in those days, my hair was itself and something else. The bad haircut didn't bother me half so much as the feeling that Margaret had withdrawn her protection. She would never have let Frank and

Mom conspire to maim me this way. Obviously, I'd lost my mind along with my hair. The Nico blaming an ugly haircut on her dead sister was no more like me than the froggy hermaphrodite frowning at me from the mirror.

My mom seemed clearer—sharper somehow—after our visit to Frank's. On the drive home, she asked if I wanted to go shopping. It was one of the few activities that seemed relatively safe. Margaret had mostly worn vintage, so she'd never come with us.

Mom and I used to drive to the Albany mall, always a little buzzed, as if something transformative might happen to us there. The same thing always happened. Mom zoned in on the sale racks. It thrilled her to find a dress by a designer I'd never heard of, and her joy splashed over onto me, regardless of how the dress looked.

As we'd swung through the racks of clothes and carried them to the fitting room, conversation was even easier than it was in the car. It was like the chatter of nursery school kids playing in separate corners. I'd talk about school, Mom might describe a sonata she was learning. Or sometimes, like all grown-ups, she felt she had to give me advice, which in my mother's case was often mystifying. I remember her saying you had to learn to exist on the line between loving the world and wanting to live in another world completely. I sensed that if I'd asked what she meant, her answer might involve more than I wanted to know.

Every so often, entirely by chance, we found a bargain that looked nice. Transformative, even. Not that it transformed *me*, but that I imagined it changing the boys in school, who would see me, in my new outfit, as a different person. A girl.

In the cramped changing cubicles, I twirled around for my mother. I knew what would please her—practical, subtle, unsexy.

And I wanted to please her more than I cared about looking pretty. Especially when nothing looked pretty. I might as well listen to her. Margaret said she didn't understand the unflattering outfits I bought with Mom on these trips. How odd that Mom's thrifty inner Puritan should choose to emerge at the mall.

Now, on the drive home from Frank's, Mom said, "Do you need anything? New sandals?"

"I don't know," I said. "What do you think?"

"The buying cure," my mother said. "That's what my mother used to call shopping. You get the joke, right, Nico? The talking cure is what they used to call psychoanalysis."

"I get it now," I said. "Ha ha."

"After my father died," said Mom, "my mother went out and bought an expensive mink coat. She wore it twice, then put it in mothballs and never wore it again. Your grandma just wasn't a mink coat kind of girl."

I hated it when my mother talked about her parents. It depressed me that she still missed them. It was worse now, because it made me realize that missing someone could last an entire lifetime.

My mother said, "What about some new summer stuff?"

Shopping was about the future. What future would I shop for? Where would I wear what I bought, and why would it matter?

"I don't need anything," I said.

My mother said, "Let's buy something to go with your cute new haircut."

"No," I said.

"No, thank you," said my mother.

"No," I said. "Bellissima, okay?"

We didn't speak the whole way home.

As we pulled into the driveway, my mother said, "I can't stop thinking about that last argument I had with your sister."

I said, "She doesn't care any more, so why should you?" It took me a while to recognize myself in the passenger-side mirror. What a terrible person I was to be so angry about a haircut.

Dad was in the kitchen, reading the paper, and when he glanced up, I understood that I looked even worse than I'd thought.

Dad said, "God, Nico. Sorry. For a second you looked like Margaret."

"Mom?" I said. "Is that why you acted so weird in Frank's salon?"

"Weird how?" my mother murmured as she moved toward the fridge. "I wasn't aware of acting weird. These strawberries are all furry."

I went to the bathroom mirror. In fact, I didn't look like myself, or like Margaret, or like the male version of me. I looked like Jean Seberg in *Joan of Arc*, lit so that the heavenly radiance shone on her upturned forehead even as her cheeks were shadowed by the silhouettes of the flames dancing up to kill her.

WE'D LOVED THE BOOKSTORE, MARGARET AND I. IT WAS OUR OWN private kingdom, which the two indulged princesses could plunder and pillage at will, as long as we read, or promised to read, whatever we took home. I'd loved Goldengrove even before I could read, when the glossy jackets seemed to call out to me, vying for my attention.

Now I loved it in a different way—superior, protective, literally above it all on the platform behind the counter from which I could survey my domain and gaze out the front window. I liked spying on the customers, catching them unawares at that undefended moment of losing themselves in a book. Or I'd watch people walk in and try to guess what they'd buy. Surprise: the ones with dirt on their knees headed straight for the gardening section. I liked the kids looking for information about brand-new pets, and the trembly, hopeful women newly interested in decoupage or sewing nylon-stocking dolls. Sometimes there *were* surprises: macho road-crew guys seeking advice on how to make their relationships work, one geeky middle-schooler with a passion for Greek tragedy and fat nineteenth-century novels.

I was glad that none of my friends, or Margaret's friends, came in. Once I thought I saw Aaron pass on the opposite side of the street. The boy, if it *was* Aaron, glanced my way and kept going. I wanted to run after him, but I didn't know what to say. All you had to do, whispered the staircase spirit, was say hello and ask how he was.

Dad went over the obvious: where each subject was shelved. He taught me how to work the cash register, which for him was the equivalent of flying a jumbo jet. After I'd mastered the hard parts, I was on my own. My father hid in his office. I'd hear him typing away. One slow day I counted an average of four customers an hour, of which an average of three looked crushed at finding me instead of Dad, and of which an average of zero needed help. So all I had to do was take their money and ask if there was anything else they needed.

Or that's how it *should* have worked. Except that an average of two out of ten felt they had to talk to me about death and mourning and loss.

Strangers knew all about me. They'd ask how I was doing, and

I couldn't just say fine. So I'd shrug, and after a silence they'd say something like, "I know. It's hard." And bang, they were off and running, telling me about grief and its life span, its half-life and its resilience, the ebb and flow, the sneak attacks, the unpredictable setbacks. They felt they had to let me know that grief lasted forever, and yet they wanted to promise me that I would outlive it. It was a kind of pep talk, I knew, but it went deeper than that. People wanted to believe that their suffering had a purpose, if only so that they could offer me the distilled wisdom of their experience.

Women told me how lovely I looked. Or they'd say I'd gotten thinner. The grief diet, they said, as if everyone knew that death was nature's magic weight-loss plan. So many of them said the same things that I might have thought that there *was* common ground, if I hadn't known that I was alone on an iceberg split off from a glacier.

I sensed that the customers were looking at me but seeing themselves—their former selves—right after a loved one died. They'd tell me their intimate stories in an urgent, confiding tone. When they wept, I cried, too, and for a moment I almost believed that my iceberg might have room for another person. For that moment, it was helpful to see that the bereaved were not only walking and talking but laughing and yelling at their kids.

People gave me useless advice. Was I getting enough exercise? Did I play tennis? Hike? Swim? They got as far as swimming, then remembered how Margaret died. A surprising number told me not to make any important decisions for a year. At least a year. They were forgetting that I was thirteen. What life-changing choices did they think my parents would let me make? I couldn't decide what T-shirt to wear, what breakfast cereal to pretend to eat, what route to take when I biked from my house to the book-store. I couldn't do or say anything without anguish and regret.

One afternoon, a woman came in. I knew I'd met her some-where. At first she didn't notice me. She seemed to be on a mis-sion. I watched her guiltily scanning the shelves, like someone searching for a book about sex or some intimate health problem. Red hair, jumpy. Roughened, papery skin. She looked like an older version of Aaron's mother. Then I realized that was who she was.

I willed her not to buy anything, but it didn't work. The book she set on the counter was called *Ordinary Grief: Helping a Loved One Survive Loss*. I looked at the title, then at her. Finally she saw me.

"Nico, sweetheart," she said. "I didn't recognize you. You look so grown up."

"Thanks," I said. When had I become "sweetheart"? I'd only met her twice. The first time was after a school Christmas concert. Margaret and Aaron introduced the parents, and then stood back and watched them squirm. Everyone knew the score. Aaron and Margaret were going out, my parents didn't approve, Aaron's par-ents weren't pleased by their disapproval. It took about a minute to run out of conversation, and then we all stood around scuffing our feet on the auditorium carpet.

The second time was after the senior show, when the tide of Aaron and Margaret's triumph practically swept both families into each other's arms. Celebrity leveled the playing field. They were the parents of stars! They still didn't have much to say, but they seemed leisurely and calm, like sunbathers basking in the light of their children's success. Were Aaron's parents at the funeral? I thought so. I couldn't recall. Their faces swam up and sank back into the black pool of that rainy day.

Aaron's mom seemed to be deciding whether or not to hug me. Don't, I telegraphed. Please don't.

"How are you, Nico?" she said.

"Okay," I said. "I guess. How's Aaron?"

Aaron's mother eyed the book and let it answer for her.

"Not great," she said. "It's been hard."

"I know," I said.

"I'm sure you do," she said.

"Say hi to him for me," I said. "Tell him to stop by the store and say hi."

"I will," she said.

"Really!" I said, startling myself. "I'd *really* like to see him."

"I will," she repeated. "Take care of yourself, dear." On her way out, she turned and gave me a thin, heartfelt smile. The staircase spirit mimicked, *I'd really like to see him.*

One afternoon, my former fourth-grade teacher walked into the bookstore.

"How are you, Nico?" she said.

I said, "Mrs. Akins! How are *you?*"

"Retired." She smiled apologetically.

I said, "You look the same."

She held out her arms, and I let myself be hugged, though it meant climbing down from behind the counter. She squeezed me until her amber beads scooped painful dents in my chest.

Kids used to make fun of her, because in the midst of a lesson she'd suddenly clap her hands and say, "Now it's time for *play!*" Then we'd fold origami cranes for world peace or make torn-paper collages. Margaret told me that Mrs. Akins used to teach her classes that the origami was in remembrance of the children who were killed or had their faces melted off when we dropped the A-bomb on Hiroshima. But the school made her stop teaching that; they said it upset the students. After that Mrs. Akins talked to us about tolerance and understanding. Some kids had trouble folding the cranes. But I felt as if the bird was already there, nesting inside the paper, waiting to be set free.

"It's so hard," Mrs. Akins said now. "When my mother died . . . you know, I think maybe you were in my class. All I remember is throwing up every day before work."

I'd always liked Mrs. Akins, though to me she was just another teacher doll that wound itself up when school began and ran down at three. I vaguely remembered she used to be Miss Something Else. We'd made her Happy Wedding cards, and when she'd returned after her brief honeymoon, the class went wild from the embarrassment of thinking she might have had sex. I'd never imagined her having a mother, let alone one who could die. I'd never dreamed she could have been grieving even as she'd ordered us to play.

Pressing me to her pillowy chest, Mrs. Akins wept, and so did I. I knew she was crying about her mother and not about Margaret, or maybe a little about Margaret, but still, we were crying about the same thing

At last Mrs. Akins released me and, fixing me with her glittery eyes, said, "There's no reason you should believe me, Nico. But trust me when I say that your sister is looking out for you. I don't know where they go, but wherever it is, they can watch us. And they can intercede. Right now, even as we speak, your sister is finding a way to help you feel less lonely. Or maybe someone to help you. Right now—"

My father emerged from his office, blinking as if he'd been writing in the dark.

"Dad, you remember Mrs. Akins?" I said.

"Of course!" Obviously, he didn't.

"My fourth-grade teacher," I said. "Remember we all made those origami birds?"

My father said, "Nice to see you, Mrs.—"

"Akins," I said.

"Mrs. Akins," said Dad.

"I'm so sorry for your loss," Mrs. Akins said.

"Thank you," said my father. "Did Nico help you find what you were looking for?"

"To be honest," said Mrs. Akins, "I just stopped in to say hello. My book club is still deciding. . . ."

"Come back any time," my father said.

"I will," she said. But I didn't believe her. I would have done anything to make her stay, to hear more of what she knew—anything but ask her, with my father watching.

Then she was gone, and in the tinkle of the doorbell, I heard the staircase spirit giggling over everything I should have asked in those few precious moments before my father scared away the messenger from my sister.

Six

IT WAS LIKE BEING UNDER A CURSE TO SPEND ALL THOSE HOURS IN Goldengrove and not be able to read. Like being in prison, unable to escape into a book. When I did read, I was only trawling for scraps of information that I found and then wondered why I'd wanted to know them.

I should have been rereading the Narnia stories I'd loved as a kid who longed to enter another dimension through a wardrobe or a snow globe. I should have stuck with the books on botany or marine biology, the ones that described how all of history and world culture had converged to produce the pepper in your shaker.

But the only books that attracted me now were the last ones I should have gone near. I pored over books about the heart. Not as in heartbreak or heartthrob or sweetheart, but as in heart attack, heart disease. As in hypertrophic cardiomyopathy. As in long QT syndrome. As in congenital coronary artery abnormalities. Every sentence confirmed my worst fears. The effect was so instant and physical, I'd have to go to the bathroom, but then I'd return to where I'd left off.

Every expert whose kindly face and spotless white coat graced a jacket flap regretted to inform me that these problems were genetic. Fortunately, the conditions were rare. Unfortunately, I was doomed. I read about the symptoms I already had, the dull ache over my breastbone, the grinding in my chest, and new ones—dizziness, palpitations—I developed as I read them. I read greedily, compulsively, and with a shame that, when a customer walked in, made me hide the medical books inside picture books on African lions and New England barns.

I'd read until I had to sit on the floor until the store stopped spinning. Then I'd scoot from the health section to the death-and-dying shelf.

I started with books that promised to help you recover from grief, books whose authors, nearly all female, looked even kindlier and more sympathetic than the cardiologists. Their motherly head shots were meant to persuade me that they knew what I was feeling and wanted me to feel better. They hoped that it might comfort me to read about the personal tragedies—a loved one's illness or death—that had made them want to help me. They'd gone to graduate school, they had practices, gave lectures, traveled the world. Every day they dealt with people suffering just like me. They urged me to reach out, talk to others in my situation. They illustrated their anecdotes with pie charts and graphs. There were workbook pages for me to jot down my thoughts, tests on which I got zero. What if I couldn't think of one activity I enjoyed? What if I couldn't find one thoughtful favor to do for someone else? The books advised me not to blame myself if I couldn't get with their programs, but they didn't offer alternate ones, which only made me feel more alone.

I paged through the book Aaron's mother had bought: *Ordinary Grief: Helping a Loved One Survive Loss*. I skimmed until the writer, a Dr. Marion Staley, PhD, described bringing home a new kitten that refused to crawl out from the sofa. She suggested that I think of the grieving relative as that poor, confused kitty. That was when I shut the book and put it back on the shelf.

I began to wonder if I'd inherited something else from my father. The only books that kept my attention were a little like the one he was writing. Not end-of-the-world books, exactly, but books that told you what people in other eras and societies imagined happened to you after death. I read *The Egyptian Book of the Dead* and *The Tibetan Book of the Dead*, and though I skipped a lot, I understood the basics. The dead passed through realms and kingdoms, worlds of dark and light, as they shed their memories and slowly let go of their love for the living. I imagined Margaret moving from place to place, each realm more hushed and peaceful and farther away from us.

My days fell into a sort of pattern—a holding pattern, I knew. But at least it was holding.

At noon, my father went into Goldengrove to talk business with Elaine before she had to go get Tycho. I left home at around the same time and biked into town and met Dad for lunch at the Nibble Corner.

The bike ride was my favorite part of the day: the gentle, curving, slow descent through the fragrant misty woods, then a dash across two meadows—one golden, one green—and by then I was on Main Street. I loved the clear air, the sun on my forehead, the landscape streaming past. My bike was a vintage dark red Schwinn that Margaret gave me when she got her driver's license. It was a part of me when I rode it, and I loved it the way cowboys in old movies loved their horses.

Every day, my father and I ordered grilled Swiss on rye with tomato. The first time, our waitress—Hi! I'm Valerie!—made cow eyes at Dad and said she'd been in Margaret's class and she was sorry for our loss. But pretty soon she'd just say, "The usual?" and Dad and I would nod. That was the advantage of always eating the same lunch. We didn't have to talk to Valerie. I didn't have to decide.

As we polished off the Nibble Corner's buttery, warm, melted cheese, my father and I concentrated on our sandwiches as if we were teasing the flesh from some lethally bony fish. I chewed slowly and without stopping, to keep my face from going slack and collapsing like a pudding. For my parents' sake, I was trying to act remotely sane. And in a way, I was. I could get through an hour or so without thinking about my sister. Then a wave of sorrow would crash into me and knock me flat.

Sometimes, when the silence thickened, my father would ask me what I was reading.

Living with Heart Disease. Surviving Loss. The Tibetan Book of the Dead.

"Nothing much," I'd say. In the old days, he might have kept asking till I came up with an answer, but now we acted as if the tiniest pressure could shatter our eggshell selves.

The only subject he liked to talk about was *Eschatology for Dummies*. I wondered if his ideas about the afterlife had changed now that Margaret might be there. I wanted to test my theory that Margaret was relocating, in stages, to a more comfortable dwelling. But it seemed safer not to ask, and besides, my father's subject was the apocalypse and not the ragged hole that one death could rip in a few fragile lives.

Though he'd been working on the book for years, he never got tired of thinking about how people coped with their fear or their hope that our planet might not last forever. He wasn't religious, he didn't have an agenda based on his own beliefs. He was simply interested, in a scientific way, in how his fellow humans imagined the unimaginable. He liked the fact that I cared about ecology and the earth. Sometimes I felt that he was planning to interview me for a final chapter about whether us gloomy, Al Gore types really believed, in our heart of hearts, that fossil-fuel emissions would strangle the planet. What would I tell him? I believed it. I didn't. I did. I couldn't.

At Goldengrove, whenever customers bought novels about the rapture, my father inquired if they just liked the plots, or if it was something they expected to happen. He always asked so politely, with such a genuine desire to know. He never went near *my* questions: Would they be raptured wearing their clothes? What would happen to their cars if they were vacuumed off the highway?

It was calming, like listening to bedtime stories, eating grilled cheese, and hearing Dad go on about the Micronesian tribe building a landing strip for the planes that would fly them to heaven, or the Siberian shamans who banged their drums until the gods destroyed the world just to make them keep quiet. Or the Aztecs who thought that they'd outlived four suns, and that the fifth would burn out unless they quenched its thirst with human blood. He spent a whole lunch explaining how the Norsemen were convinced that you could tell the end was coming because winter would follow winter without a summer in between.

"Kind of like global warming," I said.

"You got it," said my dad.

One afternoon, I sensed a change. Nothing dramatic, but noticeable enough so that when I asked my father how his writing was going, I could tell from the way he said, "Not bad," that he meant, "Really good."

He said, "Listen, Nico, I've been working on a chapter about a doomsday cult that lived around here." He was staring at me with an intensity that, for one dizzying second, made me think he'd *joined* some sect of fanatics. People did stranger things. I'd read a book about two brothers whose mother died, and they gambled away every penny of the fortune she'd left.

"When?" I said.

Dad said, "The nineteenth century. Their leader, Williams Miller, calculated that Christ would arrive to inaugurate the millennial kingdom on October 22, 1844."

"Exactly?" I said.

"Exactly," my father said.

"Cool," I said. "Smart guy."

"Nico, Nico." My father smiled.

I said, "So how many suckers did he get to believe him?"

"Fifty thousand," said Dad.

"No way," I said.

"Way. They were all so convinced that they gave away their possessions, their house and farms, their cows, their horses, their—"

"Who'd they give them to?" I said

"I don't know," said Dad. "How strange I never thought about that. Neighbors? Relatives? Friends? The faithful wouldn't be needing their donkeys when God beamed them up into heaven."

After a while, I said, "Dad . . . So how did it work out?"

"Right. On the appointed day they dressed in white robes and climbed the highest mountain and waited for the saints to pop out of their graves and witness the believers rising into the air to be married to the Bridegroom Christ. Sort of like those Moonie weddings in the baseball stadiums. They stayed on the hill for forty-eight hours. Everybody singing and dancing and playing homemade flutes. The whole crowd watching the sky."

He leaned across the table. "You know how when you're supposed to meet someone, and the person is late, and you look up every two seconds to see if the person has arrived?"

"I guess." I was trying to remember if I'd ever met anyone anywhere by myself, let alone if I'd been early. Aaron and Margaret were always on time when they'd picked me up after a movie. When I met Dad at the Nibble Corner, he was always there before me. I wondered if he meant Mom.

"That's what it must have been like. Two days of thinking that an angel was going to land any minute. Imagine the stiff necks."

I pictured the crowds of people shivering in their thin white garments, holding hands and singing hymns and leaning into each chill October breeze as if it were the headwind stirred up by the angel. I saw them swaying like wheat, like birches, turning briefly into trees and then back again into humans.

"Nico?" said Dad. "Are you with me?"

"So then what happened?" I said.

"I just told you," said Dad.

"Sorry," I said. "Tell me again."

"What do *you* think? After two days, when the angel still hadn't arrived, the elders called an emergency conference. They'd decided there'd been a miscalculation, and their leader went back to his actuarial tables so he'd get the date right the next time. Their neighbors attacked them on their way home. You know, Nico, I never realized it was probably because the neighbors assumed that they'd want their farms back. I guess I never thought about it till you asked whom they gave their stuff to. That's why I like talking to you about this—"

"Thanks," I said. "Me too." I hoped I sounded convincing.

After a beat Dad said, "When it didn't happen, when *nothing* happened, the Millerites always referred to it as the Great Disappointment."

That was what disappointed them, that they were still alive? That someone you loved could disappear—now, that was the nasty surprise.

"The Great Disappointment," my father went on. "That pretty much sums it up. Whatever you hope for, you're not going to get. I know I shouldn't be saying this to my kid, who I want to have a positive outlook. But I don't know, Nico. Sometimes, ever since . . . I keep thinking . . ."

"Thinking what?" Ever since *what*? I wanted to make him say it.

"You know what Janis Joplin called it?"

"Called what?"

"The Great Disappointment. The always being let down by life. She called it the Saturday Night Swindle."

"Who's Janis Joplin?" I said.

"Very funny," my father said.

"Margaret thought she was cheesy," I said.

My father said, "She would have loved Janis. Eventually. Another year or two, maybe."

We checked out each other's grilled cheeses, and each took small bites of our own.

"Anyhow," said my father, "the point is . . . the hilltop where they waited for the angels isn't far from here. I think the town library might have some old newspapers that might help us figure out where it was."

Help *us?* When had Dad's rapture fantasies become a family project?

"We could go there and walk around and see if we can . . . I know this sounds crazy, Nico, but maybe we'd *feel* something. Some leftover . . . vibration."

"It does sound crazy, Dad. *Vibration?*"

"Come on, Nico. It's worth a try. Just to see."

Dad's hippie-dippie project was making me want to put my head down on the table.

"Sure, Dad," I said. "That would be great. Find out where it was."

Once my father realized that I could handle the challenge of running the bookstore, he began spending more time at the library to search the archives for information that might help him pinpoint the site of the Great Disappointment. I liked having the place to myself. I could relax and read about heart disease and the afterlife without worrying that my father might catch me.

It seemed like a good sign when, for a break from the death books, I started skimming the books about sex, idly stroking the crotch of my jeans and listening for the doorbell. I couldn't tell much from the line drawings of smiling men and women twisted into pretzels, diagrams that reminded me of those pamphlets explaining how to install your new electronics purchase.

Despite what Margaret had said, I knew that sex was more than

knowing what flavor of ice cream you wanted, more than deciding how many dates you had to go on before you let a boy touch
your breasts, more than no meaning no. I understood that sex
could make anyone do *anything*, but I couldn't figure out how the
feeling I got from rubbing myself could make people ruin their
whole lives.

One afternoon, as I walked down the poetry aisle on my way to
the human sexuality section, a thick book caught my attention. It
was an anthology of poems from around the world, and at the end
was an alphabetical index of first lines.

On a hunch, I looked up "Margaret."

I turned to the page, read a few lines, and then reread them,
trying to understand and at the same time to convince myself that
I must be mistaken. I no longer cared if someone walked into the
store. I sank to the floor as I reread the poem.

Margaret, are you grieving
Over Goldengrove unleaving?
Leaves, like the things of man, you
With your fresh thoughts care for, can you?
Ah! as the heart grows older
It will come to such sights colder
By and by, nor spare a sigh
Though worlds of wanwood leafmeal lie;
And yet you will weep and know why.
Now no matter, child, the name:
Sorrow's springs are the same.
Nor mouth had, no nor mind, expressed
What heart heard of, ghost guessed:

It is the blight man was born for,
It is Margaret you mourn for.

I didn't get it right away or, truthfully, at all. Wanwood leafmeal
sounded like some kind of garden fertilizer. I knew the poem was
about grief and mourning and sorrow, about everything and everyone getting older and dying. For some reason, it infuriated me. I held
the book open before me like a cross to ward off a vampire, like the
surprise piece of evidence at my parents' trial for . . . what? What sa-
dist would name a baby after such a depressing poem? Maybe they'd
actually caused her death by naming her Margaret. Nancy or Suzie or
Heather might still be alive and well. I slammed the book shut as if it
were the poem's fault, though I knew that if I'd read the poem when
Margaret was alive, it wouldn't have meant anything beyond some
dead guy's weak attempt to sound gloomy and important.

The effort of wedging the heavy book back onto the shelf left
me so exhausted I had to lie down on the floor. I opened my eyes
to see my father leaning over me.

"Nico!" he said. "What's wrong?"

"I'm fine," I said. "I was taking a nap." I glanced at the shelves,
where the incriminating anthology had faded back into the rows
of books. I almost said, "I found the poem. I know what you and
Mom did." But what would that have led to besides a conversation
I didn't want to have, looking up at my father from the bookstore
floor?

I said, "I'm trying an experiment. A sort of osmosis thing. I'm
seeing whether if I take a nap next to the poetry books, maybe a
few lines will seep into my brain and make me understand poetry
better."

Dad said, "My little scientist. So does it work? Did anything stick?"

"Not a word," I answered.

"Too bad," my father said. Clearly, he didn't believe me. But at least he didn't ask why my experiment had left me in tears.

I HAD TO BE CAREFUL WHAT I SAID, LEST ALL MY LIES COME TRUE. My experiment in the poetry aisle had been an accidental success. *Something* lodged in my mind, so that for the rest of the day, that line, "*It is Margaret you mourn for*," bashed around inside my brain like a bird trapped in a house. I knew it was insane to think that naming my sister after a morbid poem meant that she would die young. But the line stayed with me, and I wanted to get rid of it, the way you can pass along a tune that's driving you crazy by singing it so that it leaves your head and enters someone else's.

That evening, at dinner, I kept quiet as long as I could. Then I asked, "So are you going to change the name of the store now, or what?" It wasn't what I'd said so much as the way I'd said it, the aggrieved, sullen *teenage* tone my parents hadn't heard since my sister died. They sat up and listened as if they were hearing the voice of someone they used to know.

Dad was the first to realize that it was only my former self. "Why would *that* be?" he said.

"Goldengrove," I said. "Isn't that from the poem you named Margaret after?"

My parents looked puzzled. Could they have forgotten? Did they think Margaret was just a name they'd liked when they were hippies planting vegetables by the light of the full moon?

I said, "Would you like me to bring the book home and read it to you?"

"That won't be necessary," Dad said. "I remember it perfectly well."

My mother said, "Margaret's a beautiful name."

"*Was*," I said. "*Was* a beautiful name."

"*Is*," she said warningly.

"I still think Margaret's a pretty name," said my father. "As is Nico, for that matter."

"Pretty?" I said. "Pretty?" I looked to Mom for support even as I felt my case collapse. How could I accuse them of harming my sister by naming her after a poem? Soon they'd insist on sending *me* for professional help. I wondered if Aaron's mother had told him I'd said he should come visit me at the store.

I said, "Speaking of doctors," though we hadn't been. "Did you guys make that appointment for me to see the specialist in the city?"

"What appointment?" said Mom.

I said, "I can't believe you forgot."

"Nico, sweetheart, there's nothing wrong with you," said my father.

I said, "The sooner the better, okay? The heart specialist?"

"Will do." My mother gave me a trembly version of Margaret's Ginger Rogers salute.

And though it was still early, I went to my room and got into bed.

Seven

THE NEXT MORNING, I WOKE UP DRENCHED WITH SWEAT FROM A night of troubling dreams. In one, a blotchy purple stain seeped in from the edges of my field of vision. I'd never had a nightmare like that, of gathering darkness and blindness. I was afraid to open my eyes. I opened one. I could see. Then I remembered the line from the poem.

I whispered, "Help me. I need your help. Tell me what to do."

Margaret and I used to play with a ouija board we'd found in the attic. The first few times were thrilling. The gliding, the spelling out, my gathering amazement as the letters turned into words. I'd wanted to believe that Margaret and I were taking dictation from the beyond.

The last time we did it, we'd asked the spirit what its name was.

"M-o-t-h-r-a," it spelled out.

I said, "Isn't that the monster in that horror film you like?"

"Hush, you'll scare it away," Margaret said.

The spirit spelled out "N-i-c-o." I caught my breath.

It spelled, "G-e-t y-o-u-r s-i-s-t-e-r s-o-m-e c-a-k-e."

I said, "You're doing it, right?"

"Think what you like," Margaret said.

It was easy for us to play like that, then. Whom did we think we were contacting? We'd never *met* anyone who had died.

But now, though I longed for a message, I would never have touched the board. And whom would I have played with? Instead, as I lay in bed, feeling the sun filter through the curtains, I prayed to become a human ouija-board puck. Let my sister move me.

After a while, I felt . . . something. The urge to get out of bed, a faint pressure on one elbow. I let it push me, I didn't resist as it steered me to my closet. My hand rose, and I plucked Margaret's Hawaiian shirt from the swaying clothing. I reentered my body to find it wearing my sister's shirt and feeling ever so slightly braver.

"Thank you," I said to the empty room. Or to Margaret, if she was there. In the shirt, I could face the bookstore and not succumb to the temptation of obsessively rereading the poem about death and my sister.

I slipped out of the house. I didn't want my mother to see me in Margaret's shirt.

My father was waiting in our usual booth at the Nibble Corner. When he spotted me, he looked vaguely irritated or anxious, as if I were bringing him bad news about a broken household appliance. Maybe Margaret's shirt stirred some recollection that failed to compute. Or maybe that was the default expression his face assumed that summer, before he knew someone was watching. He didn't seem to notice what I was wearing, or to connect the shirt with my sister. Evidently, Margaret's fashion sense hadn't come from Dad.

We ate our sandwiches. I went to the bookstore. I felt fine, or almost fine. The silkiness of the shirt on my skin could have been Margaret touching my arm. The palm trees swayed, hula girls danced, Margaret's ghost exerted its pressure, and all of it lulled me and kept me from seeing the hurricane heading my way. Still, I must have sensed some disturbance in the air. Because when my father left for the library, I didn't want him to go.

I said, "Have fun, Dad," in someone else's reedy voice. I felt a grinding in my chest. I needed to see a doctor! The first appointment my mom had been able to make was not for another few weeks.

To calm myself, I opened my favorite book, a volume on Sienese painting so large that I had to spread it across the counter. Each picture reeled me in, first with the bait of its story line, then with the lure of the secret beneath it. Turning the pages transported me from a candy-colored city to a hillside on which two shepherds and their dog huddled by a fire, gazing up at an angel powered by a rocket exploding from its robe. I paused at a levitating monk, rising into the air, then went on to the garden paradise crowded with joyous, reunited souls. All around were flowering plants in glorious full bloom, trees loaded with enough lemons for eternal lemonade. How glad the embracing angels were to have ended up there.

Painting by painting, I worked my way through the miraculous rescues, the saints snatching infants from the jaws of wild beasts and restoring the pink of life to the ashen-faced dead. One artist seemed to specialize in saints resurrecting drowned children. A baby had fallen into a fountain. A boy had slipped into a river. Both paintings showed the children immersed, their faces blue as water, and then in subsequent panels the boy and the baby stood, dressed in red, their tiny hands clasped in gratitude to the saint who had fished them out. I wondered if the painter had seen something like that, or if he had lost, or almost lost, a child to death by drowning.

Margaret *had* been born too late. She'd meant too late for the jazz standards, the screwball comedies, the satin gowns. But she'd been off by the centuries. Too late for the lifeguard saint.

Suddenly jealous of the families of the rescued children, I turned to the painting I loved most and saved for last, *Saint Nicholas of Tolentino Saving a Shipwreck*. Shining through the furry black sky, a celestial searchlight had picked out a boat with notched walls and towers, as if a fortified town had slipped offshore and floated onto the ocean. A storm had ripped the sails from the ship and swept them into the sky, where they whirled and snapped like laundry blown off a clothesline. From the edge of the painting, the saint flew down to save the drenched passengers and sailors huddled, praying, on deck.

Staring at the picture, I found what I'd wanted when I'd gazed into Margaret's snow globe. I left my body and entered the painting. I felt the sting of salt on my face, I heard the wind moan and the sailors' shouts, I saw the saint approaching. I focused on the heavenly laser piercing the spiraling wind, and as I cowered along with the shivering crew, waiting for Saint Nicholas to steady the boat and gather me in his arms, I imagined—no, I heard—the tolling of the ship's bell.

In fact, it was the doorbell. Someone had walked in.

Even when I heard a voice saying, almost fearfully, "Nico?" I raised one arm to ward off the lash of salt spray. I wasn't ready to leave the roiling sea for the airless tomb of the bookstore.

Someone stood in front of me. A mouth, a familiar face. It took me so long to identify it that when I finally did, my own face lit up, and I blushed. We both acted as if I'd been joking, making believe I didn't recognize Aaron. We laughed, but it wasn't real laughter. It was the noise two chimpanzees might make to express something too deep for everyday monkey language.

"Aaron! Aaron! Hi! Hello!" I was practically yelling.

"Hey, kid," Aaron said. "How are you?"

"Okay, I guess." Water bubbled out of my eyes. That's how okay I was. Fighting tears gave me something to focus on, a time-out in which to process the fact that Aaron was actually here. My standing behind the counter would have made it awkward for him to hug me or touch me. He was trying not to look at me—out of politeness, I guessed. The sight of him made me feel a stab of longing for Margaret, from which I was distracted by the startling realization that all this time, all these days and weeks, I'd been waiting for him to walk in.

"You're still here," he said. "My mom told me—"

Where else would I be? Was Aaron nervous? About seeing *me?* About seeing Margaret's sister.

"Don't cry," said Aaron. "Please don't cry. Forget I said that. Go ahead."

It was such a huge relief, not having to pretend. Weeping felt like sneezing or like falling asleep. Aaron watched me, not annoyed or impatient but, it seemed to me, grateful, as if I were doing what he would have done if he'd been a girl. Snot roped out my nose. I wiped it with the back of my hand. I wasn't embarrassed. I didn't care that he was a boy. An older guy. A relative stranger. At that moment, he was the person who knew me best in the world.

I scrubbed at my eyes and willed the tears to stop. Meanwhile, I shut the art book and slid it under the counter. What if Aaron thought I'd been looking at art just to impress him? But I hadn't known he'd come in. I'd been looking at a sinking ship, at sailors in danger of drowning. I didn't want it to upset Aaron. That a boat might remind him of Margaret made me so glad to see him that I started crying again.

By now Aaron was looking at me in a way that I mistook for curiosity about when—if ever—I might calm down. But he wasn't looking at me. He was looking at Margaret's shirt. He kept wanting to look at my face, but his eyes kept tracking down to the palm trees, then back and forth, nose hula girls, forehead coconuts, trying to put it together. Since he couldn't focus on me, I could stare at him without having to worry about him staring back. Aaron still had that golden glow, burnished by exhaustion and sadness. He looked wasted, but more attractive: a haunted, insomniac soul. I thought of Aaron's mother, and I wondered if a stranger seeing our family would think we'd aged drastically, too.

Maybe I wouldn't have noticed the change if I hadn't known his face so well, if I hadn't watched so closely as Aaron and my sister traded tastes of the pistachio that dyed their mouths a matching green. Anyone else might just have seen a handsome boy, innocent and self-admiring. Maybe a little troubled. Screw loose? I didn't think so.

"That's quite a haircut," Aaron said.

"Thanks," I said. "Thanks for mentioning it. It was my mom's idea."

"So I guess she took you to the butchers at the mall?"

How much had Margaret told him? He must have known all about us.

"You look completely different," he said.

"I *am* completely different." I wondered if I should come down from the platform behind the counter. I stayed where I was.

"I know," he said. "But different better."

"That would be strange," I said.

"Different *really* better."

"Thanks," I said. "I don't know why that would be. I feel different worse. A lot worse."

"Don't you think I understand that?" Aaron sounded almost angry. It was a little unnerving, how quickly he got annoyed. Grief was rough on everyone's nerves. Everyone was edgy.

"I'm sorry," I said. "I mean, I know you know." I'd forgotten what we were talking about. Better not to talk, better not to call attention to a girl with a bad haircut wearing her dead sister's shirt. But the longer the silence lasted, the greater the danger that Aaron would leave. Or that my father would come back. If I couldn't say, "How are you?" what were my chances of saying, "Please stay. I need you to stay"?

Finally Aaron said, "I looked for you at that meeting."

"What meeting?"

"The meeting about the pond scum."

"Oh, *that* meeting. I forgot."

"I can understand why," Aaron said.

"You can?"

"My God, Nico." He finally looked at me, at my face.

"So what's up with the phytoplankton?" I asked.

"Excuse me?"

"Phytoplankton," I repeated. "Also known as pond scum."

"Excellent." Aaron grinned and stuck up his thumb.

I watched him as closely as I dared. Was he making fun of me?

"I'm not being sarcastic," he said. "It's great that you know stuff like that."

"So what did they decide?"

"Decide? Since when has this town ever decided anything? They did what they always do. Talk and argue, dis*cuss*, blah blah, talk and argue some more, freak each other out. That's what they like best, they like to feel really scared. They've been shaking in their boots ever since 9/11, up here in the middle of nowhere, way off the terrorist radar. Right?"

"Right," I said. For a second, I wondered, Was Aaron high? I didn't think so. He just had the unstoppered sound of someone who hadn't talked in a while.

"But the thing is," he was saying, "if they're terrified, at least they're feeling *something*. Although that's not what they *think* they like. They think they like feeling *nothing*, which is why they live up here where nothing ever happens, where what gives them screaming nightmares is the fucking pond scum. And of course, your sister dying. That really blew them away."

I heard the breath catch in my throat, the only sound I could make. Aaron understood. He said, "Graduation was hell. Half the town felt they had to come up to me and say how sorry they were about Marga-ret, and I had to thank them. I knew they meant well, and all the time I wanted to kill them. I wish you'd been there, Nico."

"We didn't go," I said. "We didn't want to."

"I understand that," Aaron said. "And I respect your family's decision. I just meant for support. For me."

"Oh," I said.

"You would have hated it," Aaron said. "Everything she couldn't stand, one thing after another. There was no one I could look at. No one to roll my eyes at. Teachers and kids she didn't even *like* were pretending they were her best friends. They were all competing. Who knew her better, longer, telling their personal reminiscences that probably never even happened."

I said, "Maybe that's nice. I don't know. I'm glad I wasn't there. So what *is* the story?"

"The story on . . . ?"

"On the phytoplankton."

"Oh, right. If things keep going like they did last summer, which they will, thanks to El Fucking Niño or global warming or whatever—"

"They definitely will," I said. How I longed for that other life in which I worried about climate change. And how great that Aaron thought about it, too. I'd never realized that we had anything but Margaret in common. Margaret knew we were headed for ecological disaster, but she liked to pretend I'd invented it to be a Debbie Downer.

Aaron said, "By August we're going to be sitting on a major sinkhole. Skin rashes, eye infections, liver damage. Sulphury, rotten-egg swamp gas. It'll be like the black lagoon the creature crawls out of. At least I'm getting out of here."

"I'm not," I couldn't help saying.

"I know," said Aaron. "Sorry."

"That's all right. I don't want to leave." Only when I said it did I know it was true. Margaret and I had dreamed of going to Boston, or New York, or even Paris someday. I'd assumed we'd go together. Now she'd found a permanent home, and if I wanted to be near her, I was stuck here forever.

Aaron said, "Trust me. Nico. You'll want to leave. Get back to me in three years."

"Okay." I shrugged. In three years we wouldn't know each other. But no matter where we were, we'd always have this bond. "I'll be ready to go by then. Probably."

"For sure," Aaron said.

The effort of imagining ourselves that far into the future pitched us into a silence so deep I thought we would never climb out. Aaron looked around the shop, at the books, the floor, the ceiling, his hands, his shoes, everywhere but at me. Which was how he was able to say, "That shirt looks good on you."

"Thanks," I said. "It was Margaret's."

"I know that," he said.

Obviously. How stupid of me. Aaron had super vision.

After that we just looked at each other. Margaret's name was so powerful we expected . . . what? An earthquake to shake the books off the shelves? Actually, I expected my father to walk in and scare Aaron away and leave me alone with the staircase spirit telling me what I should have said.

I said, "My dad's at the library." Aaron understood. Whatever we wanted or needed to say, we'd better say it fast.

Aaron said, "I keep dreaming about her."

"I do, too," I said.

"In my dreams, she's always alive."

"I know," I said. "Mine, too." We were jabbering like passengers on a plane about to crash.

"I keep dreaming that they've rescued her, or that the whole thing never happened."

"That's strange," I said. "*Really* strange. I keep dreaming she's fine, and the two of you are sitting around my kitchen table."

"That's sort of like my dream, " Aaron said. "How bizarre is that?"

"Totally," I said.

"But actually," he said, "the strangest part is that she was alive and now she isn't. That's the thing I can't get past. I can't get my head around it. The absence. How someone can be here one minute, and the next minute they're gone. You tell them everything in your life and then they . . . can't be reached. Unlisted number forever. I keep thinking that this little . . . episode, this little trick will end, and she'll be back again, and it will all have been some cruel joke."

He was saying what I'd so often thought but never said out loud. I was grateful he'd said it, if only *because* no one had. I was crying again, but silently now. I closed my eyes. I was afraid that seeing Aaron cry might mean we could never be friends. Which was pointless, because we *weren't* friends. But maybe, I thought, we could be.

"I don't know what to do," Aaron said. "It's relentless. Everything I do to cheer myself up only makes me feel worse. I go for a ride, get a burger, I can't eat. I mean, how are we supposed to get through the day?"

Since when had Aaron and I become *we*? It was like Dad saying *we* needed to track down his doomsday cult. They were right. *We* were our own gang, our own separate tribe. The tiny band of survivors figuring out how to live without Margaret.

"I guess time's got to pass." I sounded like every well-meaning cornball who'd ever walked into the bookstore.

"So I hear," said Aaron. "Meanwhile I can't do anything I used to do with her."

"Me, too." I said. "I mean, me neither."

"I can't listen to music," he said.

"Me neither. I can't watch old movies."

"I can't go anywhere near the lake."

I said, "What's left?"

Aaron said. "I can't go through my entire life scared of music and swimming and ice cream."

"I've been thinking that, too."

There was nothing more to say. Aaron looked around, trying to find a book to pretend he'd come in to buy. I wondered why he *had* come in. Had he seen me through the window wearing Margaret's shirt? I'd told his mother to tell him to stop by. His mother made him do it, and now he could tell her he had.

He seemed to be getting ready to leave when he said, "I have an idea. Have you ever heard about these courses they have to help people conquer their crazy phobias? Like people scared of flying. They make them sit in airplanes parked at the gate, they play them tapes of takeoff and landing. Ease them into it, step by step. What if *we* did something like that? Did stuff together. Little by little."

I said, "There was a girl in my fifth-grade class with such bad claustrophobia she'd throw up if the teacher closed the classroom door. Her parents sent her to a special clinic. She told us she slept in a coffin. Probably she was lying. When she came back, she still got sick unless the door was open."

"Autoimmunization," said Aaron. "I read on the Internet about this guy who works with poisonous snakes, and he shoots himself up every day with teensy drops of venom, and now he can get bitten by a king cobra, it's like a mosquito bite. That's how some researcher discovered the cure for ulcers, plus another mad scientist tried it with DDT, sprinkling insecticide onto his family's cornflakes."

"That sounds sort of nuts." I wondered where this was leading. My dad had been gone a long time. If I were alone, I'd worry about him being late. But with Aaron there, I was afraid that my father would walk in and interrupt us.

"We could try doing things we can't do. Things we used to do with Margaret. We could do it together. An experiment. *You're* the scientist, right?"

I thought, Breathe in. Breathe out.

Margaret used the word *experiment* for the games she invented. Early on, she figured out that the word would persuade me to play. Once, we'd darkened our rooms and lit candles. Margaret cut a deck of cards and wrote the card down and knocked on the wall. I closed my eyes and concentrated and wrote down the card I saw. We did it fifty times, reversed direction, did it fifty times more. I didn't remember our score, but it was very high. We'd been proud of our closeness, our telepathic powers. It never made us feel crowded or spied on, the way it did when our mother knew what we were thinking.

I couldn't decide whether I should be flattered that Aaron knew something about me—I was going to be a scientist—or insulted that, once again, Aaron and Margaret were the artists and I was the boring math dweeb. I was pleased that Aaron knew I was anything at all. I liked the idea of *experimenting* with our grief and fears.

Anyway, that's what I told myself so as not to have to think about how excited I was by the prospect of hanging out with Aaron.

"Like what?" I said. "Do what?"

"Take a ride to the Dairy Divine. Have an ice cream for your sister."

All the warm fellow feeling evaporated and left me sadder than before. I dream about her, I miss her. What was *that* about? Now he was suggesting we get in the car and just go get ice cream like we used to when my sister was alive?

"I don't know if I could do that," I said.

"I don't know if I could either," he said. "That's why I thought I'd ask. I couldn't do it alone, but maybe if I had company . . . someone who knew how hard it was, what it took to walk up to the counter and order." He smiled. "You can get two different flavors, Nico. Three. You don't have to decide. It's on me."

I shook my head.

"Okay," said Aaron. "I understand why this might be tough. Think it over. Meanwhile, want to hear something else strange?"

I said, "I think I've had enough strangeness for one afternoon."

He said, "That book you were looking at, the art book—"

I touched it under the counter, like a rabbit's foot.

"I have that same book. You sister loved it. I'd been saving up. I was planning to buy her a copy for Christmas. I guess she told you that, right?"

"No," I said. "She never mentioned it." I didn't know which was more disturbing: the coincidence, or the fact that Margaret hadn't told me about the book. Whenever she found anything she loved, she couldn't enjoy it unless the whole world fell in love with it, too. One thing I'd liked about the book was its lack of

painful associations. I'd discovered it on my own. Now that had
been taken from me, and in its place was the thought that Margaret
had, as Mrs. Akins promised, helped me find someone to help. For
one shivery moment, I wondered if Aaron was lying. Why would
he lie about a book and pretend that Margaret had liked it? On
the other hand, why would someone get a book as a gift for a girl
whose father owned a bookstore?

"Come on," Aaron said. "There must have been a couple of
things about your sister that you didn't know."

I didn't want to hear what they were. I was sweating up Margaret's shirt. I said, "Do you still have it?"

"What?" he said.

"The book."

"Yeah, but I can't look at it. You want it? You can have it."

"No, thanks," I said. "I can take this one home if I want. It's so
beautiful. It always makes me feel better. Did you ever notice how
many paintings show angels saving people from shipwrecks and
saints reviving drowned children and—"

"Who gives a rat's ass about beauty, Nico? Where was that
saint when—"

My father walked in.

I said, "Okay. Sure. Let me check. I don't think we have it."

Aaron registered something I wasn't sure I liked him knowing.
I would lie to my father for him. But that was hardly news. I'd lied
to my parents every time Aaron and Margaret went out.

"Aaron, how are you?" Jolly Dad seemed pleased with himself for remembering Aaron's name. He was acting as if Aaron
were just one of Margaret's friends. Polite but distracted, the
way he always was with our friends, whose names he never re-

membered. Violet and Samantha thought my father was cute. I couldn't believe I'd liked them. The screw-loose part, the squirrelly Little Adonis part—all that was forgotten, vanished into the foggy world that still had Margaret in it. In this new world, the one without her, Dad looked glad to see Aaron.

Before all that guy-on-guy goodwill disappeared, I said, "Dad, is it okay with you if we go get some ice cream?"

My father didn't want me to go. I was his Only Remaining Child. And some part of him remembered exactly who Aaron was. He was trying to be reasonable. Maybe it would be good for me to go. To do anything. The odds—I could watch Dad persuading himself—were that I'd survive.

"All right," my father said. "But be back soon, okay? It's almost time to close up."

I didn't mention that closing time wasn't for two hours.

"Fasten your seat belt," my father said.

"The Dairy Divine's five minutes away," I said. "Less."

"Wear it," said my father.

"I always do," said Aaron. "Especially if I'm going a short distance. They say most accidents happen within ten miles of your house."

Accidents, I thought. *Margaret*. What were Dad and Aaron *thinking*?

"I know," Dad said. "That's why I always drive like hell to get out of the danger zone."

Aaron laughed. Dad said, "We're kidding, Nico."

I said, "*Three* miles. Lee Marvin says that in *Point Blank*." Neither of them got it. It made me sad to see them joking like they could have when Aaron was Margaret's boyfriend.

"Be back in half an hour," Dad said. "But don't rush. Drive slowly."

Aaron and I were already out the door. Dad was still watching as we got into Aaron's pale blue soccer-mom van, which—how had I not noticed?—was parked in front of the store. Dad, I thought, are you getting this? You couldn't ask for anything safer! Not only was Aaron so cool that he could afford to drive the world's most uncool vehicle, but he'd made it seem so cool that other kids had started asking their moms for their hand-me-down, high-mileage vans.

Then I stopped seeing it through Dad's eyes and saw it through my own. I remembered how happy I'd always been to see the van outside the Rialto. The memory knocked the wind out of me. Aaron's van was way high on the list of Margaret-related things. Everything else—music, films, the lake—slipped down a rung, like guests at a table shifting to make room for a late arrival. Aaron must already have managed to detach his van from my sister. Otherwise he could never have left the house. Maybe it was possible to decontaminate certain activities, the way flood victims wash the silt off family treasures and set them back on the mantel.

I slid in and fastened my seat belt. Aaron eased away from the pavement and drove a few blocks as if he was taking his road test. Then he hit the gas, and a warm wind roared into the window.

"Jailbreak," Aaron said.

I waited for self-consciousness to leave me paralyzed and mute. In fact I felt oddly relaxed. I didn't have to talk, because Aaron already understood the most important things: the mornings, the dead of night, the dreams, hearing Margaret's voice. It was as if his sharing the weight made the heaviness lighter. I felt free, or anyway, freer than I had in weeks. But as we rounded a curve in the road and the Dairy Divine appeared, I remembered we weren't free. We'd dragged our prison along with us.

"Is something wrong?" said Aaron. I must have looked as if I had no idea how someone opened a car door.

"No, why?'

"You seem like you're about to lose it again."

"I'm not. I'm fine," I lied.

A girl I'd never seen before was working behind the counter. She wore a long black vampire dress and a checked farmer's handkerchief tied backward over her dead, inky hair. One nostril looked red and swollen, as if from an infected piercing.

"What'll it be?" she asked the wall behind us. She didn't seem like someone who'd be patient when I took all day deciding. Nor did she seem aware that Aaron was the sole surviving member of a royal couple.

I half wanted Aaron to explain who we used to be, what we'd been through, and that this was no ordinary out-for-ice-cream excursion. That's what she must have thought. A good-looking guy was taking his little sister for a ride. Maybe he'd stayed out late last night and needed to get off Mom's shit list.

"What'll it be?" she repeated, to Aaron this time.

I adored Aaron for ignoring her. "Get what *you* want, Nico. Take your time."

"Chocolate." Picking the flavor I wanted was easier when there was nothing I wanted.

"Excellent," said Aaron.

I tried not to look at the filthy glass counter, like some bad abstract painting smeared with colored dabs. One drip of pistachio would send me racing out the door.

" 'Scuse me?" said the girl.

"The lady said chocolate," Aaron told her. "Double scoop." Then to me, "Quick thinking, Nico." He meant to sound approving. But he knew that my not caring wasn't a good sign.

The girl smashed two brown globs into a cone, handed it to me, and turned back to Aaron.

"I think I'll have the pistachio," he said.

I stared at him as if he'd said, I think I'll have the rat poison. We watched the girl dip the scoop in a blender jar of filthy water and approach the neon-green vat as if the sight of it wouldn't make the planet topple off its axis. Aaron turned toward me, without seeing me. He had a funny twitch of a smile, and his eyes looked glassy. Then he bopped himself on the side of the head. "On second thought, make that butter pecan."

The girl seemed not to have heard him and continued toward the lethal green. Then, as if she'd changed *her* mind, she spared us and swerved toward the beige.

"Thanks." Aaron put four bills on the counter.

"That's four-*fifty*," said the girl. Everything was different.

"Cost adjustment," she said, touching the inflamed nostril with the hand about to give Aaron change for a five. "Every Middle Eastern country we invade, the cost of oil skyrockets, which jacks up the price of your pecans and whatever carcinogenic shit they put in that pistachio. Plus every bomb we drop shortens the time until the next dirty-bomb attack. I figure the human race has got about another fifteen minutes, max. That's why I like selling frozen dessert. Enjoy it before it melts—along with the polar ice caps. Ha ha."

Her eyes were a pale, Siberian-husky blue, the pupils ringed with black as dark as the kohl around her eyelids. I thought she was someone I could be friends with, even though I realized her little speech had been entirely for Aaron's benefit.

Aaron said, "You can say that again." He smiled. "But don't." He toasted her with his ice cream cone, and I did the same.

"Respect," said Aaron, and the three of us fake-laughed. I loved it that the ice cream girl saw him hold the door for me on our way out.

"Can you eat ice cream and drive at the same time?" I asked. When the weather was nice, Margaret, Aaron, and I always finished our cones at the picnic table in front of the Dairy Divine. It was romantic, how they'd delayed the moment of saying good-bye.

"I could eat a lobster and drive if I had to," he said. "Come on. I want to show you something."

He headed up a narrow road I'd never been on before, though I'd thought I'd memorized every inch of the county. The road twisted up through the forest, then popped out into a clearing overlooking the mountains, their craggy silhouettes lined up in parallel rows and fading from green to purple to gray as they marched into the distance.

"I didn't know you could get this high here," I said.

Aaron said, "Well, actually, that's why people come here."

I prayed, Don't let him pull out a joint. "Does this place have a name?"

"Miller's Point," he said.

"Who was Miller?" My father's doomsday cult—wasn't the leader named Miller? I wasn't going to spoil our nice time by mentioning my dad. Anyway, Miller was practically the world's most common name.

"I don't know," Aaron said. "Some lucky motherfucker. How would you like this view to be yours?"

"Maybe he didn't own it," I said. "Maybe he discovered it, or maybe he just liked to come here and look." Maybe this was where he waited for an angel to rapture him and fifty thousand friends. Maybe this was where my dad's maps and calculations would take us. Maybe I'd have to come here with Dad and pretend I'd never been here.

"Right," said Aaron. "That's how it works. All you have to do is hang out somewhere, and they name it after you."

"Aaron and Nico Point." I was horrified that I'd said our names together.

Aaron said, "They're not going to call it that unless we both jump off."

Neither of us spoke for a while after that.

Finally, Aaron said, "I haven't been here since . . . I mean, it was always my favorite place, from when I was a kid. I used to imagine being a bird. Like every kid, I guess. But I'd always imagine flying out over my teacher's houses and shitting on their roofs."

"That's so brilliant," I said.

"I thought I would never be able to come up here again. I thought that if I came up here, I *would* want to throw myself off—"

"You don't still think that, do you?"

"Not exactly." As Aaron stared out the windshield, something in his face made me wonder if this was where he and Margaret had sex.

"Are you cold?" he asked.

"No, why?" I said.

"You shivered."

I held up my ice cream cone.

"Stupid me," Aaron said.

Aaron and I worked on our ice cream, both watching a small, solitary cloud inch across the sky.

Aaron nodded at it. "Check that baby out. What do you think it looks like?"

"A sheep?"

"I get where you could see a sheep. I was thinking Abraham Lincoln."

"I can see that," I lied.

Margaret would have seen something even odder and cooler than Lincoln. Or maybe she would have heard the cloud singing Otis Redding. And now she was gone, and here was Aaron with the dull little sister, and all she could see was a sheep. His ice cream hand clutched the steering wheel. Butter pecan trickled between his fingers.

I said, "I'm really sorry. I have no imagination." I'd never said that aloud before. Why was I telling Aaron?

Aaron said, "That's not true, Nico. That's not true at all. I'm not saying everyone has an imagination. But *you* do. I always thought you were the funniest kid. And you can't be funny without an imagination."

"I never saw it that way." Maybe I just liked to *think* I had no imagination. Because there were times I was proud of the twisty way my mind got from Point A to Point B. I just couldn't see how a sheeplike cloud looked like Abraham Lincoln.

"Look again," said Aaron. "Let your eyes go out of focus. Your mistake is zooming in too hard. That's how you get the sheep thing. But if you just let everything blur a little, you'll see the beard and the top hat."

I squinted. "I see what you mean," I lied again. "Sort of."

"It takes a while. Try catching it from the corner of your eye instead of dead-on center. Because what you've really got to be careful about is looking in the wrong direction. Missing the main event."

Listening to Aaron felt less like being part of a conversation than like chasing a runaway pet I was never going to catch. "Like what, Aaron?" It felt strange to say his name.

He thought a second. "Like . . . I've always hated magicians. Because their whole thing is distracting you, making you look away from what they're really doing. If you spend too much time watching magic tricks, you won't be fit to live in the world. You'll lose your survival instincts. You'll be like a baby bird that falls out of its nest, and the humans adopt it, and the mother won't take it back."

I wondered if he was talking to me, or if this was how he used to talk to Margaret. How could anyone spend too much time watching magic tricks? It didn't make sense, but still it seemed like the most interesting thing I'd ever heard. The cloud morphed into a Q-tip, but I didn't say so.

I said, "Have you done any paintings?" I could ask to see them, and that would be another reason for us to get together.

He said, "I can't imagine ever picking up a paintbrush again."

"You should try." I sounded as lame as Dad telling Mom to play the piano.

"I don't want to," Aaron said.

"Then don't," I said. "I mean—"

"And you know what? When people say, 'You'll get over this,' I want to tell them to go fuck themselves. Sorry, Nico."

"That's okay," I said.

"Because what will I have then?" Aaron asked as if I might know. "The world without her in it? I keep wondering what she'd say about this or that. I can't see or hear anything without wanting to tell her about it."

"Exactly," I said. "Me, too."

He said, "You know what? I quit my job. I retired before it started."

"What job?"

"I was supposed to teach art in the town rec program."

"I used to *go* to that program." It would have been fun if Aaron had been a counselor when I'd gone there.

"Everyone did," said Aaron. "I didn't feel like watching the little rug rats throw paint at each other. I didn't feel like convincing myself it's their way of being creative. I didn't feel like anything."

"Were your parents mad?" I said.

"Insane. But what's saving my ass is that they're too worried about me to get angry. They tiptoe around the house as if any loud noise might send me over the edge and—"

"And what?"

"And . . . I don't know. *Their* fantasy. Whatever that is."

Aaron's dad was some kind of contractor-builder. I didn't know what his mom did besides raise five kids. I thought about her coming into Goldengrove for a book that advised her to think of Aaron as a kitten who wouldn't come out from under the couch. Poor Aaron. His parents should have been grateful to have a son like that.

"What's their problem?" I said.

The Q-tip cloud had vanished. I'd studied the water cycle. Rain into cloud into rain into earth. The thought of it comforted me. I wished I could have told Aaron where the cloud had gone without getting lost in the maze of an explanation.

"My failure to *snap back*. They can't figure out why I can't *snap back*. So tell me, Nico. What am I supposed to snap back *from* and snap back *to*?"

"I don't know." Every time he'd said *snap back*, his lips twisted like rubber bands. He was imitating or mocking someone. Now I felt sorry for his parents. I wished he hadn't mentioned them, because now all I could think of was Dad pacing the bookstore and imagining the worst.

"I should probably drive you back," Aaron said.

"That's what I was thinking."

As we switchbacked down the road toward town, Aaron said, "Do you ever think about reincarnation?"

"All the time. Why do you ask?"

Aaron said, "Remember how your sister liked Laurel and Hardy so much? Well, I found this Web site all about these two brothers from New Jersey. Lots of people think the brothers are Laurel and Hardy reincarnated."

"And?"

"And . . . the brothers were always big Laurel and Hardy fans even when they were in preschool, and they sort of look like them, and they made this video about them, and—"

I said, "There's a movie where Hardy gets reincarnated as a horse."

He said, "I watched it with Margaret."

We passed a van like Aaron's, stuffed with kids. The driver beeped hello.

"Who was that?" I said.

"I don't know," said Aaron. "Some random soccer-mom communication. You know what I wish I could do? Watch a movie, an old one like I used to watch with your sister. Maybe we could do that. I'd thought I'd never be able to go the Dairy Divine or drive up to Miller's Point. And we did it together, Nico, and it wasn't so terrible. Was it?"

We drove by the woodstove store, then the Quikmart.

"No," I said. "It was fine. It was . . . nice."

Nice, mocked the staircase spirit.

He said, "You could come over, and we could hang out at my house and watch an old movie on DVD."

"We could?" It was one thing to go with Aaron on a spontaneous ice cream run. But making plans, watching movies . . . how would that work? Don't worry, Mom and Dad. I'm going to Aaron's to watch the kind of films I used to watch with Margaret. If they were reasonable, they'd understand that Aaron and I were just friends trying to help each other get through this. But my parents wouldn't see it that way. They'd always distrusted Aaron. Now they'd probably think he was some kind of necrophiliac child molester. If I wanted to spend time with him, I would have to keep it secret.

"Sure," I said. "We could."

"When?"

"Sunday," I said. "The bookstore's closed."

"Excellent. I'll call you."

I said, "I'm not sure my parents will go for it."

"I'm sure they won't," said Aaron.

As we neared Goldengrove, Aaron repeated, "I'll call you, okay?"

I said, "You'd probably better hang up if my mom or dad answer the phone."

Aaron grinned. "I'm good at that. I've had plenty of practice."

Eight

I TOLD MYSELF IT WAS NOTHING I HADN'T DONE BEFORE. I'D LIED to my parents every time I'd pretended to go to the movies with Margaret. But Margaret had always worked out the intrigues and the complicated arrangements.

To watch a film with Aaron would take, including travel time, three hours, more or less. My parents would worry if I said I was going to spend that long riding around on my bike. Three hours at the library? My dad spent half his day there, and it was closed on Sundays. Three hours at the movies? Even my parents knew the Rialto didn't have matinees.

I needed a friend to lie for Aaron and me the way I'd lied for him and Margaret. But I'd blown away all my friends after my sister died. Anyway, I couldn't trust them with a piece of gossip this hot. I imagined confiding in Violet or Samantha. Then I tried to calculate how long they could hold out before they told someone. I couldn't blame them. There wasn't a teenager on earth who could resist the glamour of being the first to hear that a girl she knew was hooking up with her dead sister's boyfriend. Which I wasn't, but even so, I knew how it might look.

I considered everyone I knew. Then I thought of Elaine. She was old enough, cool enough, she could keep a secret. She'd always refused to tell us the name of Tycho's dad. I'd invent a boyfriend my parents didn't like, and I'd ask Elaine to pretend that I was at her house when I was seeing Aaron—that is, the mythical boyfriend. I could ask her a favor because I was doing her one, filling in at the store till she found a sitter for Tycho. It never occurred to me that I was encouraging her to lie to her employer, probably because I couldn't imagine Dad as anyone's boss.

One afternoon, the phone at the store rang. It was Elaine, she'd forgotten a novel that she was halfway through. Tycho was home with a cold, she couldn't leave. Could I bring over her copy of *The Man Who Loved Children*?

Dad was in his office. He looked up from a book when I knocked. "Just listen to this passage. Got a minute, Nico?"

"Sure," I said. "But I need to go out. Elaine wants me to bring her a book. Can you take over the counter for a while? She's stuck home with Tycho."

"Fine. But listen." He read, " 'In one South Indian village, pilgrims come to feed the dead by throwing food into the ocean. Bearded holy men work the beach, selling packets wrapped in banana leaves, a recipe the sadhus divine the dead want to eat.' "

"I wonder what's in the packets," I said.

"Comfort food for the dead," Dad said. "Basmati rice? Vegetable curry?"

"Macaroni and cheese," I said. It had never occurred to me that

the dead might get hungry. Was there some food Margaret wanted? Pistachio ice cream, maybe.

"I wish I could use it in my book," my father said. "But it's not,
strictly speaking, about the end of the world. I wish I was smarter.
I wish I could synthesize this and Hindu eschatology and—"

I said, "You're really smart, Dad. I'm sure you can use it somewhere. But I need to go out. Remember?"

"What's Elaine reading?" my father said.

"*The Man Who Loved Children*," I read off the cover.

"I've never read it," Dad said.

"Me, neither," I said. "But if Elaine wants it that badly, it's got
to be pretty good. "

"Take your time," my father said. "I could use a break from
writing."

I ran all the way to Elaine's. I found her in the kitchen, wearing
shorts and a Jim Morrison T-shirt, her bare feet splayed across the
top of her yellow Formica table. She was smoking a cigarette, drinking iced coffee, leafing through a travel magazine. She stubbed out the
cigarette, as if I that would mean I hadn't seen it. On the CD player, a
blues singer was growling about a rabbit and a hunter and a gun.

"How's Tycho?" I asked.

"He'll live. But you know how he is. Every head cold is a metaphysical nightmare. Why should he have to suffer? Not that he
asks, exactly. But I know what he's thinking. Why can't he just
watch TV and drink juice and not chant stuff like 'Hot now!' and
'Cold now!'?"

"Maybe so you don't have to take his temperature."

"He hates it," said Elaine. "So I don't. He'd bite through the
thermometer. But what about *you*? Are *you* okay?"

I said, "I don't know why everybody's always asking me that."

"*Are* you?"

"Cramps." I made a face. I actually had my period, so I wasn't lying, not yet.

She shut the magazine. "I bet you didn't know that Zimbabwe is the new Las Vegas."

I said, "Maybe Las Vegas is the new Zimbabwe."

Elaine said, "If kids wrote these magazines, they'd be a lot more interesting."

"Thanks, I guess." I handed her the book I'd brought from the store.

"Thank *you*." She sighed. "I'll never find my place. Reading it is so painful I keep having these narcoleptic attacks, nodding off in mid-sentence. Because the father in the book is exactly like the son that my father and my ex-husband would have had if *they'd* gotten married and had a baby and the baby grew up and became a father. You should read it. But not now."

"Your father and your ex-husband couldn't have had a baby."

Elaine looked disappointed. "Metaphorically, Nico. The funny thing is, I never noticed they were alike until I read the book. Self-dramatizing sons of bitches, both of them. Men, I mean. Your dad excepted."

"Dad included. In his way."

Elaine said, "Your father's less of a motor mouth. And a million times nicer. More present and accounted for, if you know what I mean."

"Present?" I said. "Accounted for? Dad?"

Elaine said, "Maybe it's just a father thing. Christina Stead got *that* right. Hey, you want some iced coffee? Aren't you dying of heat in that? Those synthetic vintage shirts, you might as well be walking around in a plastic trash bag. Wasn't that Margaret's shirt? Sorry."

"That's okay." I fought the urge to say that Margaret told me I could have it. I could lie, but not about that.

"It looks great on you," said Elaine. "But gosh, you're losing weight. Isn't your father feeding you? Nico, how are you? Really."

I said, "I'm okay. Not great."

"Great would be bizarre," she said. "No one's expecting great. Getting out of bed is the new great. Which you seem to be doing."

"That's about all," I said.

Elaine said, "I hear you're conducting ESP experiments in the poetry aisle. I thought that was inspired—"

I said, "Can I turn down the music?" I needed a walk across the room to process the fact that my father had told Elaine something so personal and shaming. Adults entertained each other with stories about their kids. The younger you were, the less privacy you had. Well, fine. I could lie about Aaron.

"Did I ask if you want some coffee?" Elaine said. "My short-term memory's shot."

"You asked," I told her. "I said yes." I didn't like coffee. Margaret used to love it. The heart-disease books warned against caffeine. Uncaffeinated, my heart was ricocheting off my rib cage. Fear made me want coffee, the way being near a cliff can make you want to jump.

"Coffee would be excellent," I said. *Excellent* was Aaron's word. "Excellent," I repeated.

As Elaine and I chatted—the weather, her ongoing babysitter search, customers at the bookstore—I stirred three teaspoons of sugar into my thickening coffee and, sip by sip, let the caffeine and carbs get ready to do the talking for me.

"I need to ask you a favor," I said.

"I owe you one," Elaine said.

I said, "I've started hanging out with this guy."

"Oh, please, not yet," she said. "Who is he?"

"No one you know." Was that a lie, too? Did Elaine know Aaron? "Just a guy."

"What's he like?"

I waited a beat. I'd rehearsed this. "This really nice kid, in my class. Smart, considerate. You'd like him, Elaine. But my parents can't handle my going out with anyone right now. They go crazy about every little thing. I don't blame them. But no one would be good enough, and they're giving me a hard time."

"Have your mom and dad met him?"

I nodded. "It wasn't pretty."

"Why didn't they like him? Tell me the truth."

How shortsighted of me, not to have expected this, not to have invented a list of the imaginary boyfriend's alleged flaws to go with his real virtues.

"My dad says he has a screw loose."

"Which screw?" asked Elaine.

"The one that makes everything boring."

Elaine said, "This is starting to worry me."

"Please, Elaine. You *know* me. You've known me since I was born."

"Your parents aren't stupid," she said.

I said, "They'd have a problem if I was going out with God."

"Let's hope you're not," said Elaine. "Anyhow, I don't think your dad believes in God. Any more."

I said, "Come on, Elaine. Please."

"Remind me how old you are," she said.

"Thirteen. Almost fourteen."

Elaine said, "Still growing. All that sugar can't be good for you, honey."

"I don't drink coffee that often," I said. "Only on special occasions."

Elaine said, "What do you do?"

I looked at her.

"What do you and this boy *do?*"

"Nothing. We go out for ice cream—"

"Where?"

"The Dairy Divine."

"He drives?" Elaine said. "How can he be in your class?'

"We take our bikes. We get ice cream. It's nothing. My parents are paranoid. Can I say I was here with you?"

"I don't like lying to your parents."

"Listen." I paused to steady myself. "This is the first thing—the *only* thing—I've wanted to do since . . ." Elaine knew since when.

I was playing the Margaret card. I had saved it until now. It was the only thing that could make good-mom, good-person Elaine keep something like this from my parents.

Elaine stared at the ceiling. "How could that water spot be growing when it hasn't rained for weeks?" She looked at me and shrugged. "Young love. What was *that* like? Dear Lord, I can hardly remember."

"It's not *love*." I glared at her. "God, Elaine. We hang out."

"That goes with the territory. The first time it's never love. People say *first love*. Such and such a guy was my first love. But usually, they mean second love. The first time they don't know it, or they won't admit it. If you know what I mean."

I didn't. I wasn't in love with Aaron. I didn't even have a crush on him. That would have been too strange. We were friends, we were friends, we were friends, was all. I couldn't begin to explain it. But let Elaine think it was love if it made her do what I wanted.

She said, "Everyone wants to bet on young love, to put their money on first love, as if love's going up against death in some cosmic *High Noon* shoot-out. No one wants to think that love and death are working the same side of the street."

"What?" I hated how adults got cryptic when you most needed them to be clear.

"Never mind," she said. "Just two things, okay? First: Don't make any decisions for a year. I mean *any* decisions."

I said, "I've been hearing that from everyone who comes into the store."

"Well, excuse *me* for being one giant cliché. But they don't mean what *I* mean."

"Which is . . . ?"

"Don't make me get overly personal, Nico. Decisions about . . . your body."

I said, "Oh, right. Sex. I should have known. I swear we're not doing anything like that." I almost wanted to admit the boy was Aaron so she would know how wrong she was. Or maybe I wanted to hear what she knew about Aaron, what lies my father had told. But I couldn't risk it.

Elaine said, "I assume your mom had the Big Talk with you, right?"

"Sort of," I said. "Actually, yeah."

When I told my mom I'd gotten my period, she'd started crying. Then she said, "Come on. I'll drive you to the drugstore." On the way, she said, "Nico, you're a smart girl. And you have an older sister. I'm not going to embarrass us both. The most important thing is to be safe and make sure you're old enough. There's a box of condoms in the upstairs medicine chest. As for the rest . . . I don't want you to get your heart broken, honey, but I know that's wanting the impossible."

Then she'd told me about a short story she'd read in which a character says that the nature of sex is that the man is the guest and the woman the hostess. "The guest wants all sorts of things, he wants to make an impression, to enjoy himself, and so forth. And the hostess . . ."

Mom waited for me to ask what the hostess wants, but I didn't. For some reason it seemed more repulsive than something clinical and disgusting. I preferred the part about the condoms in the bathroom.

"The hostess," my mother said, "wants to be thanked."

"Was it a man or a woman character who said that?" I asked.

"A woman," said my mother. "And a woman wrote it."

At the drugstore we'd bought a lifetime supply of stick-on pads and junior tampons. The kid at the checkout counter snickered at the mother-daughter menstruation survivalists.

Elaine said, "I would have loved to be a fly on the wall when Daisy gave you the sex talk I'll bet your mother was very modern and progressive."

"I guess," I said, though neither of those words described our conversation, precisely.

"Maybe I'm less modern. But then again I'm a single mom. Living proof of . . . something. At the very least, you'll have a connection you might not want to have with that person. You can meet him twenty years from now, and no matter what else happened, he'll still be the first guy you had sex with. I don't want to be graphic, but you will have had that person *inside* you."

"Elaine," I said. "Please. That is so totally gross."

"Sorry," said Elaine. "But I don't think I can emphasize this point strongly enough."

Elaine was sounding like the sex-ed version of Officer Prozak. And I didn't need her to tell me that sex was scarier and more intimate than anything I wanted to do with a person I hardly knew. How I longed to tell Margaret about this conversation. She would have fallen down laughing, though it might have been confusing, why Elaine was warning me not to have sex with her boyfriend. I was insulted that Elaine would reduce my friendship with Aaron to instincts and teenage hormones. What had brought us together was deeper and stronger than that.

"Pregnancy's the least of it," said Elaine.

"Not really," I said.

'You're right. Forget I said that. No means no."

"No one's asking me to have sex," I said. "Not asking means no, too."

"Someone always asks," she said. "That's why they call it dating."

I said, "We're not dating. We're friends."

"Fine," she said. "Let's cut to the chase. If I'm going to lie for you, at least one of us has to tell the truth. Which brings me to the second thing. I don't want you drinking or smoking pot."

"I promise," I said. I meant it. I couldn't imagine having sex, or even a beer, with Aaron. Let her think this was love. Kissing, hurt feelings, groping, tears. Breakups, heartbreak. The whole teenage first-love drama.

Elaine said, "Okay. Fine. Don't tell me the truth. Just promise me you'll be careful."

Nine

IT WASN'T LOVE, NOT IN THE USUAL SENSE. BOTH OF US HAD loved Margaret. But someone who didn't know about our hopeless love triangle with the dead might easily have mistaken it for ordinary love. That's what someone might have thought when the phone rang on Thursday evening, and I jumped because I'd known it would ring, just as I'd known it was Aaron. That's what someone might have concluded when I took the receiver into another room so that, in an urgent, murmured shorthand, Aaron and I could arrange to meet at noon on the following Sunday.

Aaron told me twice how to reach the clearing beside an abandoned barn. I already knew where it was. Margaret and I used to meet him there. I could bike there in fifteen minutes.

"Who was that?" my father asked.

"A friend from school," I said.

Why didn't he ask, What friend? They'd always been so careful before, interrogating us on where we were going and whom we were going out with. But now they were glad I had a friend.

They wanted to believe me. They didn't want to hear that I'd just made a date with Little Adonis, the guy with the screw loose, the boyfriend they'd hated and suspected, the hero who could have saved her.

THAT SUNDAY, I ANNOUNCED I WAS GOING TO GO HANG OUT with Elaine and Tycho. My mother's faint assent barely registered above the racket of Dad's typing.

Two days had passed since Aaron called. I was sure he'd forgotten. As I biked down the sun-striped road, each tree shook its branches and whispered about my imminent humiliation. I braced myself for the pain of seeing the empty field where I would have to ward off the memory of all the times I'd gone there with Margaret. Now I would have to wait alone until I gave up and went home and tried not to think about how, in the past, Aaron had always been early.

By the time I rounded the last curve, I was so convinced that Aaron wouldn't be there that, when I saw him, I couldn't have been more surprised if coincidence had brought us there at the same moment. He'd parked parallel to the road and opened the side door so he could sit on the floor of the van with his legs stretched out in the sun. I made my graceful entrance by skidding on the gravel. He dropped his cigarette and ground it under his sneaker.

"Hi," I said, remaining on my bike until it solved the problem of whether I should shake his hand or kiss his cheek or hug him.

I slid off my bicycle, and he loaded it into the back of the van. I thought, All right. This is how it starts. Something is beginning.

"Hey, kid," he said, crooking his forearm to bump mine in a goofy soul shake.

"Good to see you," I said.

"Me, too," said Aaron. "I mean good to see *you*, too. Maybe we should get going."

"I didn't know you smoked," I said.

"I stopped. Then I started again."

"You shouldn't." Margaret's death had taught me nothing.

"Ready?" said Aaron. "Let's go."

I got into the passenger seat. This was only my second ride alone in Aaron's van, but already it seemed almost normal. Auto-immunization. I wasn't in pain over Margaret. Or I was, but just for a second.

"What was that?" said Aaron.

"What was what?"

"You made a sound."

"Did I? I'm sorry."

"Don't apologize." We both knew what the sound meant, and it silenced us for a while.

Aaron drove smoothly, with his elbow out the window, his James Dean equivalent of Margaret's old-movie steals. Oh, they were made for each other! I wondered if Aaron ever thought that he would never find someone so perfect, and that he might search his entire life for that smile, that voice, that laugh.

"Up for a movie?" Aaron said.

"Sure," I said. "Sounds good."

Which it did. Light up the small screen. Bring on the popcorn and chips. There was a TV show I used to like that made you feel as if you were sitting in a theater behind a row of space aliens watching bad, low-budget sci-fi films. That's how Aaron and I would be, *Mystery Science Theater 2000*, our tiny antennae bobbling as we wisecracked about the Martians in cheap Mylar suits emerging from their Frisbees.

Why was I so jumpy? It was only an afternoon. The minute I felt uncomfortable, I could say I wanted to leave. Aaron wasn't forcing me to do this. We were experimenting. Together.

If only I didn't have to talk to Aaron's parents! The fact that he was hanging out with his dead girlfriend's little sister would hardly reassure them about his snapping back. I imagined half a dozen ways that the meeting might go. They fussed over me or ignored me, they mentioned Margaret or didn't, I stayed calm or burst into tears and begged to be driven home.

Aaron pulled into a driveway beside a large, neat, barn-colored house. Instead of stopping, he hit the horn—It's me! It's me!— and kept going. I turned. I couldn't see anyone. I'd been spared. But for what? I hardly knew Aaron. No one knew I was here.

Come on, Nico, I told myself. Aaron was Margaret's boyfriend. But maybe her death had unhinged him, further loosened that screw. She'd warned me to be careful of him. Freaky. In a heartbeat, I'd gone from being afraid of Aaron's parents to wanting to alert them to my presence. Remember me? I'm the girl who sold you *Ordinary Grief.*

He pulled up in front of a shack covered with green roofing tiles. Margaret had told me that Aaron had his own art studio, a cabin separate from his house where he painted and basically lived.

"This is cool! Is this your studio?" My voice sounded robotic, like Tycho's. I scrambled to remember what else Margaret had said. As each of Aaron's brothers and sisters grew up and moved away, the next in line got to use the cabin as a command post from which to plot their escape. Aaron was the youngest. For now, the cabin was his.

"It *used* to be my studio," he said. "When I was *pretending* to paint."

"And now?"

"Now it's where I bake little children into gingerbread."

I did my best to laugh. Maybe *this* was where they'd gone to have sex while I waited for them at the movies. I didn't want to go inside. I wanted to go home. I could say I felt sick. Aaron would drive me back, and that would be the last time I ever saw him.

Calm down, I thought. Get a grip. Your sister's boyfriend isn't going to bake you into a cookie. You'll have fun, watch a movie. You'll be home in time for dinner. Mom and Dad will never know.

Aaron got out of the van and stretched. I reminded myself to move. The van door slammed behind me.

Aaron said, "What's wrong?"

"Nothing," I said. "Why?"

"You jumped."

"It's a hearing thing," I lied. "I'm allergic to loud noises."

One of those stone garden sculptures, like a mailbox for letters to a Japanese god, bordered the path to the cabin. Aaron's mom had put it there. I found that reassuring. This wasn't the witch's forest. This was Emersonville, with its folksy ideas about garden decor, placards of ladies bent over weeding so you could see their frilly underpants, flags with satin rainbows and unicorns, plastic reindeer at Christmas.

Pushing open the door, Aaron warned me, "Hold your nose." The shades were drawn, and a stew of putrid odors had been simmering in the dark: wet dog, pet food, mildewed carpet, cat spray, spilled beer, plus the various illegal substances that Aaron and his siblings had sneaked out here to try. Layered on top of the smell were all of Aaron's mom's industrial-strength attempts to kill it.

I'd almost stopped minding by the time Aaron found the light switch. I was flattered that he trusted me enough to take me somewhere that smelled so bad.

A window shade snapped, and a sizzle of daylight flashed along the hallway. I peered through a door that separated the corridor from a tiny kitchen. The burners were crusted black, and the sink overflowed with soda cans and yeasty-smelling bottles. The rest of the cabin was a tangle of hockey sticks, helmets, ragged sneakers, stacked magazines. A space in the center had been hollowed out and furnished with a lumpy couch and an old TV set.

"This place is great!" I said.

"Glad you like it," Aaron said. "Make yourself at home."

I wandered around, pretending to look at things, pretending there was something to look at. I searched for signs of Margaret, though I knew it would hurt if I found them. Either Aaron had obliterated every trace of my sister, or else he kept secret reminders around, visible only to him, thorns that could snag only him, so only he would know he was bleeding.

Across the room, a door led to a glassed-in porch littered with confetti. Not confetti. Paint spots. That was where Aaron painted. *Used* to paint. The easel was empty, the worktables knocked over. Coffee cans and paint tubes lay scattered, as if there had been a break-in. Break*down* was more like it. I thought about Aaron burning his paintings of the lake. There was probably still a charred patch outside on the lawn.

"Oh, look, your studio!" I said.

"Let's skip that part of the tour, okay?"

"Sorry," I said.

"It's not *your* fault," said Aaron. I jumped when he slammed the door between the main room and the porch. "Have a seat." He pointed at the couch and went into the kitchen.

The springs in the couch had collapsed so low that sitting was like having someone swipe it from beneath me. As I squirmed around, seeking a semi-comfortable place, a strip of flesh popped out from under the shirt I'd bought with the money I'd made in the bookstore. Pale yellow, with laces down the back, the shirt was nothing Margaret would have worn. I yanked it down over my stomach.

Aaron returned with a plastic bowl of potato chips and two cans of Coke.

"Gee," I said. "That's so nice of you."

"We need to keep our strength up," he said.

Greasy crumbs sprinkled everywhere as I helped myself from the bowl.

I said, "I'm making a mess."

"Don't worry about it," said Aaron. "The reason the couch has lasted so long is because we feed it."

Sipping my soda, I stared at the blank TV screen.

"What's the movie?" I asked.

"You choose." Aaron handed me two DVD sleeves.

"No. *You* pick." I shut my eyes, so I wouldn't have to.

"You didn't even look," said Aaron. "I thought we were in this together, Nico."

Ninotchka. Casablanca. Two foreign words with too many vow-

els. On one cover, Humphrey Bogart and an actress swooned toward an embrace, sharing a sort of poncho printed with a man in
a trench coat, a vintage airplane, and an exotic city skyline. The
other DVD said "Garbo laughs," and featured a painting of a
giddy, red-haired woman. I didn't want to watch either one.

"You've seen these, right?" said Aaron. "She knew them word
for word."

"No." I felt as if I'd lost some kind of contest.

"Strange," Aaron said. Like the art book, these films were private. She'd kept them for herself and Aaron. Didn't that skew our
experiment? However much pain old movies caused me, it must
hurt Aaron more to watch the ones that had belonged to them. On
the other hand, I was her sister, and he was only her boyfriend,
which tipped the scales back toward me. I would never have another sister, and he would have other girlfriends, even if he doubted that now. He still had four siblings. He won on every count.
He'd watched these movies with her. I hadn't and never would.

"Let's do it," Aaron said.

"Sure," I said. "Whatever."

"Whatever? Make up your mind, Nico. Sometimes you *have* to
decide."

"Sorry," I said.

"Stop apologizing," Aaron said.

"Sorry," I said, and we laughed. "Okay. *Ninotchka.*"

He popped a disc into the machine, then sat down at the far end
of the couch.

The credits rolled, and I braced myself to enter the black-and-
white world that I'd sworn to stay out of if I couldn't go there
with Margaret.

"Relax, Nico," Aaron said. "You look like the statues at Easter Island. If you don't want to do this—"

I concentrated so hard on unfreezing my face that I must have missed something, because, the next thing I knew, three bozos in fur hats were bumbling around an elegant hotel lobby.

"Russians," said Aaron.

"Right." I must have been crazy to think I could stand this. The scene shifted, and a woman in a fur-trimmed robe was emoting into a mirror, "It's really a wretched morning, wretched. I can't get myself right. I wanted to look mellow and I look brittle. Oh, I'm so bored with this face. Who's face would you have if you had your choice? Oh well, I guess one gets the face one deserves."

"*Now* what's wrong?" Aaron startled me. I'd been thinking of Margaret giving that speech, naked in front of her mirror.

"Nothing. Why?" I said.

He said, "You're gasping."

"Asthma." I faked a cough. "It's dusty in here."

Aaron said, "Are you having some kind of attack?"

I said, "Can we watch the other film? This one's a little boring."

"Fine. Let's check out *Casablanca*." Aaron slipped in the other disc. "Might as well go for the hard stuff."

A map appeared on-screen, and one of those human-typewriter newsreel voices rattled on about World War II, Lisbon, the Nazis. The camera waded into a crowded Middle Eastern bazaar. A murder was announced, something about German couriers, and police swarmed the market.

"*Raiders of the Lost Ark*," I said.

"Not exactly," said Aaron.

Cut to a nightclub full of international sleazes making shady deals. Zoom in on a hand signing a check and gradually move up—wrist, sleeve, white tuxedo—to the handsome, beagle-like face of Humphrey Bogart. How could I not have seen this? Margaret had made me watch everything with Bogart, everything in which brave French people resisted the Nazis.

The Germans had not only captured Casablanca but invaded the sanctuary of Bogart's club. The plot gave me something to focus on—letters of transit, refugees. And at the center was Mr. Rick, who never stuck out his neck, never drank with his customers, the hard-boiled egg with the warm liquid yolk.

A guy with bulging lizard eyes was begging Rick to help him—

"Peter Lorre's the greatest genius who ever lived," Aaron said.

The police swarmed Rick's place. Just as the uproar died down, a handsome couple swept in, as if someone had opened the door on the dusty desert night and admitted in a blast of clean, pure Nordic air. The couple telegraphed heroism, anxiety, weary sophistication. The blond actress seemed lit by a lamp inside her skull. From within the prison of her goddesslike calm, her hijacked eyes tapped out the SOS of a heart about to explode. It nearly detonated all over Rick's piano player, Sam, whom she asked to play the one song that could get him in trouble.

Aaron said, "Did you ever hear *her* sing that?"

"Yes," I lied.

"Wasn't it something?"

I couldn't speak for wishing I'd heard it. "Who's the actress?" I asked.

"Ingrid Bergman."

I said, "Rick's going to drink with *them*."

"Bingo," Aaron said.

What could Sam do? He played the song. Rick walked in and freaked until a nod from Sam redirected him to the luminous stranger. It took about three seconds for everyone except the husband to figure out the story. Ilse's eyes spilled over. Her grief had nothing to do with mine. She was weeping over love, a minor problem that could be solved, while I was grieving over death, which could never be fixed.

I gripped the edge of the sofa. Aaron pretended not to notice. Something about our being alone and sneaking under the grown-ups' radar made it hard for him to comfort me or to say that he knew how I felt. It was too scary, too intimate. We had to keep our distance.

"You know who they wanted to play Rick?" Aaron asked.

I shook my head. Why was I so tense? Didn't Aaron's question prove that we were just a couple of old-movie fans swapping Hollywood trivia gossip?

"Ronald Reagan," said Aaron.

"The worst president ever," I said.

"You weren't born yet," he said.

"What difference does that make?" I said.

On-screen, the handsome husband asked the waiter for a Cointreau.

"My man orders a girl drink," said Aaron. "That's one problem right there."

Bogart pulled up a chair at the couple's table and, surprising everyone but us, ordered a drink. Aaron smiled conspiratorially, as if we'd written this scene.

Only the clueless husband believed they were talking about immigration. Arrangements were made, agreements reached. Then the bar went dark, empty but for Sam, playing music for Rick to get hammered by as he waited for Ilse. "If she can stand it, I can," he said, as he asked Sam to play their song. That was another thing I'd learned since Margaret's death. Every song may be someone's personal implement of torture.

I said, "Aaron, are we, like, destroying ourselves?"

"We're repairing ourselves," Aaron said.

As Rick killed the bottle, and his hangdog face sagged lower, I remembered a night I'd been at the movies. Just before the film ended, Margaret slipped into the next seat. The plot concerned a cutie-pie veterinary student who rejects her high school sweetheart because he isn't rich or famous. Ultimately, she realizes he's the love of her life, and she wins him back by performing a tracheotomy on his ailing puppy. Even though Margaret had left me there so she could be with Aaron, I was embarrassed to be caught watching something so moronic.

She'd whispered, "Do you want to stay?" I did. I knew where the plot was heading, but not all the ridiculous twists it would take on the way. I said no. We went home. On the way back, she explained that they'd been at a party, and Aaron had drunk too much and gotten boring, and she'd asked a friend to drive her to get Mom's car. I never asked what boring meant. High school boys got drunk all the time. Now, watching Bogart, I recalled that last Sunday on the lake. There had been some question about their going out that night. What had she and Aaron argued about? I thought about it until I got distracted by the love that had Rick and Ilse falling apart, years later, in Casablanca.

Flashback. Car ride, boat trip, champagne toast.

Bogart said, "Here's looking at you, kid." I couldn't look at Aaron. "Kid" was what he called *me*. Maybe he'd tried it on Margaret first, and she hadn't liked it.

Now Rick and Ilse were gliding in a slow, enraptured dance. Ilse was wearing one of those silky robes that, in old movies, signal the lovers are having sex. Robe or no robe, anyone could tell. Sex was the bright bubble encasing them, and everything else was as flat as the Arc de Triomphe jiggling in the distance on their obvious-fake car trip.

Still, nothing I'd heard or read about sex explained what the two of them felt as Ilse rested her cheek against Rick's shoulder. I remembered Margaret saying that sex meant not having to think. Maybe that was it. Maybe their minds had shut down, canceling out Ilse's husband, Rick's past, the war, the Germans heading for Paris. What was a war compared to the touch of his lips against her forehead?

When Ilse told Rick to kiss her as if for the last time, Aaron flinched. Maybe Margaret used to say that. And he *had* kissed her for the last time, though he hadn't known it, no more than Rick suspected that Ilse would stand him up at the station in the pounding rain.

Aaron got a roll of toilet paper and plunked it in my lap. I tore ragged scraps and blotted my eyes until soggy wads littered the couch. This wasn't how I'd imagined our afternoon, but I didn't care. It didn't matter if my face looked like a cranberry muffin.

"So much for our experiment," Aaron said.

"No, really," I said. "I'm fine."

I knew how the story would end. Heroic Rick would send Ilse off to live with a man she didn't love but whose work was more important than running a nightclub. The plane spun its propellers, and the lovers' one chance at happiness took off into the night sky. It had nothing to do with Aaron and me. Rick and Ilse were heartbroken, but alive. Only my sister was dead. I glanced at Aaron. I could have sworn he was thinking the same thing.

He said, "I won't even bother telling you to cheer up."

"Thanks," I said. "I appreciate that."

The silence that fell seemed restful, as if something had been settled, as if more had happened than the two of us watching a film. If Aaron hadn't been there, I could have fallen asleep. I wondered if I could trust him to wake me in time to go home.

After a while, Aaron said, "But I do have something that *might* help cheer you up. Something you should try."

I didn't like the sound of *something* or *cheer* or, for that matter, *try*. Drugs, I thought. Or alcohol. I wished this weren't happening. I could say no to Aaron. He wouldn't try to persuade me, or make fun of me if I refused. He didn't want to get me drunk or stoned. He truly wanted to help. Aaron had loved Margaret, and I was her grieving sibling. But how babyish it would make me seem. No, thanks, I don't drink or smoke. I'm not brave and sophisticated like my sister. I would never have cried in front of him if I'd known it would lead to this.

He said, "It's in my room. In the house. I'll be back in a second."

Aaron was gone for long enough for me to have a complicated fantasy about him rolling a joint and getting busted by his parents. What if he'd run into them, and they'd insisted he have lunch or do some household chore, and he couldn't tell them I was in the cabin? His poor sad mom with her grief book! Her worry would spike when she learned that her son was spending the afternoon with me.

Could Aaron have forgotten me? It seemed possible, if unlikely. How strange that being abandoned made me feel trapped instead of released. I needed to plot my escape route, even though it was clear I could simply walk out the door. The truth was, I was looking for an excuse to go through Aaron's stuff. I knew it wasn't right, but it might be my only chance to find out more about him and about Margaret, maybe.

I looked out the window. No Aaron. I drifted into the studio, sidestepping the bright dots of color. All over the spattered walls were the bare, rectangular ghosts of pictures. The floor was littered with scraps of magazine pages and drawings, here a fleshy pink arm torn from a Renaissance painting, there a piece of fruit from a still life.

I picked up two halves of a picture and joined the ragged edges. A nude woman reclined on a rumpled bed, turned away so all you could see was her reddish hair and her long, dimpled, creamy back and ass. Propped up on one elbow, she gazed at her rosy face in a gilded mirror held by a fat, naked baby. I longed to run my finger along her spine, to caress each swell and dip.

A tingling ran from my fingertips to some terminal deep inside me. I was so astonished I squealed and dropped both scraps. The buzz subsided, replaced by shame at the perversion and total gayness of practically jerking off over a naked woman in my sister's boyfriend's cabin. Was that what Aaron used to do? Did he think the painting was sexy? The fact that it was torn somehow made it more exciting. Aaron had touched it, and ripped it up, and—

Aaron came up behind me. First I was glad to see him, then

nervous, then happy, then frightened. Both halves of the picture had landed faceup on the floor.

"Carracci," Aaron said. "His women always look like gym-buffed guys in drag."

Now that he mentioned it, the goddess turned, before my eyes, into a naked linebacker with a woman's head. I felt a little easier about the feeling I'd gotten from the painting. "Why did you rip it up?"

"I got tired of it," said Aaron. "Come on." As he led me back into the main room, I saw that he was carrying a delicate indigo bottle. A vintage pharmaceutical vial full of . . . what? LSD. Liquid morphine. Nightmares and permanent madness. I felt dizzy, a little sick. I sank into the couch.

Aaron unscrewed the cap, and we stared at the bottle as if a genie might fly out.

"Aromatherapy," he said. "It helps. Don't look at me like that. I wouldn't have believed it, either, Nico, but these days I'll give *anything* a shot. I don't know why it works, but it does—"

I must have looked as blank as I felt. Was I supposed to sniff it?

"Put it on," Aaron said.

How thoughtful of him to bring me perfume with healing powers, and how glad I was that it wasn't an illegal substance. I sniffed. It smelled familiar. Like baking cookies. Like Margaret.

"Vanilla extract," Aaron said. "Your sister loved it."

"It smells like her," I said.

"I know," he said.

I said, "She told me she didn't use perfume." When had she started smelling like that? Could it have been around the time she started going out with Aaron?

"It's not perfume," said Aaron. "It's a natural oil."

"Where did you get this?" I said. "The grocery store? I mean, is this like supermarket vanilla extract?"

"I got it on the Internet. It's the kind your sister used."

It shocked me that Margaret's essence was something you could order online, like a fake Rolex or a pill to enlarge your penis. Maybe the bottle *did* hold a drug, some kind of vapor or ether. Maybe crying over the film had shook me loose from my bedrock self. Or maybe I was worn out by my romantic interlude with the ripped-up painting.

"Go ahead. Put it on."

The easiest thing is to do what you're told. I tipped the oil onto my finger and dabbed it behind my ears. The cookie smell enveloped me. I sensed Margaret's presence nearby. Aaron put his head near mine, and kept it there, without moving or speaking, until his breathing synchronized with mine. Part of me thought it was creepy, Aaron sitting too close on the couch and inhaling my dead sister. And part of me truly loved it. Air flowed into and out of my lungs, each breath easier than the last. I'd almost forget that Aaron was there. Then I would remember.

"God," Aaron said. "That smells so good. It *will* calm you down, I promise."

I said, "I should probably be getting back." But I didn't move. I felt as if the scent of vanilla was only in that room, and not on my skin, which meant that I could have taken it with me. I wanted to stay where it was.

"You can have it," Aaron said. "Take the bottle home."

"Thanks so much," I said. "That's so nice of you. But I couldn't. Keep it."

"Take it." Aaron pressed the bottle into my hand, and curled my fingers around it.

"All right," I said. "Thanks."

"Don't mention it," Aaron said. "Anyway, this was . . ." He stopped. This was *fun*? This was *great*? There were no words for what this was. "We could do this again. Drive around. Come here. Hang out."

"Sure," I said. "I'd like that."

He drove me to the end of my road, and I took my bike out of his van and rode home.

Twilight was approaching. The air was moist and fragrant. From the corner of my eye, I saw dark shapes stir in the woods. I imagined they smelled the vanilla oil, and that it made them back off. I remembered Margaret talking about how the spirits of the dead emerged from the lake at twilight to make their party plans. I wondered if she was among them, if she had a date for the evening.

I pedaled hard up the driveway, dropped my bike on the lawn, and hurried inside.

"I'm home," I yelled up the stairs. A feather of greeting floated down from my mother's study. I went to my room. I didn't want to see my parents, and I didn't want them to see a red-eyed, puffy-faced Nico who smelled like her older sister.

AFTER THAT, AARON AND I MET ON SUNDAYS, AND SOMETIMES in the mornings before I went to have lunch with my father. We always met in the same spot. Aaron got there early, parked parallel to the road, and opened the tailgate so he could sit in the back, in the sun.

Mostly, we drove around in the van. He knew so many beautiful places I never knew existed. Once he stopped at a turnoff, and we hiked into the woods, and he showed me a grove of foxgloves, pink, yellow, and purple, six feet tall, standing at attention like a sentinel troupe of space invaders. Another day, we found a patch of wild strawberries so thick we ate until I felt tipsy from the fermented fruit. Anyway, that's what I pretended. Then we sat at the edge of the field, enjoying front-row seats at a duel between two hummingbirds who fought until one stabbed his beak into the other's neck, and the loser plunged into the brambles. Even though it was awful, I felt lucky to be there, as if nature had staged the death match expressly for Aaron and me.

He took me to a part of the forest where someone had piled a mound of stones. He said it was a druid grave, from centuries before Columbus. It was something Margaret would have said. Probably it wasn't true, but I didn't correct him. I didn't want him to think that he and Margaret had been the only poets.

He would never have done something corny, like whipping out a drawing pad and sketching. But every so often, he'd look at a mountain or a tree as if he was framing it in his mind, and I'd wonder if he was figuring out how it might work as a painting.

One Sunday afternoon, we were parked at Miller's Point, watching two high-flying hawks perform their suicide-courtship air ballet.

Aaron said, "You know, this is the first time I've thought about making art since . . ." That was our code-speak for Margaret's death: the silence that came after *since*.

I was so happy that being with me might have made Aaron start thinking about painting. He'd promised we'd help each other, but I'd never believed I could help him. I remembered the Senior Show, how he'd crossed in front of the screen and, for a second, Mirror Lake had rippled over his handsome face.

The van smelled of vanilla. Aaron liked me to wear the aromatherapy oil. We never had to discuss it.

At first, I'd been careful to scrub it off the minute I got home. But after I forgot a few times, and my parents didn't ask, I started wearing it constantly, dabbing it on to help me sleep and then help me get up in the morning. I was surprised, then annoyed, that my parents didn't notice. What if the smell was alcohol? They would have registered that. For all the fuss they made about their Only Remaining Child, I'd begun to feel dangerously cut loose and out there, on my own.

Putting on the oil became an addictive secret rite. Dabbing it on in the steamy bathroom, I thought, This how cutters begin. Girls who do painful things to themselves because they can't resist. The little blue vial *could* have contained LSD or Rohypnol. Why wasn't vanilla extract included in Oficer Prozak's DARE teacher-training guide?

Often, as we rode around, Aaron and I listened to music. The sweet, slow phrases flowed over us like the breeze streaming in the windows. Sometimes Aaron would replay a track and point out some smoky Lester Young lick, or how Elvis Costello communicated more than he could make himself say. Once, when Aaron played Robert Johnson, I said, "He makes the blues sound like something spilling out of him instead of anything he's doing."

Of course, we were quoting Margaret. We didn't need to say that, either. It was sad, the way the music was sad, but not so sad that we couldn't stand it.

My parents must have thought I was spending a lot of time at Elaine's. Or they would have thought that, if they thought about anything much beyond putting one foot in front of the other.

One night, at dinner, my mother announced that she and Sally had paid another visit to Dr. Viscott.

"Please don't say you're looking for closure," my father said. "It'd be like channeling Sally."

My mother said, "He gave me another prescription."

Dad said, "He's a pediatrician."

Mom said, "He listens to me. He wants to help. He says it's the least he can do."

She stood up from the table and lurched toward the bathroom. She didn't bother closing the door.

I said, "Sounds like Mom's throwing up."

"So I hear," said Dad. "I don't think it was something I cooked, do you, Nico? You're feeling okay, right?"

Neither of us moved. Finally, Dad said, "I guess Mom had better start watching that extra glass of wine before dinner."

I said, "You guys didn't have any wine."

After a while he said, "Listen, Nico. We just have to get through this. All we have to do is survive and make it to the end of the summer."

"And then?" I said.

He thought a moment. "Then we have to get through the fall."

MY FATHER WAS WORKING HARD ON HIS BOOK. THAT WAS ALL HE did now, at the store. He'd started going in earlier, when Elaine was still there. The more time he spent around Elaine, the more I worried she'd say something to make him suspect I wasn't at her house as much as I pretended.

In fact I often dropped by Elaine's so she wouldn't be totally lying. We drank iced coffee and talked about movies, about Tycho, about Tycho's dad's photographic recall for every mistake Elaine ever made and his chronic forgetfulness about child support. It was like having a friend again, except that we never discussed the things *I* needed to talk about—Margaret, my parents, Aaron.

Ever since I'd started hanging out with Elaine, I'd begun ordering iced coffee at the Nibble Corner. The first time, my father stared at my coffee glass as if it were a clue to some mysterious grown-up life I was leading without him in it. Then he said, "You know, I think I'll have one of those, too." I stirred three spoonfuls of sugar in mine, and my father did the same.

It became another ritual. We ordered coffee every day and fed our addiction to the caffeine and the sugar and the slow stirring in circles. All that sugar should have made me stop losing weight. But I kept on getting thinner and looking more like Margaret. Sometimes, passing a store window, I'd catch a glimpse of her, and my knees would go weak—and then she'd turn back into me.

One afternoon, my father and I were finishing our coffee when he told me that he was almost sure he'd found out exactly where the Millerites had gone to be raptured. Apparently, our tiny local public library had a cache of crumbling documents from the year when the cult gathered on the hillside.

"For a long time afterward," my father said, "it was known as Disappointment Hill, though I don't think they call it that now."

"Not great for real estate," I said. "Where is it?"

The map Dad sketched on a napkin passed dangerously near

Miller's Point, then turned off in another direction. I was so relieved I said, "Great!"

My father reached across the table and squeezed my arm.

"That's my Nico," he said. "Let's do it. Let's take a ride tomorrow morning. Let's find the field where they waited."

I was supposed to meet Aaron tomorrow morning.

"What's *that* going to tell us?" I said. "It's probably someone's
front yard."

"So what?" my father said. "It can't hurt to check it out. Let's
see how it feels to be there."

"How *what* feels?"

"Who knows?" said Dad. "Some leftover remnant of all that
hope and disappointment. Some aura that attached itself to the
place and is still hovering in the air."

"Aura?" I said. "Really, Dad, why not just get out the ouija
board?"

My father stared at me, confused. Perhaps my saying *ouija board*
had reminded him of Margaret, or maybe my thinking about Margaret had made him think of Margaret. All the excitement leached
out of his face and left him staring at the milky tracks on his coffee
glass as if they were tea leaves he was trying to read.

I said, "Actually, that sounds like fun. It's a fantastic idea."

Ten

HERE WAS AN OBVIOUS QUESTION I'D NEVER ASKED MYSELF
before: How could you do the same thing with two different
people, and it could be heaven with one person, and hell when
you did it with the other? I loved driving around with Aaron. Our
rides never lasted long enough. But as my father and I set out on
our Great Disappointment road trip, every mile took forever. The
houses were shabby, the barns half collapsed, the countryside depressed me.

Dad said, "Did I ever tell you that Miller got most of his information from the book of Daniel? It's an eschatologist's gold
mine. A grab bag of prophetic dreams and exploding galaxies,
tornadoes, hungry monsters rising out of a sea—"

"You told me," I said. Every time he said "Miller," I thought,
Miller's Point. I felt guilty for not mentioning it in case, with all
his poking around in the library, he'd missed some crucial connection between Aaron's panorama spot and his doomsday landing
strip. But if I told him, I might have to explain how I knew.

I couldn't believe that I, a scientifically minded person, was accompanying my father on a mission to channel the ghosts of dead fanatics. Margaret and I had made fun of Dad, but the truth was, we'd both liked the part of him that would drive to the middle of nowhere on the chance of finding some leftover ectoplasm. Once, en route to visit Gran Bradley—his mom, our only surviving grandparent, who lived with a caretaker in her rambling house in Maine—Dad detoured an hour out of our way because a Gold-engrove customer had told him about a convenience-store owner who would show you her treasure, the world's smallest cathedral. The store was shut. Dad knocked on the door. We never saw the tiny cathedral. The romance of Dad's disappointment was a major part of the drama.

But now his eccentric enthusiasm charmed me less than it used to. Now it just seemed silly and sad. Spacey old hippie theater. I told myself to enjoy it, or at least remember every detail so I could tell Aaron.

Dad said, "October. It had to be scold. Those poor suckers were out here for days, long before Gore-Tex parkas were invented."

"How do you know about Gore-Tex, Dad?"

My father didn't answer as he nosed into the traffic. Then he said, "Nico, don't patronize me, okay?"

He went back to telling me more things he'd told me before. I zoned out and tried to visualize Disappointment Hill. I pictured a ranch house with vinyl siding nestled under a buzzing web of cancer-causing power lines. Or a shack to which hermit rapists lured girls with bogus garage sales. I saw a door riddled with bullet holes, and two slobbering rottweilers whipping out to greet us.

Dad said, "Nico, look around you. Some of this scenery's lovely."

"Lovely," I said. A gas station, trees, more trees. One nice house, a cluster of trailers.

Dad said, "Before his death, Williams Miller wrote, 'Were I to live my life over again, with the same evidence that I then had, to be honest with God and man, I should have to do as I have done. I confess my error and acknowledge my disappointment.' "

I said, "Wouldn't it be better if you opened your eyes and looked where we were going?" I'd been worried about Mom's driving. Now I decided that neither of them should get behind the wheel. They had all been excellent drivers before: my father, my mother, Margaret.

"Sorry," he said. "I was trying to get the quotation right."

"I understand. But you're *driving*," I said.

"I apologized," he said.

"Anyway, I don't get it. Was the guy saying he'd do it all over again the same way, or was he saying that he wouldn't do it again no matter what?"

"I don't know," said my father. "I thought I understood it, but now that you ask, I'm not sure."

Dad kept consulting his hand-drawn map. He claimed that if you drew a line between the river and the Davenport Revolutionary War Monument and extended it into a triangle, Disappointment Hill was at the apex.

"Right," I said. *Wrong*, said the staircase spirit.

As we approached the X on the map, Dad turned onto a smaller road that heaved up into the mountains, then turned into one of those two-lane head-on collisions waiting to happen, a corridor lined with overgrown junkyards and filling stations begging to get robbed or about to start leaking and poisoning the aquifer.

"Are you sure this is right?"

"A lot happens in a hundred and fifty years," Dad said.

"I think the apocalypse blew through here, and we missed it," I said.

"Too bad," said Dad. "Certain longitudes and latitudes have a certain hard-luck karma."

"I wish you wouldn't talk like that," I said.

"Like what?" he asked.

"Like *karma*."

"Here it is, I think," said Dad.

I said, "I think not, Dad."

We'd dead-ended in a dying strip mall, five dusty storefronts lined up like an Old West town: a convenience store, a dry cleaner, a video rental place. Two empty retail spaces with white swirls on the windows. A handwritten sign propped against one boarded-over door said, "Used tires," and listed two phone numbers.

"Lovely," I said. The three battered cars in the parking lot must have belonged to the desperate losers who worked there. Who would have picked this spot to watch for a divine visitation? People whose angel didn't come. I thought of Miller's Point, and it made me feel protective of my dad, who seemed suddenly older and sadder and smaller.

He said, "I guess everybody was raptured some time in the early eighties."

I said, "This place scares me. Can't we just leave?"

"Come on, Nico. As long as we're here . . ."

We shuffled around the parking lot. The smelly black asphalt stuck to our feet. Blinding sunlight ping-ponged off the grimy windows. Anyone could have been hiding inside. I hoped no one was watching. We must have looked pretty strange, separating and wandering around and getting back together like two guests at a party at which no one else had shown up.

Aaron had warned me about looking in the wrong direction. But how did you know which direction was wrong? I looked at the sky, as the Millerites must have done as they'd waited for a distant speck to appear and grow larger. My father was looking up, too.

I said, "I'm getting back in the car."

Dad said, "Roll down the windows. I'll be there in a minute."

I kept the windows all the way up. It was broiling, broiling. I thought I might pass out. I tipped my head back against the seat. I tried not to breathe. I let the heat bake my brain until I saw the Millerites shivering in their white wedding gowns. I saw their pale lips and chapped hands. I watched them shifting from foot to foot, pretending they were dancing. To flutes, my father had said, but I heard bagpipes playing "Amazing Grace." I was lost, but now I'm found. The Millerites had stayed lost. They'd stayed here, and no one found them.

How could my father have gotten into the car without my noticing?

"Nico!" he was shouting. "Are you insane? This is how dogs die—"

I said, "Can we go home now, Dad?"

My father said, "I don't know what I was thinking, to want to come here."

"It wasn't such a bad idea. I mean it, Dad. It wasn't."

My father said, "I guess they didn't call it the Great Disappointment for nothing."

As we pulled away, my father said, "In another hundred and fifty years, this is going to be a real mall."

I said, "That's the best-case scenario. Wal-Mart's the best we can hope for."

"Meaning?"

"No ozone. No water. Poisoned soil. No air. No humans."

"That's pretty bleak," said my father. "I didn't know you felt that way."

I hadn't either, exactly. What scared me wasn't the prospect of planetary extinction but the fact that it no longer scared me. Which scared me a lot.

I said, "I don't know. You tell *me*, Dad. You're the end-of-the-world guy."

After a beat he said, "The fact that I'm writing about it doesn't mean I think it will happen. If I thought the world was ending, why would I write a book? Why would I have kids?"

He put his sunglasses on.

I said, "Dad, please, can we just drive for a while?"

We were silent for miles. How strange that my father was writing the book about the end of the world, when I was the one who believed that it was going to happen. I thought about the cult members waiting to be zoomed up into the sky. They should have been more patient. Because now they *were* there, or somewhere. But not all together. Maybe they'd joined the robed angels in the Sienese orchard paradise. Maybe they'd been sent to hell for trying to get a free pass so they could spend eternity with all their loved ones, instead of losing them, one by one. I wondered how they'd really felt on the night they went home. Maybe some of them liked their lives and didn't want leave them.

The road reminded me of the route Aaron took to the grove of foxgloves. At one point I was almost sure we were passing the turnoff. I wondered if the flowers were still in bloom. I wished we could have stopped to see. I twisted around and stared.

"What are you looking at?" Dad said.

"Nothing," I said. "How come you're going this way? It's taking forever."

"Shortcut. It's marked on the county map."

"Goldengrove," I said.

"What?" said Dad.

"Goldengrove," I repeated. "Fucking Goldengrove fucking unleaving."

We passed the feed store, then the nursery.

"I used to love that poem," Dad said. "Fleeting youth, mortality, time, age, innocence, death—the whole metaphysical enchilada. What did I think life was going to be, some kind of . . . English paper? What did *any* of that have to do with . . . this? How could we have named her that? What the hell were we thinking?"

I said, "It doesn't matter. What happens is going to happen." It was strange to hear my father saying what I used to believe. I felt as if Aaron was helping me to stop thinking that way, helping me turn back into a rational human being.

I checked my watch. I still had time to call Aaron. I could bike to our field and get back to town in time for lunch.

My father dropped me off at home. I called Aaron, he answered. I changed clothes. I'd gotten sweaty shuffling around the parking lot. I splashed on the aromatherapy oil. The bottle was almost empty. I would have to ask for more.

Aaron was waiting at our spot. He said, "You look like a train wreck. What happened?"

Maybe I should have been insulted that he would say that, first thing. But the truth was, I felt happy that Aaron knew me well enough to tell the daily train wreck from the spectacular smashup.

I said, "My father made me go to this hideous place."

"Hideous," Aaron said. "What a girl word. I love it." I made a mental note to say "hideous" as often as I could.

Aaron drove up a narrow dirt lane and parked, and we leaned against the van. The forest was stilled misted with dew, even though it was almost noon. We didn't talk and didn't talk, and then Aaron said, "What happened?"

I wanted the story to come out right. I didn't want to make Dad sound idiotic. In the end, it spilled out so fast, how could Aaron have put it together? Trolling a strip-mall parking lot for leftover doomsday vibrations? Aaron nodded when I mentioned Dad's book. Once again I wondered what Margaret had said about us. I thought, I must trust Aaron to be telling him this.

Aaron said, "Your poor mom and dad. This has got to be hard."

"I know," I said. "I forget that sometimes."

"They're in hell," Aaron said.

"They are," I said. "I forget."

"Maybe your dad wants to know what it feels like to believe in something."

"You think he wants the angel to come and take *him* away?"

Aaron said, "More likely he wants the angel to give him a reason to stay here."

I said, "That's what *I* want."

Aaron said, "That's what we all want."

I said, "How do we find it?"

After a while he said, "You know that Sienese art book? Show it to your dad. That painting of the angel appearing to the shepherds and the sailors. Heaven and hell. The Last Judgment. Isn't that what he's writing about? It could be a cover for his book, if it ever comes out. Show him the painting you like. The one with the flying saint and the ship on the ocean."

I said, "That's a great idea. I'd better go. My dad's waiting."

Aaron said, "He's probably worried the angel raptured you without him."

Dad did seem a little anxious when I showed up ten minutes late at our booth in the Nibble Corner.

He said, "That was a waste of gasoline. I apologize, Nico."

I said, "I liked it, Dad. Honestly. It had its own wacky charm."

We ate our sandwiches. We didn't talk.

As soon as we got to the store that day, I showed the art book to Dad. I paged through for my favorites, though not Saint Nicholas and the shipwreck. That one was mine, only mine. I turned to the painting of the blessed souls in the lemon-tree paradise.

I said, "Wouldn't this make a beautiful cover for your book?"

I wished I'd thought of it, I wished I deserved the gratitude on Dad's face as he looked at the citrus-grove heaven. It was as if I'd offered to *publish* his book. I was glad I could cheer him up after our sad morning. I felt like I had when Aaron said he'd started thinking about painting again. Maybe that's what I had become, a messenger of recovery, helped by Margaret to help Aaron, who was helping me help Dad. It made me feel closer to Aaron, as if he and I were siblings conspiring to comfort our grief-stricken parents.

Eleven

I WAS BEGINNING TO UNDERSTAND WHAT ANY CERTIFIED DARE graduate should have realized long before: Mom had blackmailed our former pediatrician into prescribing a ton of pain medication. It wasn't as if I hadn't noticed, but it took me a while to admit that the problem wasn't going away, or spontaneously improving. She was taking more pills every day, and they seemed to be working. Something was working. She was playing the piano again, but with fewer of the mistakes that built to the crescendo of her pounding on the keyboard. It was painful to hear those ghostly notes floating out over the lake, but at least she didn't play Chopin or Brahms, nothing mournful or lush, only the crisp Bach preludes that made me think of prairie dogs popping in and out of their burrows.

Mom and Sally were partners in crime. In the evenings when Dad was cooking, I'd hear them laughing up in her study until Sally swanned downstairs, as glassy-eyed and wobbly as Mom, only minus the apology and with twice the brassy defiance. She'd swoop past me, a salon-streaked stoner cockatoo. She'd say, "Nico, darling, how are you?" But she was only asking the air and didn't wait for the air to answer.

By dinner, the clarity that let my mother practice in the morning had melted into a puddle slicked with an oily film through which she regarded us without particular interest. The mouthfuls Dad and I ate seemed gluttonous compared to Mom's. One night, she announced that she was thinking of getting a harpsichord, which might have seemed like a good sign except that she couldn't pronounce "harpsichord." She stared us down as she struggled to get the word out, and my father and I stared back, two deer trapped in the wavering beams of her blinky attention.

I wondered what would happen when Dr. Viscott retired. Officer Prozak had taught us that addicts would stop at nothing to get the substances they craved. I'd imagined an unshaven guy in a dirty T-shirt nodding off with a needle in his arm, not my elegant, sad mother, playing Bach on the piano. It felt as if Mom had decided to go on a long journey alone, and I had to say good-bye to her, every afternoon. Sooner or later, sooner, I would have to talk it over with Dad.

One afternoon, I went to meet him for lunch, and he wasn't in our booth. I told myself he'd be there soon, but after five minutes, then ten, then fifteen, I felt as if I'd ordered a hard-boiled egg and swallowed it whole. By the time I left the restaurant to go find him, a blazing star of pain throbbed inside my chest. I wondered if Margaret had felt that pounding heat when the lake had let her in and refused to let her out. Even after I saw my father through the bookstore window, my heart took a while to slow down.

Elaine and my father were standing near the counter, checking over some papers. Dad had his hand on Elaine's shoulder, and she was smiling up at him, her face transfigured and beautified by amusement and adoration.

"Excuse me?" I said. I could have been throwing pebbles at pigeons. Dad and Elaine scattered. "Where were you? I was waiting." My father looked at his watch.

"We were going over some figures," he said.

"I'll bet you were," I mumbled.

"What?" said Dad.

"You guys go get lunch," Elaine said. "I've still got another half hour till Tycho gets home from day camp."

As the day wore on, I kept recalling the look on Elaine's face as she gazed up at my father. The more I thought about it, the more I began to suspect that Dad and Elaine were having an affair. No wonder Elaine knew all about my meltdown in the poetry aisle. But why would a handsome guy like my dad fall for lumpy Elaine? Because Elaine was serene and cheerful, everything Mom wasn't. Elaine had loved Margaret, but Margaret wasn't her daughter. Elaine still had Tycho, and every day she performed the heroic tasks—making the bed, cleaning the house—that neither my father, my mother, nor I had the strength or the courage to do. I understood all that, but it didn't make me any less furious at them both.

By dinner, the pain in my chest was so strong that I had to press both hands against my rib cage. It made it hard to eat or even push food around my plate.

"What's wrong?" Mom's spaceship docked momentarily on Planet Dinner Table.

"My heart hurts," I said. "It's hurt all day." I beamed Dad a murderous look. But he wasn't picking up on my silent communication.

After that, I made a point of showing up unexpectedly at the bookstore. I'd barge into Dad's office—Elaine did seem to spend a lot of time there—but they were never touching, never even close. My father would be sitting at his desk, while Elaine stood so near the door that several times I nearly slammed into her when I burst in. I kept mentioning them to each other, but they didn't go for the bait, or else they had perfect grown-up control over their reactions.

One day, Elaine was leaving, and my father said he'd walk her to the corner. I watched them from the window. As they said good-bye, Dad leaned down, and his lips disappeared in the frothy nimbus of Elaine's hair. Elaine's hand shot up and touched the place where his lips had been. Didn't they care that the whole town could see? Or did they imagine that the neighbors would think that this was how every boss said good-bye to his favorite employee?

In the middle of the night, I woke up wondering if Dad could be Tycho's father. It didn't seem possible, but nothing that was happening to us would have seemed possible only a short time before.

I'd imagined that Margaret's death had drawn our family closer, but now I understood that it had blown us apart. I told myself not to be angry. But they were the adults. They weren't supposed to leave me alone with my dead sister's grieving boyfriend. The truth was, I wanted that so much that I was willing to accept the risks that my parents were taking with our future. The distraction of their own problems, and their separate solutions, kept their attention diverted safely away from my secret life with Aaron.

By now, I could hardly not notice how much I thought about Aaron, how often I talked to him in my head and remembered things to tell him. And there was that trick he did with time, making it speed up when we were together and drag till I saw him again. The memory of him was like medicine: two drops in the dead of the night when I woke up missing Margaret. Then I'd remember that Aaron and I were going to watch *Trouble in Paradise*, and for a moment I'd feel better.

I'd had crushes on boys in my class. One day, a boy would be just like any other boy, and then some overnight change made my attention fly toward him like filings to a magnet. After that I always knew where he was, even in a crowd at recess. He alone stayed sharp and clear while everyone blurred around him. Suddenly, I couldn't speak when he was anywhere near. I imagined holding his hand. I pressed my lips to my wrist. Then, just as mysteriously, the crush would disappear, and I couldn't understand why I'd been foolish enough to think that one boy, that boy, was different from the rest.

It wasn't like that with Aaron. I could talk, I could think, I could be myself, or at least the version of myself that most resembled Margaret. But if it wasn't a crush, what was it? Maybe it *was* love. Not boy-girl love, not waiting-for-him-to-call love, not wondering-if-it-was-too-early-to-let-him-kiss-you love. It was something purer and deeper. No one could know how it felt to be us, to have lost and found what we had. Aaron was going away in the fall. We would only have this one summer.

On the weekends we had plenty of time. I'd pretend to be at Elaine's. Weekdays were more rushed. I couldn't just vanish for hours without telling my mother where I was going.

But gradually, the weekday visits lengthened. Dad was in the bookstore, and Mom was leaving on her drug holidays earlier in the day.

I knew the reason Aaron liked being with me was that I reminded him of my sister. I'd catch him squinting at me, searching for traces of her. I knew it, and I didn't. Some part of me believed that Aaron liked the part of me that was Nico, whoever that was. I felt as if Margaret were a plant inside me that, nurtured by Aaron, had begun to blossom. Mostly, it was fine with me, but sometimes—usually when I was tired or lonely—it scared me. I felt as if I, and not Margaret, was the one who had disappeared, or as if I'd become a petri dish in which my sister was growing. There were days when I wanted to say, "I'm the living sister." But when I ran out of vanilla oil, I asked Aaron to get me more. He always nodded and didn't talk. Those were always good moments.

One night, after my parents had gone to bed, I put on *Flying Deuces* and fast-forwarded to the end. The plane Laurel and Hardy have hijacked crashes, and as Stan crawls out of the wreckage, Ollie's ghost flutters up toward the sky.

In the final scene, Stan is walking down a country road with a little hobo pack. He looks calm and happy, his simple-minded old self. Has he gotten over Ollie? A voice calls him—it's Ollie's!—and he turns to see an irritated-looking horse with a bowler and a Hitler mustache. Ollie the horse is as foul-tempered and peevish as Ollie the person. He snarls, "Look at the mess you've gotten me into." But Stan is so thrilled to see him that he grins and throws his arms around the horse's neck. Stan hadn't gotten over his friend's death. Ollie was lost, and now he was found.

The closing credits rolled. I wasn't crying or crumpled up in pain on the sofa. I got up and went to bed and closed my eyes and slept.

MY MOTHER NEVER GOT A HARPSICHORD. MAYBE SHE FORGOT, OR maybe the trouble she'd had trying to pronounce it had dampened her desire. Now, at meals, she played with her food, extracting one shred of cabbage from the tangle of coleslaw, one curl of pasta from the mac and cheese. Then she'd lose interest and grow abstract, listening, as if a voice, inaudible to my father and me, was calling from another room. A dim gleam, a sort of fish-tank glow, would flicker in her eyes, and, waving her fork like a baton, she'd say something like, "I've just figured out the whole thing about Mozart."

We'd pause from our pretend-eating and wait, but the light in her eyes would sputter, and after a while she would ask, with rising anger, why we were looking at her.

"Because you're so beautiful," my father would say, at which point she would stand unsteadily and drift out of the room.

At those moments, I hated how grown-up I needed to be in order to keep reminding myself that they were doing their best. But their best wasn't good enough. It was in our interests to let the others hide, lest, in the flood of confession, our own secrets might spill out. It was terrible, how Margaret's death had put everything in perspective and trumped everything that might seem huge to a normal person. Margaret's death said, None of that counts. Every problem can be solved as long as the people involved are alive.

July and August mocked us from the calendar on the kitchen tackboard. Every square used to be filled with Margaret's spidery writing, notes about a party or school event, music lesson or rehearsal. It was eerie that some of the boxes were already filled. But we couldn't take the calendar down, no more than we could dismantle Margaret's room. Someone must have canceled my sister's dentist appointment.

One calendar box was marked with a new red X. I would have remembered without it. That was my appointment with the heart specialist in Albany. Every time I thought about it, I saw a gloomy, faceless person in a white lab coat telling me that I had only weeks to live.

Biking to meet Aaron, I'd think, I could die like Margaret and wind up in a ditch. If I didn't show up, how long would it take Aaron to work up the nerve to call my parents? How long would it take them to find me? The grief I felt on their behalf was so overwhelming that I had to remind myself it hadn't actually happened. Did I need to warn Aaron that my heart could stop even when we were just quietly watching a movie? In fact, when I was with him, the pain disappeared. I would have thought I was cured, if I'd been thinking about it.

Mom offered to drive me to the doctor's, but a few days before, Dad announced we were all going in the Jeep. He shot my mother a nonnegotiable look filled with information—no accusations, just facts—about her ongoing romance with prescription medication.

How could Mom have driven? It was all she could do to hold on to the directions to the hospital. Who would have imagined that there were so many ways to misplace a sheet of paper? Each time she lost it, she went insane, scrabbling under the seat, and my father's shoulders would stiffen. But I didn't think she'd taken any pills that day. She used to get nervous before. We'd forgotten what we used to be like, forgotten what was normal.

The hospital was outside the city, a short distance from the highway. I didn't get a chance to look at the shops and the traffic or to enjoy the twisted fun of my parents getting lost and fighting. But maybe I wouldn't have liked it without Margaret there to enjoy it with me.

We were all so relieved to find the hospital that we were practically ecstatic until, one by one, we remembered why we were there. As we drove through the gate, Mom said, "Abandon hope, all ye who enter here."

Dad muttered, "That's not funny."

The cement road had a bumpy stretch where a group of workers with earth-moving equipment were enlarging the parking lot.

"Good thing we brought the Jeep," said Dad.

"Brilliant," said Mom. "We need to find the Newton Pavilion. Pavilion? Whatever that is."

"I know that, Daisy," said Dad.

I thought of Dr. Viscott, and of the electric train chugging its reassuring circuit around his waiting room.

"Watch out," Mom called to me, as we crossed the oddly deserted parking lot.

Dad said, "Watch out for what?"

"Watch out on general principles," said Mom.

A cop with an orange mustache scrutinized Mom and Dad's driver's licenses as if we might be terrorists plotting to blow up the ICU.

"Picture ID?" he asked me.

Mom said, "She doesn't drive. She doesn't have a passport. Should we have brought her birth certificate? Would that have been enough?"

The guard held up his hand. Enough. He gave each of us a long, hard look. Then he waved us through.

"Thank you," my father said meekly. Mom and I glared at Dad for that, but he pretended not to notice.

"You're welcome, sir," said the cop.

As we threaded the maze of white halls to the doctor's office, all the evidence—wheelchairs, stretchers, oxygen tanks—testified to the range of disasters that strike unsuspecting people daily. Three times, my mother asked directions to Suite 14H. We could have found it ourselves.

Several doctors had their offices there, but the waiting room was empty except for a tiny boy and his mom. The boy had translucent bat-wing ears, and his skin was skim-milk blue. I didn't know if I should say hello. I pretended to read a golf magazine. If the doctor gave us bad news, I'd be spending a lot of time sitting across from Skim Milk Boy and other kids like him. Like me.

Dr. Nevins was tall and thin, with a beaky nose, dark hair in a knot, round tortoiseshell glasses. She came out to the waiting room and briskly shook our hands. She managed to make intense eye contact without seeing us, exactly. She appeared distracted, even alarmed, but not, I hoped, about me. I did sense that she was scared of me in some puzzling way. She got flustered when all three of us crowded into her office.

Mom and Dad took the chairs, and I jammed myself into the window ledge. There would have been more room for us if not for the hundreds, maybe thousands, of knickknack owls that covered the doctor's desk and filled their own glass case.

My father said, "I guess you like owls."

The doctor's twitch of a smile was pure effort, but somewhere in mid-smile she finally saw my dad, and I watched my father's handsome face work its magic even on her. She said, "Thanks. I've been collecting them since I was a little girl."

What sadistic relative first gave her one of those birds? To an owlish girl, it must have felt like being ripped by claws. I guessed she'd gotten over it and embraced her inner owl. If we'd been smart enough to consult her, and she'd saved Margaret's life, I would have found her every owl on the planet. But we hadn't bothered, we hadn't known enough, we hadn't taken the trouble.

The doctor skimmed the papers my dad had filled out. She said, "I'm a little unclear . . ." Her glance kept tracking between me and my parents, lingering on me. I grinned like mad in what I hoped was a heart-healthy way.

My father said, "Our daughter had—"

"Our other daughter," said Mom.

I'd never before seen my father shoot my mother a look like a strip of duct tape he wanted to paste across her mouth.

"Our older daughter had—" My father smoothly pronounced the name of Margaret's condition.

"I see," said Dr. Nevins. And then, all science, "How is that being managed?"

"*Was* being managed," said my mother.

"It wasn't," said my father. "She went swimming. She drowned."

"She died," mother said.

Mom, I thought. That's what *drowned* means.

"I'm so sorry," said the doctor.

"He told us there was nothing to worry about," my mother

said. "Nothing to worry about!" Amazing, how fast her tone of voice changed the tone of the conversation.

"Daisy, please," said my father.

Dr. Nevins said, "I understand your concern. These things do run in families, but the incidence of that is rarer than the chance of it happening at all. Which in your daughter's case, I know, was a hundred percent. But I'm sure Nicole's fine."

"Nico," I said.

"How can you be sure?" Mom said.

Dr. Nevins turned to me. "Have you been having any problems?"

The question was ludicrous, or would have been from anyone else.

I said, "My chest hurts. Every so often."

"Since when?"

"Since my sister died."

"O-kay," said the doctor. "Let's take a listen. And then just to set everyone's mind at ease, we'll do an echocardiogram. Painless, noninvasive. We can look at her heart on a monitor and see what's going on with—"

"Nico," I said.

"Nico," repeated the doctor.

"We *know* what an echocardiogram is," my mother said. "*Now* we do."

"—what, if anything, is going on with Nico," said the doctor. "Would you like to step next door, Nico?" Now that she finally knew my name, she couldn't say it often enough.

Mom and Dad jumped up. The doctor looked as if she wanted to push them back in their chairs.

"Why don't you relax in the waiting room—"

"Relax," said Mom. "That's what we'll do. Relax."

"And we'll come get you as soon as it's over. It's just a closet with a machine and enough room for me and Nico and the technician. I promise I won't hurt her, and I'll return her to you in one piece."

Everyone chuckled. A doctor hurting someone? What a hilarious joke. In fact, my parents seemed relieved. They'd wanted to be there for me. But they didn't really want to watch my heart, healthy or not, on TV.

I followed the doctor next door. The examining room was chilly and bare but for a table, computer, shelves, plastic gloves, gowns, a tangle of rubber tubing. A wastepaper basket with a red cross. The only light was the monitor's lunar glow.

The technician had gray dreadlocks and a calming smile. She told me to take everything off on top and gave me a short white gown flecked with pink. She smeared a blue, bubble-gum-smelling gel over my chest and ribs.

"Sorry, baby," she said. "Sorry it's so cold. We keep it like the machines want it."

In a few moments the doctor returned and asked how I was feeling.

"Fine!" I sang out, terrified and angry at myself for the wimpy hypochondria that had brought me to the point of lying half naked on a table in this icy spaceship capsule. Was it too late to call it off? I'd rather live in happy ignorance and die in the middle of life, like my sister.

The doctor listened to my heart with a metal stethoscope. The stethoscope was a formality. Her machine would tell us what we needed to know.

"This won't hurt," the doctor promised.

I jumped when she pressed the cold mouse to my chest.

"Hold still, dear," she said. She massaged it in tickly circles, concentrating on the screen. I studied her face for the wrinkle that would mean I was doomed, and when she returned to the same place twice, I knew my doom was certain. She asked me to lie on my side and ran the mouse over my ribs. I told myself to relax and enjoy my last few minutes of health.

This part lasted so long that I started shaking. I closed my eyes and asked Margaret to help me. She'd let me down about the haircut, but that hadn't counted, not compared to this.

After an eternity, the doctor said, "Looks shipshape to me." Shipshape? Was that a scientific term? It was her smile that convinced me. A weight seemed to have been lifted from her, and I understood that she *had* been frightened of having to give me bad news. I liked her when I realized that my danger had been hers, too. Suddenly she looked almost pretty to me, still owlish, but a pretty owl.

Thank you, I thought.

"Thank you," I said.

"I can't take credit," she said.

"It's a relief, is all." It was the first true thing I'd said since I got to the office.

"Were you worried?" the doctor said. "The odds were on your side."

"I knew that." I was lying again. "I wasn't worried. Not really. You know what? Science is my best subject. I've been thinking I might want to be a scientist some day. I love knowing why things happen and the scientific names and—" The staircase spirit said,

Maybe your heart's shipshape, but now she's going to make you see a
shrink.

"Oh, do you?" Dr. Nevins had started tidying up.

"Can I look?" I asked. She nodded. I got up on my elbow so I
could watch the monitor as she pulled the mouse over my heart. A
dark blob pulsed in a sea of black, contracting and expanding in
shuddery sea-creature ripples. I thought about Margaret's heart. I
wondered if it had slowed down or stopped suddenly, all at once.
Thump thump. Thump thump. Nothing.

"That's the left ventricle," the doctor said. "And see that, that's
the aorta."

"And that?"

"A vein," she said. "The vena cava, to be exact."

Already it seemed less like my heart than like somebody's science project. It was oddly pleasant, lying in the cool, dark room
with the doctor giving each part of my heart a purpose and name.

I said, "*Could* you have saved my sister?"

"Maybe," she said. "Who knows?" I could tell she thought she
could have, though maybe I was wrong. She pretended not to notice that I'd started to cry. She said, "I'm sorry about your sister."

"Thank you," I tried to say. I sat up. The doctor put down the
mouse, the screen went blank. All black sea, no island. After a
while she said, "If you really like science, Nico, don't let anybody
stop you. If that's what you want to do—" Like the bookstore
customers, she was talking about herself.

"Actually," I said, "I was thinking that if I didn't become a scientist, I might want to be a jazz singer."

"A jazz singer?" she murmured. "Interesting." She was strip-
ping off her gloves. Each finger came off with a pop. With one

glove still dangling from her hand, she paused and said, "If you want to talk to someone, I can give your parents a referral."

"About?" For a minute, I thought she meant my future in science.

"About your . . . feelings. About your sister."

I told you so, said the staircase spirit.

"That's okay," I said.

"Your parents can always call," she said.

"Thanks," I said. "I'll tell them."

My parents took one look at me and lit up as if I'd been dying and the doctor had cured me. As if I'd been dead and she'd resurrected me. For maximum embarrassment, they slapped each other a modified high five. The doctor squinted into this beacon of family bliss. She was glad to send us on our way with a positive outcome and no reason for a follow-up appointment.

The corridors and the hospital parking lot looked different than they had on our way in. My reprieve had changed them back into places where bad things happened to other people. The three of us walked to the Jeep with the duckling bounce of schoolkids who've been ordered not to run in the halls. How warm and gentle the sunshine was, how artfully the trees had been sponge-painted onto the cloudless suburban sky. I wanted to eat the air. I was overcome by a giddy lightness—weightlessness, really.

We went into the city for lunch, to an Italian place where my parents used to go when they first moved to Emersonville, before Margaret and I were born. We sat at a table with a red-and-white checked cloth, lit by a candle in a wine bottle wound with straw.

My mother said, "It's *exactly* the same."

"Time travel," said my father.

"Don't mind me," I said.

"That never happens," my mother said. "Nothing's ever the same."

"As if . . . ," my father said.

I said, "Can you pour me some water?"

The Indian waiter wasn't remotely interested in hearing how many years had passed since my mother last tasted their fabulous ravioli.

I said, "Let's order."

"Good idea," said Dad. "Our sensible Nico." I knew he was trying to be nice, but I wished he hadn't said that.

My mother ordered a glass of Chianti. My father shot her a warning look, then said he'd have some, too.

"You're driving," she said.

"Understood," said Dad.

My mother said, "It's the same menu!"

As I watched them trying to recapture that long-ago time, I gradually lost my urge to yank them back to the present. I tried to be invisible, so as not to make them wonder how they could be newlyweds with a thirteen-year-old daughter. I liked being left alone to enjoy the sense of well-being that came not so much from my clean bill of health as from the conviction that Margaret had engineered it. It was her choice that my heart had been fine, just as it would have been her decision if the doctor had told me I was dying.

For the first time since Margaret's death, I remembered what hunger felt like. I ordered linguine with clams. First I spooned up the buttery sauce, a slippery twirl of pasta, and after that I amused myself by teasing the meat from the shells. My parents' conversation was like elevator music.

Mom and Dad ordered espresso. When they asked if I wanted one, they seemed reckless, slightly wicked, as if they were inviting me to get drunk or high. The coffee shot to my fingertips. It was light-years faster than Elaine's and what they served at the Nibble Corner. When I touched the silverware, I felt as if I was discharging a mild electric shock.

My parents' good mood lasted almost all the way home. My mother reached back between the seats and squeezed my knee and said, "Thank God, honey. I mean it. If only we could all feel like this forever."

"I'll take one day of it," said my father.

"An hour," my mother said.

The hour ended when we got near town. The mood in the car took a dive. We were afraid to go home without an escape plan in place. That was when my parents got the idea of our going somewhere—Boston!—for the Fourth of July weekend. Maybe they hoped that our high spirits would burble up even higher in a bigger city.

I wanted to go to Boston with them, but not for the Fourth of July. Aaron and I had been talking about spending the Fourth together.

A few days before my doctor's appointment, we'd driven to Miller's Point. Aaron tried to make it seem spontaneous. When we parked at the lookout, he said—as if it had just popped into his mind—how awesome it would be if he and I could watch the fireworks from there.

Awesome hardly described it. I had never wanted anything so much. But I couldn't imagine getting my parents to agree. It had crossed my mind that if the doctor said I was dying, my parents would probably let me do anything I wanted. I'd knocked on wood, like Mom did. Be careful what you wish for.

Only now, a plan suggested itself, unlikely but not impossible. What if I talked them into going to Boston and letting me stay home? I would have to be cunning and patient and wait for the perfect moment.

We'd reached the outskirts of Emersonville. I pressed my nose to the window as if I was overjoyed to see each stupefying land-mark. Oh, look! The post office, the out-of-business realtor, the women's cardio-fitness gym where the pharmacy used to be!

My mother turned.

"What was that?" she asked.

"What was what?"

"I could have sworn you said something," she said.

"You're hearing things." Then I mumbled, "If you guys go to Boston, can I stay here without you?"

The question had popped out of me. I wished I'd waited and thought it through.

"Absolutely not," said my mother. "Why would you *want* that?"

My father found me in his rearview mirror.

"Watch the road, dear," said my mother.

"Look who's talking," said Dad.

"Meaning what?" my mother said.

"Nothing," said my father.

As we turned into our driveway, my mother heaved a theatrical sigh that, I suddenly realized, Margaret had learned from her.

"What a shame," my mother said. "We were doing such a good job of pretending to be a happy family of three."

Twelve

OUR TOWN WAS SO PROUD OF ITS FOURTH OF JULY, YOU WOULD have thought the Declaration of Independence was signed in the musty Grange Hall where the Cub Scouts held bake sales. A rich woman who'd spent girlhood summers at Mirror Lake had left Emersonville enough money so that, every summer, we could hire a celebrity fireworks company to help us honor the birth of our nation.

On Mirror Lake we had a tradition within the tradition. All the families who lived on the shore held parties, and everyone got into boats and floated out on the lake, from where you could see the light show in its full unobstructed splendor. As the rain of stars fell around you and rippled over the water, all you could hear were the rockets popping and the oohs and ahs of the partygoers, carried on the night breeze.

No one ever got tired of it, no one ever outgrew it. When kids grew up and left home, they'd bring their own children back to see it. Long after Margaret and I had learned to act annoyed by everything that gave our parents pleasure, we couldn't pretend we didn't love being out in that firestorm of colored light.

That summer, any holiday would have been hard, but the Fourth was the hardest. We knew we'd never convince ourselves that we should try to enjoy it, that Margaret would have wanted that, that we should think of her and be happy. I still couldn't look at the lake. I couldn't imagine rowing out on the water and feeling my sister's absence like a hole in the boat. Even if I stayed in my room, with the blankets over my ears, I would hear, or think I heard, the pop and hiss of the rockets, and the murmurs of the merrymakers too stupid to know they were a heartbeat away from disaster. But why begrudge them whatever happiness they could have before it was their turn to learn what we had found out?

Going away for the holiday would have seemed like a ideal solution if it hadn't meant leaving Aaron alone in a town full of kids who'd already forgotten Margaret. My parents had each other, I had the two of them, but poor Aaron had only me to help him get through this.

Of course, it wasn't the same for him. He'd never spent the Fourth on the lake with Margaret. My parents would never have invited him to come out on our boat. But one of his paintings at the Senior Show was of fireworks reflected in the water. Maybe he'd been on another boat, at someone else's party.

I tried to remember last summer. Had Margaret seemed distracted? Had she gazed out over the lake, wondering where Aaron was, and if he was thinking of her? The only image that came to mind was of her glowing face tilted up as if the light were rain, pouring into her mouth. The Fourth shot to the top of my list of forbidden things, another reason for Aaron and I to try and survive it together.

I did what anyone my age would have done. I invented a barbecue with all my old friends, ferociously chaperoned by a posse of paranoid parents. I told my parents I'd miss them, but I would be sadder to miss the party. I argued as if my life were at stake, because I believed that it was, that I would die of boredom and grief if they separated me from Aaron.

I said, "It'll be really fun. It's the first thing I've wanted to do since . . ." They knew since when. I'd played the Margaret card with Elaine, but not, until then, with my parents. I couldn't help noting that both times had been about wanting to be with Aaron.

I called Samantha and told her I needed a favor. If my parents phoned, her mother should back up my barbecue story. Samantha's mom always seemed to enjoy lying to the other parents, and Samantha was so happy to be able to help her grieving friend that she didn't even ask what I was really doing. She mentioned that Violet was going away for the holiday. I was glad she warned me. Violet's mother occasionally stopped by the bookstore.

Samantha asked, "Do you want my mom to say you're sleeping over?"

"No, thanks," I said. "That's okay." At that point, I was still thinking that I could stay alone in my house.

"Wow," said Samantha. "Who is it? Can I ask?"

"It's not like that," I said. "It's not what you think."

"*I* believe you," said Samantha. "Wow. Have fun, I guess."

My parents never phoned Samantha's mom. At first I was relieved that they trusted me, and then insulted that they still thought of me as a truthful child instead of a scheming, secretive teen.

They didn't think I was old or sophisticated enough to lie the way Margaret had. Anyway, they didn't need to call. They weren't letting me stay home without them.

I badgered them like a lawyer fighting to save my client (me!) from the sentence of spending the holiday without Aaron. I began with hopeless arguments, the dismissable litany of what other parents let other kids do. Kids my age babysat for infants, worked as camp counselors, traveled to Europe. My parents had always hated leaving us overnight, even when Margaret was in high school. They only did it twice, in emergencies—once when Gran Bradley had her second stroke, and once when her caregiver quit. Both times had been bliss. Tequila, old movies, loud music, falling asleep on the couch. When Mom and Dad came back, they'd seemed amazed and overjoyed to find us still alive.

The argument about the Fourth raged and smoldered for days. My mother stayed unmedicated. Some maternal instinct must have kicked in, but her determination only fueled my own.

One night, my father said, "We need to decide about Boston."

Hadn't the bookstore customers warned me: no decisions for a year? But the question of whether to go with my parents or stay in town with Aaron didn't seem to require one. I kept thinking about Margaret telling me that sex meant knowing what you wanted. This had nothing to do with sex. The very idea was repulsive. Still, I imagined Aaron and I exchanging a chaste little kiss, the airy peck that an angel might give to express some tender promise. Happy Fourth of July. Okay, not happy maybe, but we'd gotten through it.

"Nico, you look flushed," said Dad. "Are you feeling all right?"

"I'm fine," I said. "It's warm in here."

"How do you like the fried chicken?"

"Fantastic." I peeled a slippery tendon from a drumstick and dropped it back on my plate. My mother had stopped pretending to eat. She was losing weight, too. We should have been recovering. Why were we getting worse?

Dad said, "If we're going, we need to make reservations—"

"Reserve two rooms," my mother said. "We can always cancel. Reserve three rooms."

"Eat something, Daisy," said Dad.

I pictured myself in a hotel room, flipping through the channels while my parents napped next door. Or maybe they would insist that I be with them. *Together.* They would hand me the remote and pretend to be interested in what I wanted to watch. How much *fun* we were having, piled on the king-size bed! I'd torture them with MTV while I wondered what Aaron was doing.

Brandishing the drumstick like a ragged club, I said, "I'm not going. Sorry, that's it. I refuse. I don't want to leave."

"All right." My father sighed. "I guess we can all stay home for the weekend. It's not going to kill us."

My mother knocked on wood.

I said, "Mom! Dad! Don't be hasty. Think it over. You guys could use some time alone."

"We can't leave you," my father said. "Knowing you were here by yourself, we couldn't possibly . . ." What was he going to say? *Enjoy* themselves?

"Can I say something?" I tried not to look directly into their heartbreaking faces. "What I want to tell you is, how great you guys have been, how much you've helped me during this . . . during this . . . you know. . . ."

I was sincere, or half sincere. The insincere half was thinking
that I might get my way if I flattered their vanity about what good
parents they were. Which was true, and not true. They loved
me, they were good to me. But if they'd been more attentive,
I wouldn't have been trying to trick them into leaving me with
Aaron.

My mother actually nibbled a scrap of crisp chicken skin.

My father said, "Thank you, Nico. But still—"

I said, "I *want* to go to this party."

I could tell my mother was weakening even as she said, "I
couldn't stand to think about you knocking around this big house
with no one here in case—"

"In case what?" I put my hands over my ears. My parents imagined fire, lightning, crazed pedophiles, ax murderers. I hadn't
imagined anything beyond watching the fireworks with Aaron.
Only now did I picture coming home to a dark, silent house.
Maybe Aaron would walk me inside, but that would be strange,
too. I wasn't afraid to stay by myself. But what if I couldn't sleep?
What if I heard noises? What if there was a thunderstorm and
the power went out? My courage wavered enough so that I was
almost glad when my father said, "You're *not* staying here alone."

"Okay, I won't stay *here a-lone*." I imitated him perfectly, his
tone of doom and foreboding. Even as I was mimicking him, inspiration struck.

I said, "I'll stay at Elaine's." It was the perfect solution. What I
wanted, minus the scary part. The look I gave my father was pure,
flat-out blackmail.

"Hadn't you better *ask* Elaine?" my mother said. And I knew
I'd won.

Perhaps my parents were simply too worn out to argue anymore. Perhaps they welcomed this chance to let me try my wings in a limited test flight. Perhaps they were telling themselves that a new life was beginning, filled with risks and adventures, as they bravely stepped aside and let me past as I groped my way toward adulthood. Or perhaps they were simply tired of each other, of themselves, and of me.

EVER SINCE I SAW DAD KISS HER HAIR, ELAINE HAD BEGUN TO annoy me. Her voice was too loud, she smoked. I tried to come up with more irritating character flaws, but I kept forgetting and thinking disloyally that I liked her. It should have been more difficult now that I knew she was an evil homewrecking liar. I told myself that the ends justified the means of being friends with someone who could do that to my mother and me. I wondered how far I would go, how low I would stoop in order to be with Aaron.

When I asked Elaine if I could stay with her, I stressed how wonderful it would be if my parents could spend time alone. "They love each other so much. And it's been *so* hard for them. They haven't had a minute."

Elaine didn't flinch. She said, "A change of scene and a little privacy might be just what the doctor ordered. Of course you can stay over. We'll have a pajama party. I'm not doing anything for the Fourth. A picnic with Tycho rushing around and scarfing down the aluminum foil and screaming when it touches his fillings isn't my idea of fun. Fireworks terrify him."

Elaine and I were standing on the sidewalk in front of the bookstore. My dad was at the counter, waiting for me to come in and take over. She hooked her arm around my shoulders and drew me away from the window.

She said, "Does your wanting to stay home have anything to do with . . . romance?"

Romance. The word disgusted me. Especially from Dad's girl-friend.

"No," I said. "We're just hanging out. Just for the Fourth."

"Just hanging out," Elaine repeated.

"Right. I promise, okay?"

I'd promised without her prompting me. Maybe that was why she believed me. "Okay. But if I'm going to be your stand-in mom for the weekend, I want you to come home early."

I said, "What about the fireworks?"

"The fireworks? I thought you guys rode bikes. It'll be dark."

I improvised. For once, the staircase spirit would have nothing to add. "We can see the fireworks from the park. We can walk there."

Elaine said, "Fine. Have a blast, so to speak. But I want you back at my place twenty minutes after the fireworks end."

I calculated how long it would take from Miller's Point to Elaine's without speeding.

"How about twenty-five?"

"Deal," said Elaine. "After that, you turn back into a pumpkin. And I'm calling out the state troopers."

Thirteen

JULY 4 FELL ON SATURDAY. MY DAD CLOSED THE STORE FOR THE weekend. Early that morning, my parents dropped me off at Elaine's. They thought there would be less traffic on the holiday itself. They'd decided to stay just one night and come back Sunday evening. As we said our good-byes on the sidewalk, my parents hugged me and gave me so many warnings and so much last-minute advice, they could have been leaving the country or putting me up for adoption.

Dad said, "Don't go back to the house by yourself. That's the only thing we ask."

"Why would I?" I said. "Don't worry. Trust me, Mom and Dad. I'll be okay."

Underneath Mom and Dad's fretfulness was the steely resolve they could show when they thought something was good for me, even if they didn't like it. A party with other teenagers! How healthy for me to be with kids my own age! Why couldn't they just have agreed that it was good for me to be with Aaron? Like me, they had learned nothing from Margaret's death.

My parents told Elaine not to let me out of her sight and pretended they were joking. My mother kissed Elaine, and I monitored the hasty hug Elaine got from my dad, the heartfelt, grateful squeeze you would expect from one old friend entrusting another with his Only Remaining Child. I did my best to keep the two Elaines apart in my mind: Elaine my father's girlfriend and Elaine my guardian angel.

I was meeting Aaron at seven. He said he'd call around four. The rest of Saturday slipped into a lazy slo-mo trance. Elaine and I drank iced coffee. Tycho got up late. Elaine went to the supermarket, and he and I stayed home and played video games.

Maybe Tycho trusted me because I'd known him as a baby, before he became a crazy kid snorting and racing around. Or maybe it was because I'd known the rules for so long, I never screwed up: Don't look at him, don't touch him, zone out and be patient when he asks the same question over and over. Margaret used to say that Tycho was *really* born too late. Centuries ago, pilgrims would have flocked to him for prophecy and guidance. I knew that being with Tycho was sometimes difficult for Elaine, but it was easy for me. He made me laugh, and when I saw the pressure building, I'd ask if he wanted to sit on his exercise ball. He'd bounce on it and growl in his throat until he felt better, and I'd play both sides of the video game until he was ready to return.

Tycho's windows had to be closed so the sound of firecrackers didn't send him diving under his bed. I didn't mind the heat. A breeze carried the scent of lilies from a vase in the living room and mixed with the oddly agreeable little-kid smells of sneakers and half-eaten peanut butter sandwiches stashed beneath the furniture. We played Doom Invaders, then Myst. I got the hang of playing for real and still letting Tycho win. I loved the slow, unhurried passing of time, every minute delaying the hour when I would see Aaron, and by extension the moment when we would say good-bye.

Elaine returned. Did I want to watch a DVD? I asked Tycho if he minded playing alone.

"Alone!" he said. "Grand Theft Auto!"

"You let him play *that*?" I asked Elaine.

"I know," she said. "I hate it. It's so disturbing and violent. I don't know where he saw it, but he screamed for three days till I bought it."

Elaine and I watched *The Red Shoes*, and after that, *Pygmalion*.

Elaine said, "Do you realize we've just sat through the same damn movie twice? Two stories about the ways that seemingly decent men need to bully and control otherwise intelligent women. Either they want us to work ourselves to death and not have a life, or else change us into some creepo template fetish of what they think women should be."

It seemed like an odd little speech to be coming from Dad's secret love. What made it even odder was that Elaine sounded so much like my mom, saying what my mom would have said if I'd watched those movies with her. I thought, People see everything through the lens of their obsessions. To me, both films were about Aaron's trying to turn me into Margaret.

"Why did you pick *those* movies?" I said. "In general. Generally speaking."

"Why?"

"Just asking."

"God only knows," said Elaine. "I remember liking them. Why?"

"Just asking," I said. "I mean, I wondered if you knew they were connected, or if subconsciously maybe you—"

"Do me a favor," said Elaine. "Lay off the caffeine."

Four o'clock came. Aaron still hadn't called. I began to think he'd forgotten, that I'd gone through all that drama with my parents for nothing. Now I actually *was* going to have to spend the holiday with Elaine and Tycho.

"What time are you meeting your . . . friend?" asked Elaine.

"I don't know," I said. "Maybe he had to go somewhere with his parents. Maybe he got the date wrong."

"He got the Fourth of July wrong?" Elaine said. "I don't like the sound of that."

Aaron didn't call and didn't call. I wondered if I'd been fooling myself about this not being a boy-girl situation. The silence devoured the oxygen. It was hard to breathe. I played another round of Doom Invaders with Tycho, then I lay on his bed and pretended to take a nap. I could have been in Boston with Mom and Dad. Every second, I thought, Ring *now*. Tycho picked up on my mood and starting pounding the computer keys until Elaine came in and gently steered him to the exercise ball.

I'd almost given up hope when, just before six, the phone rang.

"Whoever it was hung up," Elaine said. "Probably it was for you."

"Why did *you* pick up?"

"Because I live here?" said Elaine.

"Let me answer next time, okay?" I said.

Ten minutes later, Aaron called. I said, "I thought you were going to call earlier." I sounded like a nagging insecure teenager. A nagging insecure teenage girl.

"Sorry," Aaron said. "I was busy helping my mom." He didn't know he'd stolen hours from my life, time I would never get back. He was just calling, as he always did, to reconfirm, so that neither of us would be waiting alone by the side of the road.

Even after we'd settled that, he stayed on the phone. I could tell he wanted to ask me something and couldn't figure out how.

"Could you do me a favor?" he said at last.

"Sure. Whatever you want." *Whatever you want*, mocked the staircase spirit.

He said, "You know Margaret's blue shirt with the glitter comet?"

"Sure," I said.

"What?"

"I said *sure*."

"Is it still around?"

"Yeah, maybe. Probably." It had to be in her closet. All her things were still there.

I knew what was coming before Aaron said, "Do you think you could wear it tonight?"

I said. "I'll try. I can't promise."

"Please. Please try," said Aaron. "Wear the shirt, okay?"

"I will," I said. "I mean, I'll try. See you soon."

It would have been hard enough if I'd been home and I'd had to force myself to go through my sister's clothes and put on her favorite shirt. And going to the house was the one thing my dad had specifically forbidden. Why did Aaron want to ruin everything? I told myself to stay calm. We were still going to watch the fireworks. He just wanted one little favor.

There wasn't time to bike to the house and back. Elaine would have to drive me.

"Was that the boyfriend?" Elaine said.

"He's not my boyfriend," I said, though technically she was right. It *was* the boyfriend. Just not *my* boyfriend.

I didn't want to ask her to drive me home right after I hung up. I didn't want her thinking that it might be "the boyfriend's" idea. After I'd sighed and flung myself around her living room for a while, Elaine said, "Okay, Nico. You're killing me. What's wrong?"

I said, "I forgot something up at my house. I don't have time to go get it."

"Forgot what? This had better be important."

"It isn't! But it sort of is. Elaine, are you superstitious?"

Elaine knocked on wood, like Mom. "No." She laughed.

I said, "Did you ever have your heart set on wearing some lucky article of clothing, and you knew that nothing would go right unless you did?"

It wasn't a feeling *I'd* ever had. I was borrowing from Margaret, whose wardrobe had been sorted into spheres of magical power. The red math-test sweater, the black skirt for musical performances, the blue shirt with the silver comet for special dates with Aaron. I was no longer just looking like her. I was thinking her thoughts. I felt as if I was watching myself recede into the distance until I disappeared. For a moment, I felt so shaky I almost wanted to tell Elaine the whole story of me and Aaron.

Elaine said, "If this has something to do with a boy . . . Did we, or did we not, just watch two movies about the insane, self-lacerating crap that women will do to please some guy? You shouldn't care so much about what you wear, especially at your age, when any old rag you put on looks terrific. You should know that the guy likes you even in some ratty, torn sweatshirt. He should make you feel like a princess in disguise. End of sermon."

Is that how my father made Elaine feel? He wasn't like that with my mom. Every so often, when my parents were leaving for dinner with friends—friends they never saw any more—Dad would give Mom a look. Half a look. And she'd go and change clothes. I remembered Margaret getting dressed to go out with Aaron, molting one outfit after another onto her bedroom floor. If she did that, every woman did. Maybe at this very minute Aaron was stressing about his wardrobe. I liked the idea, but I didn't believe it.

"Come on, Elaine," I said. "Don't tell me you never had some special thing you wanted to wear when you went somewhere with a person you liked? What about Tycho's dad?"

Elaine flashed me a dirty leer, as if she was thinking that she and Tycho's father never went anywhere, or wore clothes.

"Actually," said Elaine. "I *do* know what that's like. Or at least I used to." I couldn't tell if her sigh was about how much time had passed since she'd felt that way, or whether she was regretting some article of clothing she used to like and lost, or if she was sighing simply because she had to drive me home.

She said, "I guess you want a ride."

I said, "I'd owe you forever."

"You already owe me. If we're counting. Which we're not."

Which we weren't. Otherwise she'd owe *me* for not ratting out her and Dad. But whom would I tell? I couldn't tell Aaron about Dad and Elaine, or about Mom and her pills. I didn't want to make our family seem even more pitiful and damaged. The only person I could have told was Margaret.

"Look at you," Elaine said. "Let's go. I understand."

"Thanks," I said. "I'll bet you do."

"What?"

"I knew you'd understand."

"What's *with* you?" asked Elaine.

"Nothing," I said.

"I'm not your mother," said Elaine.

I counted to five, then ten, then fifteen. "Thank you, Elaine," I said.

Elaine belted Tycho in the back seat, and I sat up front beside her.

"Don't crash!" said Tycho.

"I'll try not to, honey," said Elaine. "He says that every time."

It took several tries to start Elaine's geriatric Saab, which coughed and sputtered all the way from her house to mine. Stopping at the bottom of our driveway, she said, "If it's all the same to you, I'll wait down here and keep the engine running. I'd hate to get stuck up there and have to sweet-talk some white-knight mechanic into towing me back to town on the Fourth."

My dread of not seeing Aaron trumped my fear of the empty house. Still, the driveway had never seemed so steep, and the house loomed above me like the motel where Norman Bates keeps his dead mom in *Psycho*.

I said, "I'll be out in a flash."

I heard Elaine's car choking as I fought with the swollen back door. Was Margaret jamming the lock? I pushed as hard as I could and stumbled into the silent house. The quiet was peaceful. Neutral. It was as if we had all died ages ago, and I was an archaeologist come to catalog our artifacts. The house was no longer a danger zone but a site where a civilization had disappeared, leaving behind a ruin that was better off without the humans. A piano shawl, a mirror, framed photos of a happy family on the shore of a lake. A father, a mother, two daughters. The females doing yoga.

The house was so silent I could hear the ticking of a clock I'd never noticed before, the groans of the refrigerator. I moved swiftly, like a burglar. Then the energy drained out of me, and I longed to go to my room and lie down. But I couldn't afford to be suffocated by the thick melancholy seeping from the dusty, airless rooms. I needed to stay attentive to the health of Elaine's car and to the price I would pay if I let the house win.

Margaret's room was sweltering. I walked over to the closet. The glitter comet winked at me. Margaret wanted me to find it.

I said, "I know you're not angry. I know you understand." Nothing stirred. Not a breeze. I said, "I'll take that as a yes."

I carefully folded Margaret's blue shirt and slipped it into my backpack. Then I tracked back through the house, searching for telltale signs of my presence. There were none. I hadn't been there.

"That's *it?*" Elaine nodded at my backpack.

"A shirt," I said, "I told you."

As soon as we got to Elaine's, I changed my jeans, put on Margaret's shirt, dabbed the vanilla oil—Aaron had gotten me a new bottle—behind my ears. No time for indecision, no looking in the mirror.

I timed my departure precisely. Elaine was cooking dinner. I tried to sneak past the kitchen door with a wave and a promise to come home early.

"Uh-uh-uh," said Elaine. "Not so fast. Let's see how you look."

In her new role as my substitute mother, Elaine was paying closer attention than my real mother was. Maybe people always try harder at the beginning. She called me into the kitchen and spun her finger. I twirled like the skater in Margaret's snow globe. I braced myself for the inquisition. But all she said was, "You look beautiful." I thanked her and left before *she* burst into tears, which she seemed on the point of doing.

I raced to meet Aaron, pedaling just under the speed at which I would get sweaty. The blue light of evening deepened into the satiny July night.

Aaron was leaning against the van, and when he saw me in the shirt, he couldn't stop staring. I was glad I hadn't suggested he drive me home to get it. He'd wanted me to appear like that, approaching from the distance

Gradually, he recovered and smiled. Getting the shirt had been worth it.

"Sorry I'm late," I said.

"You look beautiful," he said. That was what Elaine had said, but when Aaron said it, I almost believed it.

"Thanks."

Aaron loaded my bike in the van, and we got in front. Aaron hit the gas.

After a while, he said, "You know what, Nico? It scares me how much I still miss Margaret."

"Me, too," I said.

Aaron said, "I hear her voice, I think of some little gesture she used to make, that goofy salute—"

I said, "She got that from Ginger Rogers."

Aaron said, "I doubt that, Nico. Margaret hated Ginger Rogers."

"I know. But that's still where she got it." I hated this conversation. Margaret had saluted me before she dove into the water.

Aaron said, "I can't believe Margaret isn't here to settle this. I hear myself say her name out loud even when I don't think I'm thinking about her. I saw a girl who looked like her filling up at the Quikmart, and I followed her for a couple of miles until she noticed and got scared. I couldn't believe I'd done that. I'm not the same person I was."

"None of us are," I said.

"I'm so glad you're here," he said. "It makes me feel less alone. You're the only person I can stand to be with."

The white line ribboned toward us. Aaron focused on the road. We were speaking so straight from our hearts, we couldn't look at each other. He couldn't have known that every word was like a shiny glass bead he was trading me for having worn the shirt. He kept talking about my sister, and after a while I spaced out so that all I heard was her name. I liked hearing him say it. It clarified things, in a way.

When we reached the overlook, we tipped the front seats back, and for a long time we just sat there in the dark. Aaron slipped in a CD. A saxophone breathed a melody line as smoky as Margaret's voice, lazy, syrupy, graceful, oozing from note to note.

"Who's that?" I asked.

"Don't talk," Aaron said.

When it was over, I said, "Can I talk now?"

"Sorry," Aaron said. "You could have talked before. I was just kidding. It's Lester Young."

"What's the song?"

" 'Ghost of a Chance.' "

I said, "Could you play it again?"

"Play it again, Sam," Aaron said. I loved it that he and I already spoke a private language. We were rebuilding, word by word, the one we'd spoken with Margaret.

This time around I heard the song as the kind of conversation you have by yourself when you're all alone in a room, but you're speaking to the only person you want to talk to, the one you talk to in your head. You're explaining a hopeless love, all the stars are lined up wrong, but you have to say it, even if no one hears. And though you know it's impossible, you can't *make* someone love you, you keep thinking that the music might cast the kind of spell that makes fairy-tale characters fall in love with the first person they see.

When the song ended, Aaron said, "How are you, Nico?"

"Pretty good. And you?"

"Better. Better than I've been." He answered so quickly I realized his asking me was a pretext to get me to ask *him*. The fact he had something to tell me meant he'd been thinking about me, too.

He said, "Listen. I started a painting. Or anyway, I started thinking about a painting."

"That's awesome." The staircase spirit echoed *awesome awesome awesome*. "A painting of what?" I expected him to say a landscape, maybe of a place we'd seen on one of our drives.

He said, "Remember you told me the story about you and your dad going to the strip mall where that cult went to be raptured? I've been thinking about painting it. The strip mall and all the people—"

"What people?" I said.

"Sort of like a Sienese painting, or like the stuff the Shakers did. But this time the angel *does* show up to take them up to the sky. Appropriation, Nico. You know what that is, right?'

"Sort of," I said.

"I'm appropriating that painting you like. Saint Nicholas of Tolentino. Or maybe it's more of an homage."

It was the first time I'd heard the word *homage* since my sister died. It felt like a gift, but so did everything Aaron was saying. I was so happy that he could *do* something with our sad little visit to Disappointment Hill, that he could take our wasted morning and turn it into art. I was thrilled to be even a tiny bit responsible, if in fact I was.

Aaron said, "I've never worked figuratively before. It's a new thing for me."

"I can't wait to see it." The staircase spirit whispered, *I dare you to say something lamer.*

Aaron said, "It's still in the embryo stage. I probably shouldn't even be talking about it."

"Then don't," I said. "Finish it. It sounds great." *Great,* repeated the spirit.

"Maybe I will," said Aaron.

The fireworks began as a subsonic tremble, then a rumble I felt in my stomach before I heard the first pop. A rocket shot up, and two yellow spheres hovered above the horizon, twin suns that exploded in a hail of orange. A glowing palm tree appeared, shedding green fronds that changed into clumps of parrot feathers sifting toward earth.

"Excellent," breathed Aaron.

"*Really* excellent," I said.

Aaron said, "You can say that again."

"Really excellent," I said, and we laughed, and then stopped laughing as the geysers of light shot up to form a Liberty Bell. A tolling boomed, as if from inside the sky, and a crack in the bell appeared, and the bell split open and showered us with streamers of red, white, and blue.

Aaron said, "Did she ever play you that Leonard Cohen song?"

"I love that song," I said.

"I always thought that song should be our national anthem."

"That's what I always thought," I said.

Pop-pop. Hailstorms of comets crossed. A fizziness frothed up inside me. From time to time, I glanced at Aaron and caught him looking at me. I knew he was looking for Margaret, but I didn't mind, or tried not to. The way the lights trembled before they broke up reminded me of her smoke rings. If I'd said that, he would have known what I meant. I didn't say it. I didn't have to.

Then everything exploded at once, so fast that if you blinked, you missed whole galaxies, Milky Ways, flaming planets, and shooting stars. It was like having a ringside seat at Armageddon.

A new volley of pops and booms signaled that the end was approaching. I tried to memorize every light, to hold on to it longer, but each flash erased the one before it, until the explosions stopped. We waited for more. There was no more. The last Roman candles had left a bright green smudge on the blackboard of the sky. We stared at it, without talking, until it disappeared.

"What are you doing tomorrow?" Aaron asked.

I said, "I don't know. Nothing."

He said, "Maybe we could hang out. You could come over to the studio and watch a movie."

I said, "I could do that. My parents aren't getting back until to-morrow night."

"You could see my painting," Aaron said.

"I'd love to," I said.

"Can we meet early? Around eleven?" Aaron patted my shoul-der. Or maybe he was just stroking the shirt, and my arm was in-side it. No one had ever touched me so gently, but my skin burned where his fingertips had rested.

I said, "Elaine's waiting. I've got to get back."

It took him strangely long to hear.

Then he said, "Let's blow this clam shack," and started up the van.

Fourteen

I KNEW THAT IT WAS SUNDAY BEFORE I KNEW WHERE I WAS. WHY was I lying under the ceiling, and whose ceiling was it? For an instant I imagined I'd levitated and gotten stuck in the air. Then I heard Tycho snurfling in his sleep, in the bunk bed beneath mine. I lay perfectly still, trying to extract some oxygen from the coffin of space and convincing myself that I could get through another Sunday. I'd play video games with Tycho, watch a DVD with Elaine. Somehow I'd manage until my parents came and got me.

None of which accounted for the faint thrum of excitement, an echo from a time when I still looked forward to things. Until a flare of fireworks burned off the last wisp of fog. I *was* looking forward to something. I was spending the day with Aaron.

He didn't call until ten thirty. But this time I didn't worry, or anyway not as much. This time Elaine let me answer the phone. When I told her I was going out, she seemed disappointed, as if she'd been looking forward to spending the day with me. Or maybe she wasn't disappointed so much as alarmed by some signal she was picking up from my secret life.

She said, "Isn't that the shirt you went home to get? Didn't you wear it last night? Don't you have anything else?"

"It's my favorite shirt," I said.

"You smell good," she said. "Is that perfume?"

"Aromatherapy oil," I said. "It calms me down." I gave her a look meant to remind her why I might need calming.

"Have fun," she said. "But please, promise me. Get back soon in case your parents come home early. How would it look if I didn't know where their daughter was? I'd hate for your dad to fire me for being such a lousy babysitter. Er . . . chaperone."

Liar, I thought. Slut.

"Thanks," I said. "See you later."

Outside, the hot air clung to my skin like scraps of cellophane. By the time I biked to our meeting place, my armpits were soaking wet. I penguined my elbows against my sides. But the second I saw Aaron, my hand shot up, and I waved. I could tell he was glad I'd worn Margaret's shirt without his having to ask.

He gave me an awkward hug and let his hands linger on my shoulders. He said, "I don't want to mess up your shirt."

I had to recover from his saying "your shirt" before I noticed that he had paint all over his hands. I sat next to him on the tailgate while he finished his cigarette.

"I guess you've been working," I said.

"A little," he said. "Pushing paint around on canvas."

"Can I see? Hey, if you want to paint this afternoon, we could hang out some other time—"

Aaron shook his head. For an artist who'd just started working again, he didn't seem as cheerful as I would have expected.

"There's not much to see. But sure. I'd like that. No one else has seen it yet. Now for the bad news. Ready?"

I nodded.

"The air conditioner in the van is broken." Maybe that was why he looked glum.

"That's fine. I like the heat," I said.

"Right," said Aaron. "See if you still feel that way in a couple of minutes."

We drove with the windows open, the hot wind slapping the windshield like those fat soapy strips in the car wash. A band of dust hung over on the fields. The corn was parched and stunted. I'd always slumped down in Aaron's passenger seat, hiding, but now I sat up straight. No one was out driving or walking or mowing their lawns. We passed a few houses with lines of cars parked out front, but the heat had driven the guests inside or around to the backyard pools. Whiffs of charcoal and charred meat were the only signs of human existence.

A neutron bomb could have fallen during the night. Or maybe Martian invaders had used the fireworks as cover for their attack and kidnapped our neighbors. I thought about my father, wandering around the doomsday parking lot. Maybe the end times had come and gone while he and Mom were in Boston.

Of course, the world hadn't ended. Aaron's parents' cars were in his driveway. He hit the horn—*beep beep*, hello—and drove to the cabin out back.

The heat made the cabin smell worse than it normally did. I thought how little it took to make the most putrid pigsty seem like a refuge, like home. It was cool inside. I was glad to be safe indoors and out of the roasted dead world.

Someone had cleaned up the cabin since the last time I was there. All the junk had been herded into lumpy mounds under sheets. Light streamed in from the glassed-in porch where, from the doorway, I could see an easel and a table with brushes in coffee cans and tubes of paint lined up in rows like bright, exotic candy. The scraps had been swept off the floor.

"Can I go in?" I said.

"Please. Please do," said Aaron.

I edged into the studio. One wall was covered with a patchwork of postcards and reproductions from books: *Last Judgment*s, *Resurrection*s, *Ascension*s, angels descending from heaven and saints rising up to meet them. Everywhere were blue firmaments dotted with cottony clouds and winged cherubs, like fleshy pink blimps, hovering in the air. It reminded me of Margaret's room, but more animated and sweeter.

I said. "I can't believe you put all this stuff up since . . ."

"That's just research. Go ahead. Look." Aaron nodded toward the easel.

At first all I saw was syrupy black, but as I approached, dabs of color appeared, and two figures—a man and a little girl—hopped out of the background. They were looking up, with their arms raised. The sky was stitched with fireworks, and the man and the girl seemed to be trying to gather the light in their arms. It didn't resemble us all that much, but I knew that it was me and Dad wandering around the blacktop on Disappointment Hill. Except that, in the painting, we *had* seen the heavenly sign. The rockets were the volley of the angel army come to save us.

Aaron said, "I had most of it sketched out. And then last night, after the fireworks, I stayed up all night, and it kind of came together."

"You didn't sleep?"

He shook his head.

That explains it, I thought.

"What's wrong? Don't you like it?" Aaron said. "Maybe I should tear it up and quit even trying."

"No, it's beautiful!" I said.

"Beautiful?" said Aaron. The staircase spirit chortled. "That's all you've got to say?"

"I mean it's *really* beautiful," I said.

"That's better," Aaron said. "I don't want to put you on the spot, but you're the only one who's seen it. I need to know what you think."

I wondered whom he was talking to: Nico or her sister? I focused on the painting and tried to forget he was there. Once more I poured my energy into crossing the border between the real world and the picture, and becoming that girl in the landscape. But the problem was, I'd *been* her, and it wasn't like that.

"I love it," I said. Which I did. So why did I sound so fake? Aaron would see into my heart. He would know what I meant.

I said, "What movie are we watching?"

Aaron said, "Jesus, Nico. This is the first work I've done since . . . and I show it to you, and you want to know what *movie* we're watching?"

"I'm sorry," I said.

"Forget it," Aaron said.

"The painting's really great," I said.

Really great. Really great.

"Right. I got it, Nico. Listen. There's something I want you to hear."

Across the porch from Aaron's worktable was a portable CD player. He rolled up a chair and motioned for me to sit down and came around and stood behind me. Close behind me. Too close. I kept thinking he'd move away.

For a moment, I was afraid that he was going to play a recording of Margaret. The final stage in our experiment. I didn't want to hear it. But Aaron would never do that, not without asking me first. Aaron would never hurt me. He cared about me. He was good and gentle and kind.

He hit the remote, and for a moment we stared at the silent speakers. I heard some static, then a few timid notes. Someone tinkling around on a piano. A deep voice said either, "I'm going to eat it," or, "I'm not going to eat it." A murmur rose from the crowd, which seemed to know something awful was coming. At least it wasn't Margaret.

"Where is this?" I asked.

"Tokyo," said Aaron. "Hardly anyone in the audience speaks a word of English."

"Who is it?"

"Don't talk," said Aaron. "Can't you do that, Nico? Can't you keep quiet and listen?"

I did what he said. I tried not to wonder why he sounded annoyed. I recalled that he'd been edgy before, and it hadn't been about me. The piano repeated the same arpeggio. The singer kept missing his cue, or maybe he was stuck like those drivers who panic on freeway entrance ramps.

"*My Funny Fah-leen-tine.*" The crowd made a sound that somehow managed to combine a scream, a moan of pleasure, a snicker of disbelief. Did the weirdly familiar voice belong to a man or a woman?

Aaron was still behind me. I could feel the heat from his hips and the brush of denim through Margaret's shirt. Was this supposed to feel *sexy*? I guessed it did, in a way, the sexiness of being singled out, the hot light of his attention. At the same time I felt trapped. A wide belt banded around my chest, pulling tighter and tighter. I was glad I'd found out that my heart was okay.

"Who is it?" I said. "I know that voice. Tell me—"

"Listen," he said. "Just listen. Relax and let it wash over you."

I turned back toward the music. Where had I heard that singer? Margaret had played me every version of "My Funny Valentine." Ella Fitzgerald, Chet Baker, Nina Simone, Rickie Lee Jones. I would have remembered this one.

The voice was broken and wobbly, with a heavy accent. *"Vaaah-len-tine . . . loffable . . . unphotogroffable. . . . My favorite verk of art."* The words were only vehicles for the desperation, the reaching and stumbling off pitch, the loopy crescendos on *"favorite"* and *"smile,"* the bravado or terror with which the singer got louder just before the phrases I listened for, dreading the gap between the right note and the note I was going to hear. The voice kept trying to punch through the song, the voice had burned through everything else, and there was nothing left. No sex, no age, no home, no time. Ashes. Sorrow and courage. Alcohol, drugs, cigarettes. Recklessness, there was that.

The piano tried to pretend it knew where it was going as the singer lurched along. But on one of those high notes— *"when you O-pen it to speak"*—the voice was off by so far it knocked the piano off, too. After that the piano stumbled around in the dark as the voice let the ballad beat it up. I felt proud and embarrassed for the singer slicing through to whatever made the song so tragic. My mother was right about those being the cruelest lyrics, ever.

I said, "Is that person *dying*?"

Aaron gave me the thumbs-up sign. Meaning, I assumed, good question. Or anyway, good enough to make him hit the pause button.

"Not at the moment," said Aaron. "But soon. Soon after this show."

"Who is it?" I said, almost pleading. "I know that I know."

"Listen." Aaron hit the play button again. "Shut up."

And now it was like hearing someone *actually* dying of whatever ruined that voice in the first place. When my sister sang the song, it was all about love and sex, but this version was pure death. When the voice sang, "*Stay little valentine, stay,*" it was pleading with life itself. Or maybe the singer was crooning to laughable, unphotographable death, asking *it* to stay, which put a whole new slant on things—a song like a suicide note. Not even my mother could object to this, because no one could imagine that the owner of this voice could feel superior to the weakest mouth, the most un-Greek figure.

"Who is it?" I repeated.

The voice limped on. The accent thickened. "*Each day is Fahlintine's day.*" The piano attempted a chirpy exit and failed. The audience applauded.

Aaron said, "They sound like passengers clapping when the plane lands after a bumpy flight."

"Who was it?"

Aaron said, "You know."

I hadn't wanted to know. I didn't want to think about someone with my name turning my sister's song into a serenade from hell.

"It's Nico," he said.

"I know that," I said.

"I knew you did, Nico," said Aaron. "It was one of her last concerts. Not long before she died. She was riding a bike and had some kind of aneurysm, and her brain exploded."

I said, "I saw *Nico Icon* with Margaret."

Aaron said, "You did?" Everything stopped for a second. Then he said, "It's a rare recording. I listened to it the whole time I was working on the new painting."

I was ashamed for having imagined I'd inspired Aaron with a silly story about me and my father playing Ghostbusters in a strip mall when Aaron's real inspiration was a German junkie's love song to self-destruction.

I said, "Did my sister ever hear that?"

"She played it for me," said Aaron.

"How come I never heard it?"

"Maybe because it's so fucking depressing. Maybe she was protecting you. Did you ever think of that, Nico?"

"Did she like it?"

"She hated it. But she thought it was kind of great."

"It *is* kind of great."

"Are you going to cry?" Aaron said.

"I'm trying not to," I said.

"Don't," said Aaron. "I'd really appreciate it if you wouldn't cry."

"Okay, I won't," I said. It was time for him to move away, to back off and give me room. Aaron's nearness radiated into my back and shoulders.

I heard him say, thickly, "Sugar." I was afraid he'd called me something he used to call Margaret. Maybe he had, because he stepped back and spun my chair around and looked as if he was wondering who I was and how I got there.

"Excuse me?" I said, meaning, *Me*. Nico, the girl whose parents named her after that voice. I pictured my mom and dad window-shopping on a tree-lined Boston street. I willed them to imagine me in this steamy cabin with Aaron. But they couldn't, they didn't need to, they couldn't get here in time. I wanted to play the song for them, not to make them feel what I was feeling but to ask them why Aaron would want me to feel this way. Screw loose, said my father. Little Adonis, said Mom. Freaky, said Margaret. Watch out.

Maybe the thought of my parents had telepathically introduced some specter of adult authority into the room, because now Aaron seemed almost normal as he said, "Right. Sugar. This is one of those situations that calls for a massive dose of *sugar*. Nico, why are you looking like that? What part of *dessert* are you not understanding? I got us something to eat."

Sugar. Dessert. What was wrong with me? How thoughtful of Aaron to have gotten us a snack. And how glad it made me that there was an *us* he'd gotten it for. I'd overreacted to the song, and to Aaron standing behind me. Everything was better. The good Aaron was back.

"It's in the kitchen," he said.

I followed him out of the studio and went to wait on the couch. After a while he returned and sat next to me with a cardboard container and two spoons. His smile was wicked and beautiful.

"Ice cream," I said. "That's so *nice*."

Our friendship had started with ice cream. It was like an anniversary present.

Aaron said, "I don't want it to melt."

"Oops, I'm sorry," I said.

Aaron said, "I hope you don't mind if I made the flavor decision for once." We laughed. We had a history. We shared private, unfunny jokes.

Of course, I knew what flavor it was before he took the lid off the Dairy Divine pistachio.

"Want some?" he said.

"Yes," I said.

I reached for a spoon, but he pulled it away. He looked into my eyes. Gravity dragged me toward him. He filled the spoon with ice cream.

"Open up," he said.

"I can't," I said. "It's hideous."

"Don't be silly," said Aaron. "You like it. Come on. Baby bird."

I watched myself from a great height, sucking the cool metal spoon. Ice cream slid between my lips, shockingly cool and smooth. I'd braced myself for the dish-detergent taste. But taste was the least of it, really. I opened again. I took the spoon. Ice cream slipped down my throat. Delicious.

I could tell that Aaron wanted me to look at him while he fed me. But it was already too much, being fed and eating and keeping the ice cream off my mouth. The next spoonful came too fast. Ice cream dripped from my lips. Aaron watched it. His eyes drifted shut and then opened again.

I knew it was ill and perverted, but I didn't want him to stop. At the same time I needed to see if I had the power to stop him.

I said, "I used to hate pistachio."

Aaron said, "I know. But you're not the same person, Nico."

"Well, actually, I'm kind of still *me*."

Aaron said, "Don't talk." He filled the spoon. "Please, Nico, don't say anything."

"I *really* don't want any more," I said.

"For me? Just another bite," Aaron pleaded.

"All right," I said. "One bite."

I opened my mouth just wide enough for the tip of the spoon to part my lips.

"Okay. One last bite and we're done," said Aaron. I thought, Fine. I can do this. I'd seen TV programs on which contestants gulped down pails of grubs. It was just pistachio ice cream. Nothing more, nothing worse. It wasn't drugs or poison. Autoimmunization.

The next spoonful was so large I had to stretch my mouth wide.

"Brain freeze," I said.

"Swallow," Aaron said.

I tried to swallow. A green bubble blipped from between my lips. Aaron put down the spoon and, with his fingers, smeared the sticky green all over my mouth and chin. He sat back, admiring his work. Then he took his finger and put it in my mouth. Astonishment fractured me. I split off from myself. Half of me watched the other half sucking on Aaron's finger.

He took his finger out of my mouth, dipped it in the ice cream, and painted my lips with his finger. And before I could wipe it off, he swooped in closer and kissed me.

I kissed him back, gently at first, and then a little harder, trying out different ways, as if he might get bored if I did the same thing for too long. The pressure of his lips against mine melted every cell in my body.

"Jesus." Aaron's eyes were closed. He didn't seem to be talking to me.

He kissed me again. His tongue touched my lips.

"I said, "Is this . . . ?" What was I going to ask? Was this still my first kiss? Or was it already over, lost and buried beneath all the subsequent kisses? The only first kiss I would ever have. And it wasn't even mine.

Aaron repeated, "Don't talk."

As his kisses grew more intense, I veered between sleepiness and alertness. At moments I was ashamed that Aaron was in the room when I was having these feelings. I seemed to be shedding layers until the problem of *me* no longer mattered. I wasn't me. I was a pair of lips that existed to find Aaron's.

Aaron pulled away and looked at me. His mouth was a bruised, candy-lipstick red, glowing beneath the pistachio. It was terrifying and funny, or it would have been in another situation. I wondered what Aaron saw in *my* face. I didn't want to wonder if Margaret kissed better than I did. Of course she had. She'd had practice. They'd had sex. This was just kissing.

Now I remembered why Aaron needed to know that I wasn't my sister.

A seismic growl of nausea stirred in the pit of my stomach. I jumped up, crashed past Aaron, and sprinted for the bathroom. The housecleaning hadn't gotten that far. The bathroom smelled like generations of drunken teenage boys pissing everywhere except the toilet. I vomited, then crumpled to the floor and lay my cheek against the gritty tiles. I didn't care how filthy the floor was.

I knew I should probably wash my face, but the sink was repulsive. The mirror was grimy and smeared, but not so that I couldn't see that my mouth and chin were still green. I went back to the other room and perched on the arm of the couch.

I said, "You must be totally grossed out."

Aaron said, "I'm trying not to take it as a comment on my kissing."

"It's my fault," I said. "It's—"

"Let's not talk," he said.

"We need to," I said. "You need to know. I'm not Margaret, I'm Nico."

"I know who you are," he said. "I'm not crazy, Nico. Or if I am, we both are."

I said, "We shouldn't do this."

I expected him to ask me why, or to say I was being overly dramatic, to say that we were simply friends helping each other get over Margaret's death. But kisses were a marker. Kissing drew a line. My first kiss and my first breakup were happening at the same time.

"You're probably right," said Aaron. "We probably shouldn't hang out at all."

"Probably not," I said. The staircase spirit would have given anything to take it back.

We couldn't look at each other.

Aaron said, "Damn if this doesn't feel like channeling Adam and Eve."

I loved him, I loved him for saying that. No one else would have thought it. No one, that is, but Margaret.

I said, "I know what you mean." The worst, I knew, was ahead of me, like when you get stung by a bee, and at first it's not so bad, but you know the pain is coming.

"I should probably take you back," Aaron said.

"Probably," I agreed.

We didn't talk on the drive to town. When Aaron dropped me near Elaine's, he didn't say, as he usually did, that he'd see me soon. I might never see him again, our paths might never cross. It would be hard but not impossible, even in our little town. He was going away to college. He should have known better than to do what he'd done. It should have been illegal to dress a girl up like her sister and kiss her and make her physically sick. And to make her want more.

"Bye," I said.

"Bye," he said.

Bye, said the staircase spirit. The spirit said, *Maybe we should talk one more time.* But it was already too late.

I found Elaine in the living room, watching *Law and Order.* Aaron had left me alone with Elaine and a crime-show rerun.

"Where's Tycho?" I said.

"Day-camp picnic," she said. "I'm waiting in case they call and ask me to come take him home. What's that stuff on your mouth?"

"Ice cream," I said.

"What ice cream is that *color?*" she said. "Nico, sweetheart, what's wrong? Crème de menthe OD? Don't tell me you and the boy were drinking some crappy kid-shit at two in the afternoon."

I could have said "pistachio." I wanted to tell Elaine. I wanted to hear how the story sounded if I said it out loud. I wanted to ask Elaine if it was normal to get your first kiss from a guy who made you eat ice cream so your mouth would taste like your sister's. Had something like that ever happened to her?

Elaine said, "Let's try it another way. Where did you get the ice cream?"

"At Aaron's." I gave the word time, testing to see if the world would end.

"Aaron as in *Margaret's* Aaron?" said Elaine. "Please tell me it's some other Aaron."

"That Aaron," I said.

"My God," she said. "Is *that* the boyfriend you've been seeing?"

"He's not my boyfriend," I said.

"Forget that," she said. "The guy you've been hanging out with?"

I nodded again.

Elaine said, "This is creeping me out. Oh, my God, you poor baby."

"I'm not a baby," I said.

"Sorry," she said. "I realize that. Nico, what *is* that on your mouth? It looks like battery acid."

I said, "That's sort of how I feel."

"You're kidding, right?" she said. "I knew this girl who tried to kill herself by drinking antifreeze."

"I'm kidding," I said. "About that."

"What's going on?" said Elaine. "Sit down. Tell me everything. Begin at the beginning. No, wait. Go wash that stuff off your mouth. Pour yourself some orange juice and bring it over here."

The bathroom mirror showed me how wasted I looked. I scrubbed my lips till they burned. The orange juice tasted vile. Maybe the fake pistachio had ruined my taste buds forever.

Elaine said, "Start from the beginning."

I said, "Only if you promise you won't tell my parents."

"I can't do that," Elaine said.

"Then I can't tell you."

Elaine considered the options. "Fine. But I don't like it."

I speed-talked my way through the story, surprised by how much I had to say and how long it took to tell it. I heard how creepy it sounded: Aaron getting me to wear my sister's shirt and her perfumed oil and making me taste like her before he kissed me.

Elaine said, "The kid's a pervert. He's four years older than you. He's a graduating senior. You're a ninth-grader, Nico. The guy was *way* out of line."

I said, "It wasn't like that. I wanted to be with him. It felt like he was my age. He knows me, he knows what I'm going through."

Elaine said, "I'm glad to hear it. Tell that to the cops."

"He didn't rape me. Kissing's not a crime. He kissed me, I kissed him back. It was sort of like we were in love. Except that what he really wanted was for me to be Margaret."

Margaret's name still worked magic. Elaine went blank for a while, then said, "Nico, it's so sad I can hardly stand it. Listen, there will be other guys. Not all guys are like that. This was off the charts." She shook her head. "You know what? I just realized what this reminds me of. God, Nico. You've been Judy-ed."

"Judy-ed?" How could there be a *word* for my situation?

"It's an expression my friends use," said Elaine. "It comes from *Vertigo*. I can't believe you never saw it. I thought you and your sister liked old films. It's my favorite Hitchcock—"

"What's it about?" I asked.

"Jimmy Stewart's a private detective hired to tail this woman . . . I don't want to spoil it for you. Anyway, what I mean is . . . sometimes, certain guys want you to *be* someone else. Some sexy aunt or grade-school teacher they got imprinted on, like ducklings. Some old girlfriend who broke their heart, some Victoria's Secret model. They keep edging you in that direction. And you want to please them. But you'll never be that person. Sooner or later they figure it out, and that's when they dump you."

"What's the Judy part?" I said.

"That's the woman Jimmy Stewart tries to turn into someone else."

"Was the someone else dead?"

Elaine said, "I don't know how I overlooked *that* little plot detail." She took both my hands in hers. "Hang on. The video store has to have it. I'm sure it's in. No one in this town ever borrows anything decent."

Margaret used to. And Aaron. I missed them both. I was sorry I'd told Elaine, if it meant I couldn't see Aaron.

"Thank God they're open on Sundays now." Elaine rushed out the door.

The video store was two blocks away. Elaine's absence gave me long enough to remember kissing Aaron. The memory brought back that melting sensation. It was shaming to feel like that, alone, in Elaine's apartment. I wanted to feel it with Aaron, this time without the ice cream. But I'd ruined any chance of that.

Elaine came back with the DVD. As she hit the play button, I thought how silly it was that Aaron and I had made a sacred love-memorial séance out of watching a film. If it turned out that Aaron and I could still be friends, we could simply watch a movie without it being so heavy.

We got through the FBI warnings and fast-forwarded through the previews. The spiraling credits spun us into Jimmy Stewart's panic attack.

"Margaret never liked him," I said.

"Not *my* type," said Elaine.

Cut to Scotty's recuperation and the cheer-up visit from perky, butch Midge.

"Poor Midge," said Elaine.

A man wanted Scotty to follow his wife, Madeleine, who had a bizarre fixation on a dead woman named Carlotta. Madeleine haunted Carlotta's favorite spots. A cemetery, a boardinghouse.

"Believe it or not," said Elaine. "I had a film history professor in college who wrote a book on how Madeleine symbolized the cookie from Proust."

I laughed, even though I wasn't sure who Proust was. Scotty was staking out a fancy apartment building. An elegant blonde swirled out the front door and into the driver's seat of a luxury sedan.

"Kim Novak," said Elaine. "She is so hot."

Moments later, a panicky Scotty was fishing Madeleine out of the bay. The near-drowning was hard for me. Elaine noticed and felt guilty, so things were a little tense until the action shifted from the shore to Scotty's apartment. Madeleine was waking up in his bed.

"Is she naked? Did he undress her? Isn't *that* a little perverted?"

"A *little*?" said Elaine.

As Madeleine and Scotty played out their star-crossed romance, I couldn't look at Elaine. I kept thinking of her and my father, and I didn't want to hate her. So I must have missed a beat, because now Scotty was chasing Madeleine up the tower of a Spanish-style church. I screamed when she fell.

"Everybody screams the first time," Elaine said. "But watch. Here comes the Judy part."

My whole body tensed defensively against the look on Scotty's face as Judy emerged from the dressing room in Madeleine's gray suit. I needed to tell Margaret that Jimmy Stewart was a better actor than we'd given him credit for. Somehow he knew exactly how a guy looked at that rare—no matter what Elaine said, it *had* to be rare—moment when he's transformed a living woman into a dead one.

I said, "I can't believe it's something that . . . *happens*."

Elaine said, "That's the point. It's not personal."

I felt a lurch of nausea and burped up some pistachio-tinged acid. The room began to spin lazily. Vertigo was catching.

Elaine said, "That's the thing about art. Each time, you see something new. I'd always assumed the film was about men's sexual weirdness. But it's also about grief and how crazily grief can make people act. It can totally unhinge them. Sort of like *Last Tango* . . . Don't see that one for a while, either."

I said, "Elaine? I think I'm getting the flu. I think I need to lie down."

Elaine said, "You look pale, honey. Can I get you something? A Tylenol? Water? Herbal tea?"

"Nothing, thanks," I said. "I'll be fine."

"Do me a favor. Don't give whatever you've got to Tycho," Elaine said. "Lie down on *my* bed, all right?"

"Don't worry," I told her. "I'll go out back and lie in the hammock."

I let the hammock swing me through the hot, still afternoon. I concentrated on rocking so as not to think about Aaron. I tried to empty my mind so completely that when a mosquito landed on my forehead, I didn't have the instinct or the energy to swat it away. Let it have a big gulp. I deserved to be bitten. Every so often, Elaine would come out and check on me and put her cool hand on my forehead.

"You're not running a fever," she said. "Thank God."

Early that evening, my parents came back, wired from their vacation. They swept into Elaine's place as if I were a hostage they were liberating from a safe house.

"What's that bump on your forehead?" my mother asked, first thing.

I had to think a minute. "Mosquito bite," I said.

"I can't believe I didn't notice," Elaine said. "Put some aloe on it. Here."

"That's all right. It's only a bug bite." Now Mom was the calm one. Elaine seemed completely frantic.

Dad said, "Gee, Elaine, it's not malaria."

"Let's hope not," said Mom.

Elaine said, "I don't know what I could have done. That bug repellent is poison. Tycho can't stand the smell."

"He's the canary in the coal mine," said Dad.

Elaine said, "Put some ice on it, Nico."

Mom said, "Don't worry about it. Thanks, Elaine. We can't thank you enough."

I liked my mother saying *we*. Too bad for Elaine if it hurt. Elaine was nice, she'd been kind to me. But now it was me and my parents, the three of us against the world. Elaine was on the world's side. I wanted my father to understand that.

My father said, "Nico, we missed you so much. We're so glad to see you."

They took turns squishing and kissing me. I checked out Elaine's reaction. She adored our sitcom reunion. She was as good at hiding whatever was going on with my father as I was at hiding my secret life with Aaron. I didn't need to hide anything now. All of that was over.

"What did you guys do?" asked my dad.

"We watched movies," said Elaine.

"Which movies?" my father asked.

"*Vertigo*," Elaine said.

"I love that film," my mother said.

"I don't know," said my father. "It kind of gives me the willies."

Mom and Elaine exchanged looks that said, Men. What can you expect?

"Toughen up," Elaine told Dad. For a few seconds, no one knew how to react, then everyone laughed. Except me.

"Did you like the film?" Mom wanted me to say yes.

"I did," I said. "I—"

Everyone waited.

"I got tired. I took a nap in the hammock."

"Kids," my mother said. "Nico, darling, see it again in a few years."

"Sure. Maybe sooner," I said. Oh, if she had any idea! I shivered. Was it fever or fear? My secret was no longer safe. The staircase spirit rattled off the lies I should have told Elaine.

It took a certain cool on Elaine's part not to mention that I'd felt sick. I'd tell them if I had to. In fact, I felt almost recovered.

We thanked Elaine and left. Driving home, my parents chatted about the fabulous time they'd had in the city. The Greek street fair with the homemade baklava, the fife and drum corps, the hip-hop group in the park. They didn't ask about the barbecue or the fireworks. They weren't ready to return to the subject of Emersonville and Margaret.

Not only had they gone shopping, but they'd found the perfect presents. Fancy olive oil for my father, sheet music for my mom, a Bach toccata she hadn't been able to find online. A first edition of *Two Serious Ladies* for Elaine. A new video game for Tycho. They should have given the book and the game to Elaine, but the gifts were packed in their suitcase. My father would give them to her later.

"The game's based on the Brothers Grimm," said Dad.

"Excellent choice," I said. Tycho would never play it. Hadn't they brought me a present? I'd made them go without me. I couldn't complain if I'd slipped their mind.

Mom said, "Boston was so beautiful. I'd forgotten how much I love it. Your father and I were wondering why we ever left the city. Maybe we could move back there sometime, find a way—"

"Good idea," I said. And it was. A new life with all new kids who wouldn't think of me as the dead girl's sister. I could have some control over how much strangers knew about my past. I would never see Aaron again. Unless he missed me and found me.

Dad drove home as if the road was taking us into that glowing future. But the bright road dead-ended at our darkened house.

For me, the first rush of grief at being home was diluted with worry that I'd left some trace when I'd come to get Margaret's shirt. But my parents weren't looking for signs of me. They were remembering where *they* were. My mother put her music on the piano but didn't open it. When I went to the kitchen for water— I still wasn't feeling well—I found my father staring at his new olive oil as if he'd forgotten what it was for.

"Oh, Nico," he said. "We got you a present, too. I can't believe we forgot."

I said, "I was wondering. But I didn't want to ask."

My dad said, "What a terrific kid you are!"

"Thanks, Dad," I said.

He called my mom, who came into the kitchen with a long, narrow box. Inside was a watch. On its white face was a black spiderweb. The hour and minute hands were spidery black needles, and the second hand was a tiny black spider that hopped around the web, one hop per second.

I loved it. It was more than a watch. It was proof that they knew me well enough to know what I would love. They'd bought it for me, only me. It wasn't a bottle of vanilla oil or a shirt or a frozen dessert for a ghost that a crazy guy wished I was. A guy who'd been driven crazy by the death of my sister.

I said, "It's perfect. I love it."

"We had a feeling you would," Dad said. "Your mother picked it out."

My mother was looking at me, and for the first time in a long while, she actually seemed to see me. I remembered what it used to be like when I'd thought she was reading my mind. She knew that something had happened to me, but she couldn't have known what it was.

I concentrated on the spider, hopping round and round without hope of peace or escape until the battery died. It reminded me of the Hitchcock movie, and of the sticky net that trapped us all: my parents, me, Elaine, Margaret, Aaron. Probably even Tycho. All I could see was the barren desert of time ahead, the minutes and seconds I would have to fill without Aaron or Margaret to help me.

My parents were still staring at me.

"It's perfect," I repeated.

I managed a watery smile. And then, as both of them watched, I turned away just in time to vomit on the kitchen table.

Fifteen

I RAN A FEVER FOR A FEW DAYS. ELAINE BLAMED HERSELF. MY parents felt guilty for leaving me. I overheard my father telling my mother that we should call a doctor, and my mother saying that, in case he hadn't noticed, we no longer *had* a doctor. To which my father replied that he'd noticed she had two. I knew whom he meant: Dr. Dawson, the arthritis specialist she'd given up on, and Dr. Viscott, who'd been giving her drugs, but whom she didn't trust enough to press a popsicle stick on my tongue.

"Neither of them knows anything," I heard my mother say.

My father diagnosed the flu. Eventually, my fever subsided. But I'd lost my appetite again, and there were lingering symptoms. Misery, for one. I realized how waiting to see Aaron and then seeing Aaron and then thinking about the last time I'd seen him and looking forward to the next time—how much that had structured my time. Without that simple armature, the days imploded around me.

My illness demoralized us all. Even when I felt physically better, I kept the covers over my head. I burrowed beneath the light summer quilt to muffle the sound of the world, which was silent enough, except when my mother practiced the Bach toccata. Eventually, the mistakes would start, and she'd begin furiously picking out one-fingered nursery rhymes—"Old McDonald," "London Bridge." Or I'd hear her and Sally laughing. Every so often, the sad voice of the loon would echo over the lake.

My father spent all day writing at Goldengrove. When I said I wanted to quit working there, no one argued. After Elaine left in the afternoon, my father carried his Selectric to the front of the store and wrote between customers.

And so began the worst time of all, ferocious and unexpected. Grief seemed to have outlasted us, and, besieged, we surrendered. I lay in bed, I lay on the couch. I thought about Margaret and cried.

From time to time, I heard the faint hiss of a whispered conference that I knew was about me. Separately, my mother and father asked if I wanted to *see* someone. I wanted to see Aaron and tell him that my parents were doing the same thing his parents had done.

Elaine found a new babysitter. I was glad not to have to see *her*. I didn't want her nagging me to tell my parents about Aaron. When she heard I was sick, and then that I wouldn't get out of bed, she called and made me swear that Aaron had only kissed me.

She said, "I trust you, Nico. Correct me if I'm wrong."

I said, "I told you the truth, Elaine," and hung up the phone.

Day turned into night and then day again. I couldn't sleep or wake up. I dreamed about Aaron, vague dreams from which I awoke with the warm feeling of having been chosen, singled out of a group. In my dreams he was always sweet, always thoughtful and tender.

I'd loved Aaron. I could say that now that the danger had passed. And what did love mean, exactly? I had no one to ask. I needed to ask Margaret. But how would *that* conversation have gone? I've fallen in love with your boyfriend, who tried to bring you back from the dead by turning me into you. I could almost see the face she would make and hear her chiming laugh. Would she blame Aaron? It wasn't his fault, or mine. Love was love. We'd loved her. Neither of us could help it. Maybe when enough time had passed, Aaron could love *me*. Maybe he would appreciate what made me unlike anyone else.

But I'd forgotten what that was, what was me and what was Margaret. It had been so much easier when she was alive and I could compare us, side by side, and measure the distance between us.

One night, I dreamed that the phone rang. I picked it up. It was Margaret.

She said, "I have something for Aaron. Go into my room and get it. Tell him it's from me."

I awoke with Margaret's voice in my head and the unshakable conviction that she wanted me to call Aaron. She knew about the ice cream, the kiss. She was telling me to get in touch with him. You couldn't ignore the dead's wishes. All I had to do was figure out what she wanted me to give him.

I went into the hall and stood in front of Margaret's door and asked her to guide me. I walked in and turned on the light. It was sad, but I could stand it. I prayed for my parents not to wake up, and I froze till my prayers were answered.

I remembered Margaret teaching me how to swim. We'd started with the back float. She'd held me under my arms and skimmed me over the surface of the lake, like a water bug. Once more she held me and moved me, but now tears streamed down my face as I leaned on whatever force was pushing me across the room.

This was what I'd wanted. This was what everyone wanted. The sailors on the storm-tossed ship, the believers on Disappointment Hill. They prayed to be lifted and set down where they belonged. The only thing that spoiled it was my confusion about how I could be having a miraculous out-of-body experience and at the same time wondering how I would describe it to Aaron.

Margaret's spirit steered me to her bulletin board, where she'd tacked up her idols. The ones who remained were the winners: Bessie Smith, Lester Young, Sam Cooke, Jimi Hendrix.

I dried my tears with the back of my hand. The collage came into focus. I saw something I'd never noticed, a snapshot of Margaret and Aaron. His arm was around her, and both of them were smiling into the camera. Aaron was wearing a jacket and tie. He looked purely happy and years younger than the person I knew. Margaret wore her blue glitter T-shirt and a short pleated skirt. In the background, dressed-up strangers were eating at tables with white cloths. I couldn't have been more surprised had I found a marriage license. How had I never noticed this clue to my sister's life with Aaron? When and where had they gone out for such an elegant meal, and who took the picture?

I studied Margaret's face, then Aaron's. Then I made myself turn away, ashamed to be feeling, all at once, grief and longing for my sister, yearning for her boyfriend. Was she warning me to be careful? Or was I supposed to call Aaron and say she wanted to give him the snapshot?

Then something—Margaret, I told myself—drew my eye to the upper corner of the picture, and to an orange origami crane dangling from a pushpin. I flinched, as if the faded bird had brushed my face with its wings.

It was one of the paper birds we'd folded in Mrs. Akins's class. I had no idea where my crane had gone. But Margaret had kept hers. This was what Mrs. Akins meant. The message from my sister. I was sure that the origami crane was what my sister wanted me to give Aaron, though I didn't know how I knew.

I waited to phone Aaron. Once I did, it would be over. I'd know if he wanted to see me. I put it off till I couldn't hold out. I dialed. Aaron answered.

"It's Nico," I said. The silence was like a conversation. Every so often, he'd inhale as if he were smoking, or about to speak.

"I know who it is," he said. "What do you want, Nico?"

"Can I see you? Something strange happened."

"I had the flu," he said.

"So did I. Maybe we were both getting sick, maybe that was the problem." More likely we'd *made* each other sick, exchanging some virus along with the ice cream.

"Strange how?" Aaron said wearily.

I said, "It's about Margaret."

"What isn't?"

"Sorry," I said.

He didn't bother asking what I was sorry for. He didn't say, Don't apologize. He said, "Can't you tell me on the phone?"

He must really have hated me. My eyes watered. I focused on sounding calm.

I said, "There's something I need to give you."

"What is it, Nico? What do you want? Quit screwing with my head."

"I'm not," I said. "I wouldn't do that. You know I wouldn't do that."

"Right," he said. "I got that."

"You're the only one," I said. "The only one who could understand."

"Understand what?" he said. "I don't—"

I said, "I dreamed about Margaret."

"So what. So did I."

"What was *your* dream?" I said.

"I don't remember," he lied.

I said, "I dreamed she called me on the phone."

A silence. Then, "What did she say?"

"She told me to give you something."

"What?"

If I'd said, an origami crane, it would have ended there. He would never have believed that Margaret would bother contacting me about something so childish and trite.

"She told me to give it to you. I need to see you in person."

This time the silence lasted so long I thought the line had gone dead. Then Aaron said, "Okay. When?"

I pretended to have plans for that afternoon. We arranged to meet the next day.

I soaked for an hour in the tub, I splashed on vanilla oil, I used Margaret's hair dryer and a little of her makeup. I put on her blue comet shirt. I kept getting it tangled as I slipped it over my head.

The morning was misty and cool, and the air had a smoky late-summer sweetness. My eagerness to see Aaron made me cheerful and optimistic even as I told myself not to get my hopes up.

I biked past a cornfield, where, I was shocked to see, the stalks were tasseled and taller than I was. Somehow the summer had slipped away when I wasn't looking. I was glad that it was ending without having done even more damage than it had.

Reaching into my back pocket, I checked for the paper crane I'd pressed between two pieces of cardboard: my magic charm, a real one this time, not like the Hawaiian shirt. Margaret had chosen this one. I told myself that Margaret would keep me safe, that she knew where this was headed, toward one final gesture of friendship and goodwill that would let me and Aaron have fond, unembarrassed memories of each other. Though I couldn't help wondering why I imagined the dead saw further from their vantage point under the ground. I needed to think like Margaret, like a poet and a believer. I felt like a girl in a fairy tale on a mission that depends on not allowing cowardly thoughts and only thinking brave ones.

Aaron's van was in the usual spot, except that he'd always parked parallel to the road and waited for me in the open tailgate. Now the van was backed up into the field, and Aaron sat behind the wheel with the doors and windows shut. Something made me want to turn and leave before he saw me. But he'd already seen me. I couldn't just ride away. We were friends who'd been tricked by grief into making a mistake, and now we'd learned our lesson, and we could be friends again.

I eased my bike onto the grass and walked around to the driver's side. Aaron eyed me blankly, then rolled down his window.

"Hi," I said. "Nice to see you."

"*Hi?*" he said. "*Nice to see me?*"

"I don't know, Aaron. I don't know why I said that. How are you?"

"Nice to see me." He shook his head. He had paint on his T-shirt and jeans. So what if he hated me? He was painting again. He had to give me some credit. At least he could be pleasant.

I went around to the other side and let myself into the van. The van smelled a little like alcohol. Not heavy, but it was there.

"So what is it?" Aaron said at last. "What did she tell you to bring me?"

Why was Aaron sneering? He was making me feel like his stalker.

"Oh," I said. "I'm sitting on it." I should have taken the cardboard folder out of my pocket. I had to lift my ass to slide it out of my jeans. Aaron watched me, watched my ass. He sighed. The alcohol smell got stronger.

I said, "Aaron, are you okay?"

"Why wouldn't I be?" he said.

"I don't know," I said.

"I'm great," he said. "Never been butter."

"Butter?" I said

Aaron's eyes were as flat as poker chips. He said, "Better. I never felt butter."

"I feel a lot butter myself," I said. Aaron stared at me.

"So let me have it," he said.

"What?" I said.

"The so-called present your sister told you to give me in the bullshit bogus dream."

"It's not bullshit," I said. Tears of outrage popped up in my eyes. I was bringing a gift *from my sister*. "I'd never lie about something like that."

"No one said you were lying, Nico." He made it sound like an annoying thing I did all the time. It was amazing, how fast you could go from being friends to this.

I said, "Here. I'm pretty sure this is what she meant."

Aaron watched me peel the origami crane from between the cardboard layers. I thought his expression was how I must look when I accidentally saw a photo of Margaret, or heard music when I wasn't expecting to, or caught a glimpse of the lake.

He said, "You knew about this, Nico. Margaret told you. So this is a joke, right? It's a bitch thing to do."

"Knew about *what*?" I said. "We all made those birds in Mrs. Akins's class. I did. You did too, Aaron. Remember?"

"Swear to me you didn't know," he said. "Swear it on your eyes. Swear you'll go blind if you're lying."

Had Margaret mentioned the crane? If I woke up blind tomorrow, I would know I had forgotten.

"I swear," I said.

"Then that's that. End of story."

"What story?"

"Just keep quiet a minute, okay?" He tipped back his head and shut his eyes. I knew I should get out of the van and get on my bike and go home.

Aaron said, "We called it the carrier pigeon. Your sister always wanted to play these little . . . games, these dramas with secret codes and signals. She'd gotten the carrier-pigeon thing from some cheesy spy film. When she could meet me that evening, she'd slip the bird between the grates of my locker door. And I was supposed to give it back so she could use it again."

"Why couldn't she just have *told* you?" I asked. "You were in the same classes. Why couldn't she have called you, or e-mailed?"

Aaron winced, just as Margaret used to when I was too literal-minded, too one-thing-after-the-next. It hurt my feelings, just as it always had. I considered telling him about Mrs. Akins coming into Goldengrove, but he'd just think it was another lie I'd made up as an excuse to see him.

"I guess she means you to have it now." I noticed I was talking about Margaret in the present tense.

Aaron draped the bird over his rearview mirror like angora dice.

"You knew about it," he said.

"I didn't," I said. "I promise."

"What else did she tell you?"

"Nothing," I said.

Aaron grabbed the paper crane, yanked it off the mirror, crumpled it, and put it in his pocket.

"Hey, I should probably go," I said. "My parents are expecting me back. I just sneaked out for a minute. I can bike home from here."

He said, "You got somewhere you have to be?"

"No," I said. "Not really."

"Good," he said. "Because I've got something to show you. A little surprise of my own. Let's go."

"My bicycle," I said.

He popped the hatch and got out and walked around and threw

my bike in the van. He'd always treated it so tenderly. Did he know it used to be Margaret's?

Aaron got in and started the engine. He took the first curve too fast. I wanted to tell him to slow down, but I couldn't speak. We drove through an insect storm. Winged corpses slimed the windshield. Aaron didn't mean it. The bugs didn't want to die.

"Where are we going?" I asked.

"Where do you think?" said Aaron.

I faked a stupid-me laugh. I opened the glove compartment. I wanted soothing Charlie Parker sliding from phrase to phrase. I pulled out a handful of CD cases. Aaron had gotten totally new music. Gangstas in leather jackets and chains scowled into fish-eye lenses. Every cover had its shiny parental-advisory sticker still attached. In one photo, two women in thong bikinis were draped, caveman style, over a fat man's shoulders so that their asses looked like epaulets.

"A little mood music?" Aaron said.

I nodded. Anything was better than silence. Aaron took one hand from the wheel, and with the other slipped in a CD.

Music blasted out of the speakers. I reached for the volume control.

"Leave it up," said Aaron. "That is, if you don't *mind*, Nico."

The bass thrummed through me, shaking every inch of flesh that was capable of wobbling. Someone was going to fuck up the bitch and she wasn't going to like it. Where was silky Lester Young? Where was dying Nico?

Aaron said, "Not your kind of music. Not your sister's music. What's the matter, Nico?"

I said, "Isn't it great how the guy uses his voice as a rhythm instrument?"

"What the fuck does that mean? It sounds like something your sister would say." He tromped harder on the gas. We nearly missed another curve. I thought, Margaret wants us to join her.

"Where'd you get that watch?" Aaron said.

"You like it? My parents got it for me in Boston."

"Boston. I've got a full tank. We could go to Boston."

"Please, no," I heard myself say.

"I was joking, Nico," Aaron said. "Can't you take a joke?"

Was I being kidnapped? We still had to drive through town, through two traffic lights. One would stop us, and I could jump out. Unless Aaron ran a light. I watched the bookstore slip by. Elaine stood behind the counter.

We stopped at the second traffic light, in front of the public library. Two mothers, chatting over their strollers, were probably going to story hour. My mother used to take us there. Grief pinned me to the seat.

We spun into Aaron's driveway and pulled up to the cabin. Aaron followed me down the path. All the curtains were drawn, and in the humid darkness, the cabin smelled worse than ever. How bizarre, that I used to find this stench so touching and romantic. Aaron paced the room, throwing open the curtains, then led me to the glassed-in porch.

"What happened to the postcards?" I said. "All those pictures of the Last Judgment and—"

"I took them down," said Aaron. "I didn't want that tired crap getting into my head. Anyhow, forget about that. Look at my painting."

On the easel was the painting of my father and me in the doomsday parking lot. Aaron had totally ruined it. The fireworks had been painted out and replaced by angels. That should have made it *more* like the painting of Saint Nicholas saving the sailors at sea, except that the angels, the man, and the girl had grotesque, monstrous faces.

All the hope and sweetness were gone. I wanted to cover my eyes. But I kept looking, then gasped when I saw that one of the angels was a dragonfly with a human face—a clownish cartoon of Margaret. I'd thought it would have been hard to make someone so beautiful look so ugly, but Aaron had found some part of her that was witchlike, harsh, and vengeful. It was if I was seeing back through the years to when we were little kids and had knockdown physical fights, and I saw her enraged, implacable face growing larger as it came toward at me. As the dragonfly-angel dive-bombed the man and the girl, its mouth drooled pistachio green.

I couldn't look at it anymore. I turned toward Aaron. He was crying.

"I fucked it up," he said.

I touched his arm. I said, "Can't you fix it?"

The staircase spirit said, *Tell him he didn't ruin it. Tell him it's better than before.* But I hadn't thought quickly enough to lie, and now the spirit sat down on the stairs and watched, delighted by the harm that a few words can do.

Aaron flushed red from his hairline down, until the blood had nowhere to go and pooled in the whites of his eyes.

"Fix it?" he said. "Fix it? How would I do that? Roll back time to the day she drowned and bring her back to life?"

"I just meant the painting," I said.

Aaron went into the living room and sat down on the couch. I sat beside him and leaned my head against his shoulder and talked

into his sleeve in the voice I'd used with the little kids who skinned
their knees when I'd worked at my old nursery school.

"Everything will be all right," I said. "Right now we don't believe it, but time will pass, we'll get over this—"

It made no difference what I said, or that I didn't believe it.
What mattered was the soothing tone, the silky reassurance. He
could fix the painting, or he could paint something else.

I said, "It's only a painting."

"Only a painting? Come on, sugar," he said thickly. "Look
who's talking. What would you say if I said to you, It's only a
song? Only a performance."

I said, "Aaron, I'm not Margaret. I'm Nico, remember?"

"Whoops," he said. "Sorry about that."

Why didn't I get up and run to Aaron's parents' house and beg
them to save me from their drunken, screw-loose son? Maybe because of the pitiful way Aaron's shoulders slumped. I was afraid
to leave him. I felt as if he was falling, holding on to my hand, and
if I let go, he would plummet into the abyss.

After a while he shook himself and remembered I was there.
He half fell, half lunged at me. His fogged-over eyes didn't seem
aware that his lips were smashing into mine. He pushed me into the
couch. I struggled against the solid wall that Aaron had become.
Holding my shoulders, he fastened his lips onto my neck—first
like a nursing baby, then like a bloodsucking vampire. I went limp.
I couldn't stop what was happening. I just had to get through it
and pretend I was somewhere else.

I didn't know where to pretend I was, so I let myself be carried back to that last afternoon with Margaret on the lake. I heard
our mother's piano rippling over the water. I watched Margaret

blow smoke rings. We talked about suntans and weight. I asked her about sex, which seemed doubly weird, now that it seemed I might be about to have it with her boyfriend. She stood and gave me that inscrutable look and that funny salute. But this time I understood that she was waving good-bye. She was telling me I was on my own. She was making a promise. Everything would turn out all right. What was lost would be restored.

But it would be up to me. I had to take credit or blame. Responsibility, maybe just that. I had wanted to come here. I didn't really believe in ghosts, so if you subtracted dreams and spirits from the equation, it meant that calling Aaron had been *my* idea. I'd wanted to be haunted, but I'd failed even in that. Margaret was gone. I saw that now. It was time for me to wake up from the long fever dream in which my sister sent me messages for her boyfriend.

Aaron was squeezing my breast the way he'd squashed Margaret's paper crane.

I yelled, "Wait! This is totally twisted!"

Aaron didn't hear me, but the pain in my breast receded as I slipped back into the rowboat where Margaret was still waiting. I felt as if I were floating into some ethery state in which I could hear her singing "My Funny Valentine."

Is your mouth a little weak? Is your figure less than Greek?

Was it a hallucination, or was I dying? Was this the sound track behind the scene of your dear departed loved ones waiting in the white light at the end of the tunnel? This time, Margaret didn't sound sexy so much as confident and funny. This time, the song was all about laughter, and a future in which every laughable unphotographable person found someone to love.

Aaron stopped grabbing at my shirt. He froze, as if he was listening, too. And then he let me go.

I checked my clothes. He hadn't undone a button or zipper.

We sat side by side on the couch, like strangers waiting for a bus.

Without looking at me, Aaron said, "Let me tell you something about your sister. This was maybe a year ago. We were hanging out on the dock by your house, and I said I couldn't imagine painting anything as corny as a lake. She laughed. You remember that laugh. She said, 'It depends how you do it. You can make paintings of the lake that are total works of genius. Let's make a bet. You paint the lake, and everyone will love it. And I'll take some sentimental piece of crap like "My Funny Valentine" and sing it so the whole school has one big collective orgasm.'"

Did I believe him? Ninety percent. True or not, it was what Aaron remembered.

Then he said, "The night we had that conversation was the first time we had sex."

I said, "I don't want to hear this."

He said, "There's no one else I can tell. Every time we had sex, I could never figure out if your sister was actually getting off or if she was working out some amazing new way to sing that song."

Aaron fumbled for my hand, and I thought the whole thing might be starting all over again. I wasn't even scared anymore. I just felt tired and sad.

"Aaron," I said, "I'm Nico. I'm the sister, remember? You've got to leave me alone now. This has got to stop."

Aaron said, "I know that, Nico. I know perfectly well who you are. You're the younger sister. I always thought you were cute. I told your sister I'd want to date you if I wasn't dating her. She got really mad at me, and she stayed mad even after I told her I was kidding."

"When was that?" I asked.

"Not that long before she died. *Right* before. That morning, actually."

I said, "Were you going out that night? The night she died?"

Aaron said, "I don't know. She was still mad at me. She was supposed to call, and she didn't. And then . . . Jesus Christ, Nico, imagine how I feel about that. I *didn't* really think you were cute."

"Thanks," I said.

"You were *sort* of cute. I mean, you did those cute movie-star imitations."

So that was it. I did imitations. I could imitate Margaret.

"But not cute *that* way," Aaron was saying. "Not like cute as in *hot.* I never thought that, believe me. I just said it to piss off your sister."

I said, "Aaron, I'm thirteen."

"Screw that," said Aaron. "In most countries you'd be married. You'd have two kids already."

Aaron reached under the cushions and pulled out an ancient pink rubber ball and threw it across the room. We watched it bounce away. I thought, Even the ball doesn't like me.

I said, "Why did you want to piss her off?"

Aaron put his face in his hands. "I don't know," he mumbled through his fingers. "I guess I got sick of feeling that if she had to choose between me and her music . . . She'd already chosen. She was going to Ohio."

Aaron was leaving, too. But before I could point that out, he lifted his head and said, "Sometimes I think that's the worst part. That we were fighting when she died. I didn't have time to say I was sorry. You know what I mean?"

I did. But I didn't want to say so. Not to Aaron. Not now.

The cabin smelled sweetish and rotten, like a dead mouse in the wall.

"Can I open a window?" I said.

"Go ahead," said Aaron.

It was hard work, unsticking the window from the blistered frame. Hot air flowed in through the dusty screen, along with the smell of bacon. Was Aaron's mother cooking? The thought of bacon made me think there might be a reason to go on living.

From across the room, Aaron said, "Maybe you rowed right over her body. Did you ever consider that?"

"I did," I said. "I mean, I thought of it. But I don't think it happened. Aaron, I have to go now."

Something or someone—a force—propelled me toward the door. Not Margaret, not Saint Nicholas of Tolentino. It was me, only me. I walked out onto the shady path. I popped the latch on Aaron's van and got my bike out of the back. I considered stopping at Aaron's parents' house. I decided against it. I hoping they weren't watching as I detoured around their yard, then pedaled as hard and fast as I could down to the end of the driveway.

When I heard a car come up behind me, I dragged my bike into the woods and hid behind a tree. I had to lean over and grab my knees because I felt so faint. But it wasn't Aaron's van. If Aaron was coming after me, he would have caught up already.

Maybe he'd fallen asleep or passed out, or maybe his better self had talked him out of doing whatever he was planning to do. I would never know what that was. Maybe he didn't, either. I would never have to know, and I didn't want to.

My face was soaked with sweat and tears. There was nowhere I wanted to go and no one I wanted to talk to. I looked at my new watch. The spider's jerky, regular hop from second to second calmed me. It was almost two thirty. My dad would be at the bookstore. I couldn't imagine telling him. My mother was probably home, but our house was twice as far, and she'd probably already left on her daily drug vacation.

Then I thought of Elaine. She'd be home by now. For the first time, I was almost glad that she was having an affair with my father. It meant that I could confide in her and she couldn't judge me. It meant that neither of us could pretend that people did things for good or intelligent reasons, or for any reason at all.

I didn't deserve to find Elaine at home, but there she was, at her kitchen table. She hadn't washed her hair for a while; the soles of her feet were black. She smiled when she saw me, and her face was as lovely and serene as those of the painted saints being thanked by the resurrected children.

"Is Tycho around?" I don't know what possessed me to pretend I'd come there, streaky and out of breath, to hang out with her kid.

"In his room," she said. "Jesus, Nico, where have you been? What have you been doing?"

"Riding my bike," I said. "Can I talk to you?"

Elaine said, "Oh, my God, Nico. I thought you were finished with that asshole."

"*Now* I am," I said. "Believe me."

"I believed you the last time," she said.

I told Elaine what had happened. She listened patiently till I was through, then waited to make sure there wasn't more.

"What a mess," she said. "Swear to me, Nico, *swear* to me it wasn't worse than you told me. Swear to me he didn't—"

"He didn't. You're not going to tell my parents, are you?"

"You have to," Elaine said. "You should have told them already. And you *will*. Immediately."

"They'll kill me," I said.

"They won't," she said. "I promise you that. Do you want some iced coffee?"

"Sure," I said, though what I really wanted was a break in the conversation. Elaine brought me a glass. I was glad I could focus on stirring the sugar when I said, "Elaine, don't get mad, but I need to ask. Are you having an affair with my dad?"

"No," she said. I glanced up. Her expression reminded me of how my mother had looked when I'd asked her if they named me after Nico. The look of an adult teetering on the needle edge of a lie.

"I'm not," she said. "It's nothing like that."

"But?"

"But nothing."

"But something. Something happened."

"All right. Once. Your dad and I were sort of involved. For about a minute."

"When?" I said.

"Years ago. Years and years ago. Tycho wasn't even a twinkle."

"Was I a twinkle?"

Elaine didn't answer.

"Before me? Tell me, Elaine."

Elaine hesitated. "Just before you were a twinkle. Maybe you were. But I don't think anyone knew it."

"How *could* you?" I said.

Elaine pushed the hair out of her eyes and blew at it until it fluttered. "I don't know how to explain. What excuse I can make. You dad was so good-looking. It felt like something I *had* to do. It didn't seem like a choice. We were all young. I mean, younger."

"And?"

"And nothing. Nothing happened. Nothing was going to happen."

For a moment, I almost wanted to slap her friendly big face. Then she turned back into Elaine. And she was right. My father hadn't left us. Had my mother been pregnant with me? Nothing happened. That was a lifetime ago. My whole lifetime, in fact.

"Why did Dad do it?" I said.

Elaine said, "I'd prefer to think because he liked me. But I don't know. I really don't, Nico. I never asked. I didn't feel I *could* ask. Who knows why anyone does anything?"

I said, "I know what you mean."

"I *bet* you do," said Elaine. "Anyway, it stopped as soon as it started. He was in love with your mom. I mean, *is* in love with your mom. And you. With your family. I don't know, Nico. It's past. It's like it never happened. We're friends. Why didn't you ask me earlier? Do you think it would have been easy for me, covering for you and letting you hang around here if I was sleeping with your dad?"

I couldn't do the math. I had to ask, "Is Dad Tycho's father?"

Elaine looked truly horrified. "Jesus, Nico, what kind of person do you think I am? Have you ever *met* me? Do you think I could not tell you something like that and then one day say, 'Oh, by the way, meet your little brother.' For the record, Tycho's dad's name was Casey. *Is* Casey."

"Where is he? What does he do?"

"He taught environmental studies at the community college up in Edgemont. Then he got a better job somewhere else."

"I didn't know they had environmental studies at the community college."

"They do. Or they used to. But don't even think about going there."

"Does he ever see Tycho?"

"A couple of times. It didn't work out. They didn't get along."

Neither of us spoke for a while. Then Elaine said, "What I *will* say is that I'm probably the only person in the world who's read your father's book"

"How is it?" I said.

"Really interesting. Maybe a little more than you want to know about the end of the world. But a page-turner, sort of. And we're not going to let him call it *Eschatology for Dummies*, are we?"

"No," I said.

"My God, Nico, you could have been hurt. That lunatic could have raped you. What the hell were you thinking? That guy could have killed you. So let me say it one more time. You need to talk to your parents. I'm calling your father right now."

"Go ahead," I said. "You might as well. I'll hang out with Tycho till they get here."

"Tycho would like that," said Elaine.

I found Tycho in his room, lying on the floor, staring up at the ceiling.

"Hi, Tycho," I said.

"Hi, Tycho," he said.

"What's up?" I said.

"What's up?" he said.

"Don't you get bored doing that?" I said.

"Don't you get bored doing that?" he said.

"You don't look all that happy," I said.

"Hi, Tycho," he said.

"Never mind," I said. I waited for him to repeat it, but instead he said, "Hi Nico," which, from Tycho, was the equivalent of a bear hug.

I said, "It's suffocating in here."

"I hate the breeze," he said.

"Why?" I said.

"I hate it on my face," he said.

"You need to breathe," I said.

"I do," he said. "I breathe all the time."

"Okay," I said. "Whatever. Want to play Doom Invaders?"

"Doom Invaders," Tycho said. "Yeah!"

"Okay, let's," I said.

Tycho got up. We played Doom Invaders. I let him win. He would have won anyway. I kept looking over at him. He was inside the game. He and the keyboard were one. Leaving his body and entering another dimension wasn't a fantasy he was trying out, and failing. I knew his life was hard, that he went to special schools and camps because he'd been beaten up by kids at the public school. But for a moment I envied him, though I couldn't have said why.

Tycho said, "Your sister died."

I said, "Yeah. She did."

"I know that," Tycho said.

"It's sad," I said.

"Please don't touch me," he said.

"You know I won't," I said.

We played more video games. Tycho won every time.

Finally he said, "Your father's here. I hear him."

But it was still ten minutes before my father showed up.

MY FATHER SHUT THE STORE FOR THE DAY AND DROVE ME HOME.
Luck was finally on my side. Sally wasn't at our house, and Mom
seemed almost normal. We went out to the porch.

By then, I was calm enough to tell them the least alarming version of the story. I said I'd been hanging out with Aaron, things
had spun out of control. Nothing serious, finally. Just a bit scary
and strange.

"I'll kill him," said my dad.

"That's not helpful," my mother said. "Finish, Nico What do
you mean, *a bit* scary and strange?"

"It was like I had a crush on him."

"A crush? What does *that* mean?"

"Nothing. That's it. That's all." They couldn't have handled
the details. They both would have wanted to kill him.

My father said, "This can't go on, Nico."

I said, "It won't. I swear. I swear it on my eyes."

"You swear on your *eyes?*" my mother said. "Where did you
learn that superstitious crap?"

Dad said, "Shouldn't we call the police? Shouldn't we talk to a
lawyer?"

I said, "I need you not to do that. If you do, I'll deny it all. I'll say nothing happened."

For the rest of the afternoon my parents and I sat on the porch. It would always be the porch on which we'd waited for them to find Margaret. I wondered if I'd ever confront my father about what Elaine had told me. She was right. Nothing happened. I didn't want to know more, no more than I'd wanted to hear about Aaron's sex life with my sister.

Outside the crickets were singing, a regular performance, syncopations, call and response, a cricket hallelujah chorus. I imagined they were singing to us, and that when they stopped, my parents and I should applaud or somehow let them know how much we'd enjoyed it. That was how Margaret would have thought. I imagined correcting her, telling her that the crickets were either calling or courting, the loud chirp was the come-here call from the male to the female, the quiet chirp was his courting song when she was finally near.

During an intermission in the cricket symphony, my father said, "How about pasta with calamari and zucchini?"

"Zucchini?" said Mom.

"Trust me," said Dad.

"Sounds delicious," I said.

My father said, "Good. Because that's what we have."

Then I said, surprising myself, "I think I'll go for a swim."

"Really?" my father said. "Are you sure?"

"Really," I said.

"Be careful," Mom said. "The algae . . ."

"I'll be careful," I said.

I went and put on my bathing suit, which was too big for

me now. I'd have to buy a new one. I'd have to gain back some weight.

The water slid apart for me. It was happy to have me back in. It stroked my skin and kissed me. The lake seemed to be whispering in my ear, telling me what I already knew. It said it wasn't the water's fault. It hadn't meant to hurt Margaret.

I flipped over onto my back and skimmed the surface, like a bug. Then I raised my head so I could see the beach. My parents were watching me from the dock. They waved, and I waved back.

Sixteen

LITTLE BY LITTLE, WE SURFACED FROM THE DARK, GLUEY DEPTHS of that summer. Bobbing into the blinding light, we had to relearn how to breathe. Missing Margaret was still painful, but the agony subsided, and someone—perhaps some compassionate angel— had lowered the volume of the siren song that so nearly took us down with her.

I no longer expected Margaret to contact me from the beyond, and I stopped trying to analyze each new stage of my relationship with her ghost. It was hard, letting go. But if I'd learned anything that summer, it was how essential it was to hold on to the here and now, the one thing after the next.

Mom made us go with her to the town dump, where she scattered her pills like ashes. Neither Dad nor I bothered asking why she couldn't just have thrown them out or flushed them down the toilet.

"Bye-bye," she said, when the last bottle was empty, and somehow I knew she meant it.

Her friendship with Sally ended. I wanted my father to throw Sally out of the house, like a saint casting demons out of a madman in a Sienese painting. Dad said exorcism wasn't required, and he turned out to be right. Mom got rid of her prescription meds, and Sally stopped showing up.

Once more, Officer Prozak proved to have been a deep well of misinformation. My mother's recovery was less difficult and more permanent than the DARE program had warned.

Near the end of summer, we decided to take a vacation. And even though school was starting, we left for two weeks in Rome.

From the moment we got through security, where a guard pulled my underwear out of my backpack for the whole airport to see, everything delighted me, everything made me happy. I loved the gauzy light of the plane filled with glowing passengers waiting to be raptured and set down amid the tall umbrella pines and the pointed shrubs. On the cab ride into the city, we sped past a fountain of writhing serpents spitting diamonds into the traffic.

Our taxi driver stopped and waved us into a market stocked with glossy fruit, iridescent fish, plump attractive vegetables that didn't exist at home. An old man was demonstrating a vegetable peeler that turned carrots into pig's tails. At the edge of the market was our hotel, where they were expecting us, and where the handsome young desk clerk let his gaze hover ever so lightly on me, and then flashed me a smile so quick that only I saw it.

None of us were sleepy, and we left the cool lobby and headed back into the broiling city where no one knew us, no one pitied us, no one knew what we'd lost.

I loved the arches, the Colosseum, the monumental reminders of how time layered over everything, cementing in the gaps, repairing or covering over what was cracked and broken, pressing it down into the earth and building on top, and on top of that. At every moment, or, to tell the truth, every *other* moment, I thought how Margaret would have loved it. But Margaret had never been there, and no matter how hard I tried to see it through her eyes, I was the one who twisted through the dark alleys and squinted when a plaza went off like a flashbulb. By the time I blinked, the open space had become a circus. Fried artichokes, mosaics, incense, the spires and domes of churches. Even the car exhaust was sexy. I felt that the city was revealing itself in glimpses that I alone saw—sights saved for me, intended for me, as if the city knew me, because I was someone who *could* be known, who would love certain things and not others.

We were lost more often than not. My father had read all the guidebooks, but Mom had control of the map. Dad and I tried not to fidget or feel embarrassed as we stood on a corner and she turned and turned it.

I was only annoyed at my parents once, for their starchy New England opinion that St. Peter's was gaudy. Gaudy! I worshipped each curve and scallop, the way the vaulted ceiling sucked the thoughts right out of my head. I even liked the disturbing sexual buzz I got from gazing at the smooth marble arms of the dead Jesus in Michelangelo's *Pietà*.

In the Sistine Chapel we sat on benches and looked up. I raised one finger like a lightning rod, as if I could make the God of Creation bypass Adam and lean down and touch me. I couldn't imagine leaving my body and entering *that* painting. What portal would I have gone through? After a while, my eyes began to feel gritty, as if the saints were scratching their dandruffy beards above me.

Our visit to the Vatican was a pilgrimage of sorts. My father had come to see Fra Angelico's *Last Judgment* in the Pinacoteca. I almost hoped we wouldn't find it. I was afraid that the picture might remind me of my Sienese art book and all its shaming Aaron-related associations. But the husks of those memories must have dropped away over the ocean, and the *Last Judgment* was only itself, shimmering and enchanted. How astonishing that one painting could tell so many stories. If you'd been good, you died with perfect skin and hair, and you shuffled—with maximum dignity, considering you were naked—in an unhurried airport line ascending into heaven. If you were bad, you burned in hell. The sinners were still wearing their clothes and had just that moment figured out where they were going forever. Salvation, redemption, the afterlife. Aaron would have loved it. Where was my sister in all this? Nowhere, and right beside me.

My father said, "*That's* my cover." At first I had no idea what he meant. I'd forgotten about his book. I recalled him saying he wanted to use the painting of the lemon-tree paradise, but he didn't remember, and I didn't remind him.

"Good idea, Dad," I said.

The Roman Forum was my favorite place. It was love at first sight. The first time we went, it was twilight, the air had a bluish cast, and we had to rush because the gates closed an hour before sunset. I didn't want to leave. I wanted to spend the night there. My parents promised we could come back, but I said I'd meet them in twenty minutes and took off running, like a kid.

I ran and speed-walked till I was out of breath. I leaned against a railing and had a mini-hallucination.

Slowly, the Forum repaired itself, like an animated cartoon.

The pillars rose, the weeds receded, the walls piled brick on brick, the Senate and the streets and basilicas recovered their shimmering glory. I saw how the imperial center had looked when men in togas had strolled along the cobbled avenues and plotted assassinations and made plans to rule the world.

The cartoon ended. I got up and wandered around. Every stone was glowing, every patch of moss, every shred of garbage. It was a playground, built and knocked down to my exact specifications, a pleasure garden designed just for me, historic but unhaunted. I wanted to go there every day. I wanted to spend all day there.

The city had risen around it, two, maybe three stories high. That seemed at once amazing, comforting, and scary. The Forum was physically lower than anything in Rome, and maybe that was why we were drawn there, like water, by its gravitational pull. It was where we'd suddenly find ourselves when we'd thought we were lost.

Our hotel was nearby, and my parents let me go to the Forum alone in the early morning if I promised to be careful crossing the traffic circle. On those mornings, the Forum was my own ruined city, and later in the day I managed to feel alone there even when it was crowded.

My father had the *Blue Guide*, and when we went to the Forum together, I had to listen to him read aloud, what god had been worshipped in this temple, what that pillar had supported. It was boring. I felt I knew it somehow. I could have recited it along with him. If I'd believed in previous lives, I would have been sure I'd lived there.

One day, while my dad was droning on, I noticed a woman moving strangely around the Forum, ducking and weaving and looking behind her as if she was being followed. I was sorry she saw me watching. The woman had witchy lamp-black hair and wore an elaborately tied, printed scarf and a shiny silver raincoat. She approached us and said, in a heavy New York accent, "You guys wanna guide?"

"No thanks," said my father. "We're fine."

I liked it that my parents wouldn't dream of making me take a tour, standing there, not knowing where to look, pretending to listen to an overly talkative stranger. And then at the end there might be some embarrassment about money.

The woman said, as if to someone behind us, "Assholes. They think they know shit about the Caesars." Then she stalked away.

My mom said, "I think she liked you, dear."

"Great," said Dad. "I'm flattered."

A little later, I wandered away from my parents. As I turned a corner, I thought I heard someone mumbling. I tracked the sound toward a mossy cave that reeked of mildew and rot.

Inside the cave was the witchy guide, bowing toward a stone altar, chanting some gibberish incantation. The sky had darkened. The air smelled of rain. I heard a growl of thunder. Crisscrossing the altar were long-stemmed roses in cellophane tubes, like flowers that boys might buy their dates for the senior prom.

I backed away. On my way out, I stopped to read a plaque. The grotto was the altar on which they'd lain Caesar on the night he was stabbed in the Forum.

As I hurried to find my parents, I had the strangest sensation. It seemed to me that I passed myself, hurrying in the other direction. The filthy, hungry-eyed Nico rushing toward the cave was the girl I'd been that summer. She was running because she'd read about the Roman oracles and because she thought that the crazy guide might have a message from her sister.

I waved to my other, earlier self. I pitied her. I wanted to help her. But I wasn't her, not any more. I was going the opposite way, and not even the staircase spirit could have convinced me that I was headed in the wrong direction.

In the fall we returned home. The minute we walked into the house, all three of us knew we couldn't live there any more.

The lake smelled like a sewer. The algae had won, after all. The water looked like spinach left to blacken in the fridge.

I went to school for a couple of weeks while our house was on the market. That was when I discovered how short people's memories are. I was just Nico again, not the girl whose sister had drowned. I wasn't the same person, but it was too hard to explain.

We sold our house to a retired couple, who bought the book-store along with it. We moved to Boston. Somewhere along the way, Margaret's possessions were absorbed or disappeared or went into storage.

Things turned out all right for us. As well as could be expected.

My father's book was published. It was called *The End of Days* and had the Fra Angelico cover. People bought it and liked it. My mother got a job giving piano lessons in an after-school program for kids. Her arthritis, or whatever it was, went into remission. Every so often my father wondered aloud if her illness had come from the dampness at the lake, and we would all fall silent and wait for the breathlessness to pass.

I finished high school, I went away to college. I looked more like Margaret, and then less like her as I passed the age at which anyone could have said what she would have looked like. There were terrible days, even weeks, when I felt her spirit haunting me, and not in a friendly way. I came to understand that Margaret's death was an entity, separate from Margaret. My sister would always love me. But her death was a monster that would rip me apart, if it could. Time passed; the monster aged and lost some, but not all, of its power to ambush and wound me.

Occasionally, a stranger would ask if I had siblings. For years, I felt compelled to say I'd had a sister. I used to explain that she had drowned when I was a teenager. I hated the responses. Discomfort and pity, mainly. I started simply answering no, which was, strictly speaking, true. The question was in the present tense: Did I have any siblings?

I moved, changed cities, moved again. Until, after a while, people had no idea I'd ever had a sister.

Of course, my husband knows, as do my close friends. I told my children when they asked about that photo my father took of their grandmother, their mom, and that other girl doing yoga by the lake. My children never asked again, and we don't discuss it.

I dream about Margaret from time to time, dreams in which she and I are the age we were when she died. Sometimes I wake up in tears. More often than I would expect, I catch sight of her on the street of a city where she never was. There ought to be a word for that: seeing the dead in a stranger. Some special phrase, like déjà vu, or the spirit of the staircase.

When I was pregnant, and everyone in the supermarket felt free to predict the baby's sex or offer child-raising advice, I'd think of the bookstore customers who told me not to make any decisions for a year. It makes sense that birth and death are what people have in common. They want to think it can teach them something they can pass on to someone else.

The memory of my romance with Aaron faded into a detail of that summer. I never saw him after the day I ran away from his cabin. For a brief period, while my parents were selling the house, I hoped and worried that I might run into him, in town. I have no idea where he went or how his life turned out. I've searched for him on the Internet. Maybe he left the country.

My husband and I are geologists. It's crossed our minds that, after all the trouble I had early on with water, my attraction to earth and stones might not be accidental. But I think it has more to do with my lifelong worry about the planet and my lifelong desire to help stave off the end of the world.

Our work takes us to foreign countries. For years, we brought our children along. And so it happened that, one afternoon, my husband and I, our daughter and son, found ourselves in a small museum in a provincial French city.

It was one of those sleepy museums in which the smell of dusty velvet, old varnish, and floor polish induces a swampy exhaustion that makes walking from room to room feel like trudging through water. The paintings were grouped, as they often are, by subject matter, so that the many slight variations keep you from focusing on any one floral explosion in a roomful of bouquets, any one windmill or velvety cow grazing by a stream.

Most of the galleries were dim, as if to mimic gaslight. But finally we entered a room in which a flat sheet of sun raked through a skylight at such an aggressive angle that, as we stood in the doorway, each frame took turns flashing back a rectangle of glare. Then a cloud must have crossed the sun, and, as the dazzle faded, the paintings revealed themselves, one by one, as ordinary landscapes.

Perhaps it was a trick of the light. My husband suffers from optical migraines, spiky hallucinations brought on by the strobe of driving past a forest. Maybe I experienced some stationary version of that, a neurological phenomenon that sent me into free fall. Or a verbal association, some complex chemical brain pun. At any rate, the glass over the paintings seemed like a series of mirrors.

One of them drew me over. A painting of a lake.

I no longer knew where my husband and children were. I lost track of my surroundings. I approached the canvas with that long-forgotten childhood desire to separate into molecules and reassemble inside it. From across the room, I knew that it was somewhere I had been. It was Mirror Lake. The view I'd seen from my window until the day I'd stopped looking.

For the first time in decades, I thought of Aaron's paintings, the ones he'd destroyed. The closer I got, the more the parquet floor seemed to pitch and slosh beneath me.

A lake. It could have been any lake. Behind it was a mountain, bare red rock stubbled with whiskery pines. On the shore of the lake were four figures, four shadowy brushstroke columns.

It wasn't our lake. It was nowhere I'd been. The brass plaque read, "Un Lac en Provence. Ca. 1890." A nameless lake that a nameless artist had painted a century before I was born.

Yet something—the image of the lake, or the four figures beside it—had awoken in me that old longing to be inside the painting. I told myself, Children think like that. Adults know you are stuck in your body. Any attempt to leave would mean knocking on a door that opens only once, only one way. Even so, even knowing that, I kept staring at the landscape.

It was nowhere I'd lived as a child. It was only a painting.

That was what I told myself, and how I let down my reserve, and then how I forgot myself, and let the painting take over. How could it have done that, such a modest little landscape? How could it have so overcome me that I was unaware of anything but the painted lake and the four figures and the mountains behind them and then my own shockingly grown-up face, reflected in the glass?

I felt myself slip out of my skin and become that girl watching her sister dive into the water. I lost myself in the time before, and in that innocent landscape, until the spell was broken by a museum guard, shouting.

He was speaking a foreign language, but I understood. He was saying I'd gotten too close. I'd let the current pull me. I'd allowed myself to drift into that hushed and watery border zone where we live alongside the dead. I was grateful to him for calling me back and reminding me where I belonged, in the clamorous, radiant, painfully beautiful kingdom of the living.